Praise for Linda Winfree's *What Mattered Most*

Joyfully Recommended "*What Mattered Most* is one of those stories that twists your emotions ...With her first book Linda Winfree knocks it out of the park."

~ Melissa, Joyfully Reviewed.

5 Hearts "The tension and suspense were perfect ...a phenomenal piece of work from this author."

~ *Tera Cuskaden, The Romance Studio.*

5 Cups "...a highly charged tension grabber that locks onto the reader and does not let go until the conclusion ...Linda Winfree develops incredible characters, a roller coaster ride of events and a great plot that makes this read extraordinary in every way ...an explosive read."

~ Cherokee, Coffee Time Romance.

"...the heart-breaking story of betrayal, pain and second chances ...A strong emotional tale, head over to Samhain and pick up WHAT MATTERED MOST."

~ *Jennifer Bishop, Romance Reviews Today.*

What Mattered Most

Linda Winfree

A Samhain Publishing, Ltd. publication.

Samhain Publishing, Ltd.
512 Forest Lake Drive
Warner Robins, GA 31093
www.samhainpublishing.com

What Mattered Most

Print ISBN: 1-59998-421-0
Digital ISBN: 1-59998-266-8

Editing by Jessica Bimberg
Cover by Anne Cain

First Samhain Publishing, Ltd. electronic publication: February 2007
First Samhain Publishing, Ltd. print publication: November 2007

Dedication

For Rick, who always believed.

For Carol, my IR. Without you, this book wouldn't be what it is.

And for SB, for loaning me his name.

Chapter One

Desk duty sucked. With a sigh, Lanie Falconetti dropped the last flyer on the huge pile taking up half the desk. She missed the unpredictable nature of patrol, and if she had to look at one more schedule, report or freaking bass tournament flyer, she'd scream. Addressing advertisements for the department's annual fundraiser was *not* why she'd gone into law enforcement.

A folder hit the desktop and sent shiny, four-color pamphlets everywhere. They slid over the desk, and several fluttered to the floor. Anger sparked through her, and after a slow count to ten, she looked up.

Steve Martinez, his black hair windblown, grinned at her and dropped into the chair opposite the desk. "Incident reports to be filed. God, Falconetti, your stomach is huge. How much weight did you gain this month?"

Only the bond of a five-year partnership and the fact she wouldn't want to deliver her baby in prison kept her from killing him then and there. She bared her teeth in a semblance of a smile and shot a pointed glance at his midsection. He was in good shape, but sported a distinct thickening around his waistline since she'd gone on desk duty. The rookie he now partnered obviously didn't discourage him from super-sizing his value meals the way she always had.

"Well, Martinez, at least I have an excuse for getting fat. What's yours?"

A flush crept over his sharp cheekbones, and he cleared his throat. "How'd the appointment go?"

"Like they always do. I pee in a cup, they prick my finger, I get naked, and Dr. Shaw pokes and prods me. You want all the gory details of my pelvic exam?"

"No." Steve picked up the tacky tourist's water globe from the desk and shook it, sending metallic pink flamingos dancing along a plastic beach scene. "Did O'Reilly show for this one?"

Lanie flipped the incident report folder open and dropped her gaze from his. The urge to cry, which she'd been fighting all afternoon, rose again, and she squashed it. "No. He was called out on a multiple homicide early this morning, and when I phoned this afternoon, his precinct said he was out doing witness interviews."

"Yeah, Cameron needed help with those." Dry sarcasm coated the words.

She glared at him. "I know where you're going with this. John missed a doctor's appointment because he was busy. Big freaking deal. Remember when we had that huge pile-up on the bridge? You forgot your own sister's wedding."

He laughed. "Man, was my mom pissed or what?"

She didn't bother to answer. The whole reason she'd buried herself in addressing brochures was to help her forget John had stood her up again. A cold knot of hurt lodged in her throat, and she swallowed against it.

"Why do you let him get away with this?" A frown pulled Steve's dark brows together and he shrugged. "You wouldn't tolerate it from anyone else."

"It's his job, Steve. Is he supposed to just bail on an investigation because of my routine doctor's visit?" She shook her head, smothering the part of her that wanted him to do just that. With a quick glance at her watch, she pushed to her feet. "It's after three. See you later."

"Yeah. Be careful."

A couple of deputies greeted her in the parking lot, and she endured more good-natured teasing about her rapidly-expanding figure on the way to her car. "Kid," she addressed her stomach as she slipped behind the wheel of her SUV, "I will be so glad when you finally get here."

Glad no one could hear her carry on a one-sided conversation with a fetus, Lanie pulled out of the parking lot. Despite the cold, she let the windows down, loving the damp, salty air on her skin. The circuitous coastal highway was her route of choice for the short drive home. The island, tucked into the bay north of Galveston, had avoided commercialization and maintained a small-town air. Gulls dipped and swooped over the choppy waters of the Gulf of Mexico, and a lone sailboat drifted along the cloudy horizon. She loved this drive, loved this small island off the Texas coast with its gorgeous views and friendly atmosphere.

Within minutes, she drove into the driveway of the two-story cedar and glass contemporary she shared with John. The next couple of hours belonged to her before she could expect him home. Time enough for a long walk on the beach, the daily exercise her obstetrician insisted on, then a long soak in the tub before she and John went out for the evening.

As she unlocked the door and disarmed the security system, Lanie suppressed a sigh. She wasn't looking forward to tonight's gathering. Any other time, dinner with John and her friends at Emerson's, one of Cutter's beachfront dining and dancing hotspots, would be irresistible. But not tonight. Not with Caitlin and her all-seeing eyes. Lanie could convince Steve that John's seeming lack of interest in their child didn't hurt. She wasn't sure she could hide that pain from her intuitive cousin, and Caitlin wouldn't keep quiet about it either.

They were too much alike, Lanie thought. She discarded her slacks and sweater and pulled on sweats, followed by her tennis shoes and a light windbreaker printed with the logo of the Haven County Sheriff's Department. If Caitlin was headstrong and quick to speak her mind, so was Lanie.

Except when speaking her mind involved giving John hell about missing doctor's appointments. Hands tucked in her pockets, she started down the beach, the damp sand crunching underfoot. She wanted to give him hell—she wanted to rant at him. Only that meant acting like her mother, and that was not an option.

So what if he missed the sonogram, missed seeing the awesome reality of their baby just weeks from birth? She'd show him the video, and somehow Lanie doubted this sonogram would be the last since Dr. Shaw seemed intent on monitoring the location of the placenta right up until delivery. He'd make the next one. She wasn't going to kick up a fuss, make a scene about it, the way her mother always had when her father missed a school function or a family outing.

How different would her mother's life have been if she hadn't been prone to the emotional blowouts that drove Lanie's father's crazy? For what had to be the thousandth time that year, Lanie swore to be different. She already was. John couldn't say she was overemotional.

Buoyed by the thought and the peaceful quiet of the beach, Lanie rested a hand against her stomach. "Okay, kid, promise number one hundred and twelve that Mom is going to keep or die trying—a peaceful, secure home life."

ଓଃଈ

Lanie was going to kill him, and he deserved it.

John O'Reilly draped his coat over the back of the leather couch. He hadn't really forgotten the doctor's appointment. He'd remembered it—an hour too late, while he was wrapped up in trying to question a near-hysterical witness. That interview had given them a lead begging to be followed up, and he *had* forgotten to call and plead for forgiveness.

Guilt curled through him. The kid wasn't even here yet, and already he was a lousy father. What would he do when the baby was a reality instead of a lump that nudged him in the back every night?

The scents of vanilla and cinnamon wafted through the entire house. Following the aromas, he took the stairs two at a time, knowing just where he would find her. The weariness of a fourteen-hour day tugging at him, he stripped off his tie and suit jacket. In the bedroom, ivory candles flickered on every available surface—the nightstands, the bureaus, the long, low table at the foot of the bed. Tossing his tie and jacket on the plush chair in the corner, he stepped out of his shoes.

More candlelight drew him to the open bathroom door. Just as he'd expected, mounds of scented bubbles filled the large tub. Cinnamon and vanilla hung in the hot, moist air. Eyes closed, Lanie lounged in the tub, her dark hair piled in an untidy knot at the top of her head. Just above the bubbles, he could see the upper slope of her breasts, droplets glistening in the line of her cleavage.

John inhaled the sweet, spicy air. This was why he couldn't even walk into a bakery anymore without getting hard. Unbuttoning his shirt, he continued to watch her. She lifted one long leg, pointing red-polished toes in a feline stretch. God, she was graceful, even with the basketball-sized bulge of their baby poking above the water. His shirt fell to the hardwood floor in a soft rustle of starched cotton.

"Evening, Deputy Falconetti." He knelt by the tub and reached for her foot, kneading the muscles in a soft rhythm. Her ankle, slightly swollen, called out for a kiss, and he obliged, bubbles tickling his nose. "I'm a jerk. Scum. Lower than dirt."

"Is that an apology, Detective O'Reilly?" Her soft, lyrical voice wrapped around him. She propped her other foot on the edge of the tub, and he reached for it, treating it to the same massage.

"Yeah, it is." He pressed his thumbs into her arch, and she moaned, her pleasure zinging through him. "I'm sorry, Lanie. I know this was important to you—"

"And your job's important to you." She said the words without rancor, but they seemed too smooth, too practiced. "It's okay, John."

Okay? That was all? He ran his hand up her calf, watching her face. She closed her eyes and sank a little deeper in the water. "You don't want to yell at me or anything?"

"No."

He opened his mouth and closed it again. Why the need to push the issue? If she said it was okay, it was okay. Only it didn't feel right. She didn't feel right.

"Would you care to join me?" She reached out a languid hand to brush a finger down his chest.

"Aren't we going to dinner?" He had to push the words out, his mouth dry with a sudden rush of arousal. The doubts fled.

"I thought we might have dessert first." She opened her eyes and stunned him with the desire burning in the golden hazel depths. With a lazy gesture, she beckoned him closer, bubbles and water sliding over her smooth skin. "Are you coming in or not?"

"What do you think?" He shucked his slacks and briefs in one smooth movement. Chuckling, he tugged off his socks, tossed them aside and joined her.

ঔৣ

Sleep drifted away, and John opened his eyes. Candlelight flickered around him still, reflected on the large glass doors, obscuring the twilight view of the Gulf. Lanie's soft, even breathing blended with the roar of incoming waves. One of his arms lay beneath her neck, the other draped over her waist. Under his hand, the hard, rounded bulge of her stomach felt warmer than the rest of her body. A flurry of activity shifted against his fingers.

His son.

John tasted the words, seeking the pride and affection he knew they should engender. He closed his eyes, frustrated when the effort failed. He *wanted* to be the father his son needed; he just didn't know how. What was he supposed to do? A vision of playing catch in the backyard rose in his mind, thanks to a ton of sappy commercials, but there had to be more to it than that. With his background, he didn't have a clue.

The baby moved again, kicking harder, and Lanie sighed and shifted in her sleep, her bare bottom pressed into his groin. A harsh groan escaped him, and his hand slid up to her swollen breast. All paternal thoughts fled his mind. He wanted her again already.

But he wanted her all the time, ever since the first time he'd met her. Even with the unisex deputy's uniform, bulky bulletproof vest and severe hairstyle, she'd been the sexiest woman he'd ever seen. His thoughts had taken a dive for the erotic and stayed there since. They'd ended up in bed during the first week of their acquaintance, and a month later, he'd taken her up on the laughing suggestion that he just move in, since half of his stuff had migrated to her beachfront home.

The sex had been plentiful and incredible.

The baby had been a kick to the jaw, thanks to a faulty condom.

He rubbed his palm over her distended nipple, his erection nestled against the cleft of her bottom. God, she felt good. Even heavy with child, she drew him like no woman ever had. His lips brushed her shoulder, traveling up the slope of her neck. Pure desire shot through him, mixed with gratitude for the simplicity of their relationship.

He wanted her, she would be the mother of his child, and she didn't make demands he couldn't fulfill. Lanie had not asked for his love, and that was fine with him. Look what giving away his heart had gotten him before—he had to live with that failure on a daily basis.

While his mind shied from the thought, he nipped at her ear. "Lanie? You awake, honey?"

Lanie shifted again, pressing closer. Her drowsy murmur vibrated over his skin. "John... We have to get up. We were supposed to be at Emerson's at seven."

His hand trailed from her breast, over her side, and between her thighs. He grinned at her sudden intake of breath. "Are you sure you feel up to it? Maybe you're running a temperature. You feel awful hot to me."

She writhed against his hand, her fingers a warm caress at his wrist. “I’m always hot with you. Lord, O’Reilly, I don’t think I’m supposed to want this so much right now.”

With a growl, he pulled her up against him and entered her with slow precision. Her body closed around him, hot, tight, wet. “Really? When did you start caring about what you weren’t supposed to do, Falconetti?”

“I said I didn’t think I was supposed to,” she gasped, her body arched to bring them into closer contact. His slid his hand up to her breast again. “I didn’t say anything about caring—”

“Still worried about being late?” He almost pulled out, teasing them both.

“Are you kidding?” She pushed back against him, seeking him.

Laughing, lost in the scent of cinnamon and vanilla again, John gave her what they both wanted.

Steam silvered the bathroom mirror, and John wiped it away before smoothing a comb through his hair. Beside him, Lanie pulled her thick, dark tresses into a casual knot. She shot him a cynical glance. “We’re over an hour late. Everyone’s going to know what we’ve been doing.”

Affection thrummed through him, and with a grin, he pulled her into his arms. Her stomach bumped into his lower abdomen, the fit not quite as perfect as in the past. “We could stay in. Order Chinese and sit by the fire. I’ll rub your ankles.”

Temptation lurked in the golden depths of her eyes. “No, we can’t. She’ll only be here two days.”

With a sigh, he let her go and walked into their bedroom. Sitting on the edge of the bed, he pulled on socks and his shoes. “Which cousin is this, anyway?”

“The perfect one.” Disgruntled affection colored Lanie’s voice.

John chuckled. “Is she really perfect?”

“No.” Returning to the room, Lanie lifted a silver pendant on a long chain from her jewelry box and slid it over her head. The pendant, a stylized infinity swirl, nestled between her breasts and shone against her black tunic sweater. “She was just smart enough not to get caught.”

An emotion John couldn’t quite decipher shimmered in her voice, just below the surface. Resentment? Regret? He couldn’t be sure. Either way, he could think of better ways to spend an evening than sitting around while Lanie caught up on old times with her faultless cousin. Like sitting in front of the fire, Lanie in his arms, and the quiet of the house wrapped around them.

While putting on small silver stud earrings, Lanie met his gaze in the mirror. “Are you ready—”

His cell phone’s shrill chirp cut through the air. Shrugging in silent apology, he grabbed the phone from its charger. “O’Reilly.”

“John?” His partner’s voice greeted him and sent a shiver over his nerves, as it always did when he was unprepared. And even sometimes when he was prepared, when they sat close together in the unmarked unit, and he remembered the way it had been between them. Once upon a time when they’d been more than just colleagues and friends.

“Hey.” *Beth*, he mouthed at Lanie’s quizzical look. She smiled and turned away, dabbing an expensive, rarely-used perfume on her pulse points. “What’s up?”

"I know you and Lanie are going out tonight, but I need a favor." Apology hovered in Beth's voice.

"Name it."

"I'm at the sitter's, and my damn car won't start. Could you—"

"I'll be there in ten minutes." Lanie glanced up at him, a question in her eyes, but none of the resignation and anger he knew lots of cops saw in the eyes of the women who waited at home.

"Great." Relief pushed the apology from Beth's tone. "I'll drop you at Emerson's on my way home."

The line went dead, and he clipped the phone on his belt. "Beth's at Sally Gilbert's place, and her car won't start. I'm going to walk over there and see what I can do."

Lanie shook her head, affectionate acceptance sparkling in her eyes. "Why doesn't she trade that piece of junk in? With what she spends on parts monthly, she could buy a new car."

John shrugged into his leather jacket. Memories of making love to Beth one long ago night in the battered Ford clicked through his mind. Guilt tore through him, and he shoved the recollection away. His focus should be on the woman in his embrace, not the one who didn't want him anymore. "She loves the damn thing."

"It's not safe." Lanie tilted her head back to smile up at him, her arms going around his waist. "I take it you're going to meet me at Emerson's?"

He dropped a kiss on the corner of her mouth. "I am."

The baby moved, a hard kick that vibrated through John's own abdomen. Lanie smiled, her golden gaze warm. "Be careful."

"You, too." He pulled away, nervous tension already settling in his stomach as he prepared to pretend to be just Beth's friend, just her partner. "I'll see you later."

ᏅᎵᏒ

Once he'd tightened the battery cable, John stepped back from the car. "Try it now."

The motor fired to life on the first try, and he dropped the hood to find Beth grinning at him from the driver's seat. "You're wonderful," she said as he climbed into the car.

Adjusting his seatbelt, he glanced over his shoulder at Nicole, drowsing in her booster seat. The five-year-old clutched an old, ragged stuffed bunny. John shook his head, remembering what the bunny had looked like brand new. He'd bought it for her, a couple of Christmases ago. "Don't you ever wash that thing?"

Beth laughed, steering onto the street. "Have you ever tried getting it away from her? Just wait until your son gets here. That kid is going to get a double dose of stubborn from you and Lanie."

"Yeah." He looked away, uncomfortable talking about this with her. Work. A nice, safe subject. Nothing with emotional teeth there. "Did you request a copy of that incident report?"

She glanced at him, eyebrows lifted. "I did. And stop trying to change the subject. How did Lanie's doctor's appointment go today?"

"Okay, I think."

"You think? John, I swear, to hear you, someone would think you didn't even know she was having a baby." She reached over and patted his knee. "You've got to get your act together or you're going to forget to show up at the hospital while she's in labor."

The brief contact spread comfortable warmth through his body, and he shrugged away. *Think about something else. Baseball. The Yankees in the World Series. Autopsies. Remember that last body, the guy who stepped in front of a semi. Lanie. Think about* Lanie, *for God's sake. You know, the woman who's having your baby, the woman who's everything you've ever looked for—smart, beautiful, independent, sassy as hell.*

Except she wasn't the woman sitting in the driver's seat. She wasn't the woman he'd sworn to protect with his life. She wasn't the woman he'd loved without hope for years.

"John?" Beth's quizzical voice brought him out of the reverie. She glanced at him, a wide grin curving her full bottom lip, and heat flushed his cheeks.

"I was thinking." He hated the defensiveness in the mumbled words.

She laughed, shaking her head. "I won't ask what about. God, do you two ever make it out of the bedroom?"

"Yeah." *But not very often. Because when I'm with her, she makes me forget about you.* He watched the dark silhouettes of trees and houses whiz by. He'd never understood why Beth wanted to live in the country, in the middle of nowhere, after spending her entire adult life in the constant movement of Manhattan and El Paso. Although, he'd grown to like living on the beachfront with Lanie, having the peace of the Gulf in his backyard.

Beth slowed to make a turn onto McCollum Road, the sparsely populated cut-through to the beach area. "You know, I'm really glad you found her. She's perfect for you. Didn't I tell you that you'd find the right woman one day?"

"You did." The night she'd told him it was over, right after he'd poured out his heart, offered to be Nicole's daddy and tried to get her to forget the man who'd ruined her life.

"You don't have to sound so happy about it—"

Her sarcastic rejoinder faded as the car lurched and sputtered. Beth's low curse filled the darkness. The engine coughed one last time and died. As she steered to the shoulder, she slammed her palm against the wheel. "Damn it, not again."

With a low chuckle, John released his seatbelt. "Face it, Cameron, the car's possessed."

"She's just temperamental."

He tossed her his cell phone. "Do me a favor. Call Lanie on her cell and tell her where we are while I look under the hood."

"You're so domesticated, O'Reilly."

The teasing chafed his already raw nerves. Lifting the hood, he surveyed the engine. What the hell was he supposed to look for? A loose battery cable, no problem. Anything more complicated than that? He didn't have a clue.

He dropped the hood, the latch snapping closed. "Hey, when you get Lanie, ask her if Burnett's there—"

"Don't move, O'Reilly." Doug Mitchell's gruff voice, instantly familiar, sank into John's consciousness, and the hair lifted on his body. He'd known this would happen one day. He'd known Mitchell would come back—for Beth. The distinctive click of a round being chambered in a semiautomatic handgun strangled the breath in his throat.

He reached for his own gun. "Beth! Lock the doors and stay in the car!"

As his fingers closed around the butt of his gun, stunning pain slammed into the back of his head. He slumped, trying to shake off the disorientation, hearing Nicole's panicked crying.

He tried to push up to his feet, his head throbbing. He had to get up, had to stop Doug Mitchell before he finished what he'd started three years ago. Had to stop him before he killed Beth. He reached again for the gun that was no longer there. "Mitchell, you son of a—"

Mitchell's foot connected with his ribs. The bones gave with a sickening crack, agony exploding in his chest. Adrenaline surged in his veins, and he pushed to his feet, launching himself at Mitchell's black silhouette.

The gun butt smashed into his face, and he sank to his knees. Still struggling to rise, he gasped for breath while fury and pain gripped his body. Another kick pushed the air from his lungs.

"John! Doug, don't do this!" Beth's scream mingled with Mitchell's curses in the still, cold air. Darkness sucked at John, and he heard two things before the blackness pulled him under—Beth calling his name, followed by gunshots.

଩ଓଠ

Half-listening to the conversation swirling around her, Lanie checked her watch again. Forty-five minutes. Where the hell was John? Probably still at Sally Gilbert's, talking shop with Beth.

Lanie leaned forward, rubbing at her lower back in an effort to ease the mild ache, her constant companion for the past month. The dull throbbing continued, and she stood. "I'm going to step outside for a minute."

The oceanfront deck that jutted over the beach was deserted in the frigid evening air. Emerson's boasted three levels, and as usual, people packed the place tonight. However, few dared to venture out of the restaurant's warm cocoon.

Lanie pulled her cell phone from her small purse and dialed John's number. The voice mail picked up, his clipped Manhattan accent wrapping around her. "John... You're late. Call me."

After disconnecting, she punched in Sally Gilbert's number. Sally answered on the third ring. "Hello?"

"Sally? It's Lanie Falconetti. Is John still there, by any chance?" She leaned against the railing, watching the white-capped waves roll ashore. The baby moved, a strong jab to her ribs. She rubbed at the spot, the knobby outline of a foot beneath her fingers.

"No, he left with Beth about thirty minutes ago." Worry entered Sally's voice. "You don't think they broke down again, do you?"

Unease shivered over Lanie's skin. "I doubt it. They're probably just talking shop. I'll try Beth's place. Thanks, Sally."

Ending the call, she hit number seven, Beth's home phone stored in her speed dial. No answer. Where were they? She tapped the phone against her lips. She'd give him five minutes then she'd corral Steve or somebody and go look for them.

"God, it's freezing out here."

Startled, Lanie jumped at Caitlin's husky voice. She glanced at her cousin, who leaned on the railing next to her. Caitlin pulled her jacket closer and rubbed at her arms. Lanie smiled. "Then what are you doing out here?"

"Checking on you while you check up on him."

Lanie didn't like the implication in her cousin's words. "I'm not checking up on John. He's late, and his partner drives the flaming car of death. I'm worried, that's all."

One of Caitlin's perfectly shaped brows rose. "Do I detect a note of defensiveness there, deputy?"

"No. You detect a note of annoyance."

"With me or the absent detective?"

"Cait, stop interrogating me. He's late. He's late a lot. It's no big deal."

"I never said it was. You *are* tense, though, Lane."

Lanie sighed, tucking her phone back into her purse. "I don't know why I'm so irritable. Chalk it up to hormones or something."

"Chalk it up to your Falconetti temper, and maybe a change in circumstances," Caitlin teased. "I mean, I never thought I'd see the day when you'd actually commit to a man."

"Who said I was committed?" Lanie wanted to call the words back the instant they left her lips. Who was she kidding? She'd been committed to John O'Reilly since the first time she'd gone to bed with him.

"You're having his child. I'd call that a pretty big commitment. The next thing you know, you'll be sporting a wedding ring."

Hardly. Lanie remembered John's offhand offer of marriage when she'd told him she was pregnant. She'd refused, thinking she didn't need the ring or the paper. He loved her, even if she didn't have the words. She was sure of it—the emotion was there every time he touched her. And if sometimes a niggling doubt raised its ugly head, whispering she should have taken the offer... Well, she squashed it ruthlessly.

John loved her. She loved him. They would share a child, a family. That's what mattered most.

"Lane? You still with me?"

Lanie blinked, hating the teasing, knowing expression in Caitlin's green eyes. That was the problem with having a cousin who was closer than a sister would be—she couldn't hide anything. The baby jabbed her again, and she winced. The kid was going to break one of her ribs before he was born. "Don't you have anything better to do than harass me? Like write a profile or chase down some psychopathic serial killer?"

"I'm on—"

"Lanie." Steve strode across the deck, his never-serious face set in grim lines. Foreboding trickled down her spine, especially when Caitlin stiffened, too.

"What's wrong?"

He stopped in front of her, his dark gaze intent. "Preston just located Beth Cameron's car, disabled, on McCollum Road."

Lanie relaxed, a relieved sigh escaping her. "Well, that explains why he's late again—"

"Beth and the little girl are missing."

The apprehension returned, grabbing her spine with an icy hand. "What? Where's John—"

Steve darted a look at Caitlin, who edged closer, her hand warm at the small of Lanie's back. "He's being taken to Cutter General. Estimated arrival is in five minutes-"

"Oh God." Lanie covered her mouth, nausea pitching in her throat. Her other hand slipped to her stomach, curved around her baby. "What happened? Is he—"

"I don't know what his condition is. But he's alive."

Hysteria tried to take her voice. "Steve, damn it, what happened?"

"He's been shot."

Chapter Two

Lanie hated the antiseptic smell of a hospital. The harsh mingling of disinfectant and illness triggered memories of sitting and waiting, hoping her mother would get better, realizing she never would. The detested scent wrapped around her again, and the same fear grabbed at her chest while she stared at the doors of the emergency unit.

Somewhere, John lay on the other side of those doors marked *No Admittance*—his ribs cracked, a gunshot wound to his shoulder. She pressed icy, trembling fingers to her lips in a futile attempt to suppress a horrified moan. He could have died, and she'd never told him she loved him, never told him how much he'd changed her life.

"I'm going to get some coffee." Beside her, Steve shot to his feet. He never could sit still, and Lanie was surprised he'd managed to stay in the chair as long as he had. "You want something? Juice, milk?"

She wanted to run this night back like a bad movie and start it all over again. Pitch one of those feminine fits John detested, insist he call the auto club for Beth and come with her to Emerson's. She wanted him safe and whole, with her. Without removing her gaze from the gray double doors, she shook her head. "No, thanks."

"Will you be okay until I get back?" Steve hovered, hands jammed in his pockets.

She shot him a look, part of her wishing again that Caitlin had accompanied her to the hospital. One thing her cousin never did was ask stupid questions. "I'm fine."

Steve didn't question the lie and sauntered down the hall. Lanie clenched her fingers in what remained of her lap. Lord, how long was this going to take? The minutes without news stretched, making her want to scream. *Please, please, someone come through those doors and say he's going to be all right.*

Tension keeping her nerves taut, she pushed to her feet and paced to the window. Below, the parking lot stretched to the road, bright halogen security lights reflecting off the car tops. From the fourth floor, she could see beyond the busy street to the oceanfront district. Emerson's remained brightly lit, and if Lanie tilted her head to the side, she could just make out the tiled roof of her house. Out of sight was McCollum Road, which would be flooded with patrol units and swirling red and blue lights.

Arms hugged around her stomach, she rested her forehead against the cool glass. Where were Beth and Nicole? And who wanted them badly enough to shoot John to get to them?

The bitter aroma of vending machine coffee preceded Steve into the waiting area. He joined her at the window, and Lanie lifted her head. Taking a cautious sip of his coffee, he shot her a smile. "Come on, Falconetti. Buck up. He'll be fine. He's a tough guy."

"I know." She closed her eyes against a burning wave of tears. She'd gotten a glimpse of John as he was unloaded from the ambulance, and the images blazed on her closed lids—his straight nose bruised and swollen, a cut still bleeding at his hairline, his wonderful blue eyes closed, dark lashes fanning across the unnatural pallor of his skin. A shudder traveled through her.

Please don't let him die.

In her womb, the baby—John's son—stirred, and Lanie pressed her hands to that promise of life. Steve was right. John was the quintessential tough guy. Invincible. Superman. A smile trembled at her lips as she remembered how pleased he'd been with the framed comic book art she'd given him at Christmas. Her fingers drifted up to toy with the infinity pendant, his gift to her.

Forever.

He'd never said the words, but the significance of the pendant whispered volumes. At the time, Lanie had thought the *I love you's* unimportant. Now she ached to hear the words, ached to whisper them against John's ear.

She would, she promised herself with fierce hope. As soon as he woke up.

The double doors whooshed open. "Lanie?"

Hope fluttering in her chest, Lanie spun to face her other perfect cousin, the one who'd graduated with honors from med school. "Sheila? Is he okay?"

Sheila tucked a dark curl behind her ear. "He's having his shoulder stitched up. The wound isn't a through-and-through. It's a hotline, more of a graze than anything else. The pain killers knocked him out, but you'll be able to see him in a half-hour or so."

"Oh, thank God." Lanie sagged against the wall, aware of Steve's supportive hand at her shoulder. "Can't I go in now?"

Sheila shook her head. "When they're finished with his stitches. It will only be a few more minutes."

"Oh." Lanie wrapped her hands around her stomach. How could the idea of minutes feel more like years?

A soothing smile curved Sheila's mouth. "Dr. Lott will put him on IV antibiotics and tape his ribs. He has a mild concussion, but his CT scan was clear. No bleeding. The man must have an incredibly hard head."

Lanie laughed through attacking tears. "You have no idea."

"He has four hairline fractures to his ribs, not to mention his nose, but there's no reason why he shouldn't make a full recovery. We shouldn't have to keep him but a couple of days." Sheila reached out and brushed tears from Lanie's face. "Hey, none of that. I promise, he's going to be fine."

She'd be more convinced when she could see him, touch him, hear his voice. "Promise you'll come and get me as soon as he wakes up?"

Sheila hooked her pinkie through Lanie's, the way they'd done as children. "Promise."

ଔଓ

John swam in a thick grayness, somewhere between light and dark. His body felt as though he should be in pain, but the sensation hovered just out of reach. The cold was real, and shivers racked him.

"John?" A lyrical voice soothed over his nerves, a familiar touch stroking his jaw. He turned toward the warmth. Lips brushed his. "I love you."

He struggled to open his eyes. "Beth?"

Warm fingers linked through his. "No, it's me."

Weighted lids lifted, and the grayness receded in the piercing fluorescent light. He recoiled then focused on the face above him. Warmth and peace trickled through him. "Lanie."

"I wondered if you were ever going to wake up." She blinked, tears sparkling on her long, dark lashes. What had happened to bring that look of strain to her face? Her fingers danced over his jaw again. "I love you, O'Reilly."

The reality of her words slipped away as remembrance flooded his mind—Beth's screams, Mitchell's curses, the bullet burning his shoulder. He struggled to sit up, and the lurking pain tore through his chest. "Beth. Oh my God, Beth. Got to find her—"

Lanie's hands pushed at his arms. "Stop. You can't—"

He thrust her away, his arms heavy and uncoordinated, agony shooting through him with each movement. He ignored it. "Damn it, I've got to find Beth."

"Everyone's looking for her. John, you're going to pull out your—"

A sharp stinging tore through his hand, and he stared at the blood spurting from his skin, the intravenous line lying useless on the bed now. He shoved to a sitting position, his head swimming.

"Oh hell." Lanie tried to push him back again, reaching for the call button at the same time.

"He'll kill her. I've got to find her."

"John. Stop it." Lanie took his face in her hands, her hazel gaze holding his. He stilled, breathing hard, impatience and terror pounding under his skin. "The FBI is here. The Texas Rangers, too. They've sealed off the county, and a door-to-door search is underway. They're going to find Beth and Nicole. I promise."

Screams and pain filled his mind again. He pulled her hands away, blood dripping down his forearm, and shook his head, trying to clear the dizzy fuzziness. "You don't understand. She needs me."

"I do understand. And you can help her best by getting better." Lanie's soothing tone grated against his ears.

"You don't understand." He snarled the words at her, and she stepped back, a startled expression crossing her face. "You can't."

A nurse materialized at his bedside. She exchanged a glance with Lanie. "Mr. O'Reilly? Lie back and let me put your IV line back in."

Nausea and panic clawed in his throat. "No. I don't need it."

"Yes, you do."

"John." Lanie's voice slipped from soothing to authoritative, the tone he knew she used with recalcitrant suspects. "You are not leaving that bed. Now, you can either let her put the line back in, or we can strap you to the bed and *then* she can put it back in."

He glared at her, almost hating her for standing between him and Beth's safety. "You wouldn't dare."

Her golden eyes narrowed. "Try me. Steve's on the other side of that door, and I know he has his cuffs with him."

With a growled curse, he subsided and allowed the nurse to replace the line. His gaze remained locked on Lanie's throughout the procedure, although dizziness attacked him again. When the needle was in place again, Lanie smiled grimly. "Now. What did you mean, he'll kill her? Who is he?"

Agitation crawled along his nerves. "Doug Mitchell. Beth's ex-husband."

Startled confusion settled on her face. "I thought—"

“I need to get the hell out of here.”

“You need to rest. If you’ll be a good boy, I’ll go see if there’s any news, okay?”

The brief struggle had exhausted him. The gray depths pulled at him, and he fought the sucking heaviness. He had to stay awake, had to help Beth. He had to—

“Rest.” Lanie’s whisper and her gentle touch washed over him once more. “I’ll be right back.”

The gray rushed in on him, and awareness vanished.

Tears rushing to her eyes, Lanie sagged against the wall next to the recovery room door. He was alive, alert, and she should be thankful for that. Fear curled through her. She closed her eyes, pushing the tears down. Just reaction. And damn hormones again. Not because he’d lied to her about Beth’s past. Not because he’d asked for Beth first.

“Lanie?” At the sound of Caitlin’s husky voice, Lanie opened her eyes. Sometime during the night, Caitlin had swapped the leather jacket she’d worn earlier for her black duty jacket with FBI emblazoned on the back in large, white letters.

Hope flaring in her chest, Lanie pushed away from the wall. “Did you find them? Are they okay?”

Caitlin wrapped her hand around Lanie’s. “Not yet. Deputies are searching the woods, and we’ve set up roadblocks. The Rangers from A Company are going door to door.”

Lanie sank onto the bench against the wall. Confusion tightened her throat, leaving her voice a harsh whisper. “God, Cait, why is this happening? Where are they? John says Beth’s ex-husband did it, but there is no ex. She’s a widow. Beth told me her husband died.”

"She lied." A manila folder balanced on her knee, Caitlin sat next to her and pulled a mugshot from the file. She held the photo out for Lanie's inspection. "This is Douglas Mitchell. They divorced four years ago."

The photo shook in Lanie's grip. Malevolence glowed in the man's dark eyes. "What was he arrested for?"

"Domestic abuse. Assault. Child endangerment. Violating a restraining order. He jumped bail three years ago while awaiting trial in New York on those charges."

Lanie swallowed hard. "John said Beth's life is in danger."

Caitlin nodded. "It was an ambush, very systematic. Beth's car was tampered with, and there's a second set of tire tracks on the shoulder, up the road from where the car died. He had to have been watching her to know what route she would take."

"Beth was armed. Why didn't she—"

"Fear does awful things to people. Trust me, she had reason to be afraid of this guy."

"He left John to die, to bleed out alone."

"From a graze wound? I don't think so. The previous assault charge stemmed from an altercation between the two. According to the NYPD report, O'Reilly interrupted Mitchell's attack on Beth."

Caitlin's odd tone sent shivers along Lanie's stripped nerves. "What aren't you telling me?"

"Nothing."

Lanie cupped her fingers around the bulge of her stomach. The baby lay still, and a detached part of her mind remembered reading that infants slept in utero. The idea of her baby sleeping, protected from the chaos around him, comforted her. "You're a lousy liar, Cait. Now what don't you want to say?"

“If Mitchell wanted John dead, he had the opportunity to kill him instantly. He chose not to.”

“But—”

“Tell me about John’s relationship with Beth.”

The shivery unease intensified, and her fingers tightened on her stomach. She remembered whispering of her love to John as he awakened, and his first thought had been of Beth. That was only natural under the circumstances. It didn’t mean anything. “What relationship? They’re partners.”

“Is that all?”

Anger curled along her skin, pushing the apprehension aside. “Damn it, Cait, what are you implying? They work together. Show me partners that aren’t close friends.”

“When John stopped Mitchell’s attack on Beth, they were sharing an apartment.” Caitlin pulled a copy of a report from the file.

“You just said she’d left an abusive marriage. He’s her partner—maybe she went to stay with him.”

Caitlin shook her head, and Lanie turned away from the sympathy lurking in Caitlin’s green gaze. “In New York, maybe. When they went to work for the El Paso P.D., they rented the apartment together. Both names were on the lease.”

“God, what did you do, wake the landlord?” She held onto the anger, using it as a shield.

“Yes, I did, and he wasn’t happy about it. They leased the place for a year, until Beth moved here. O’Reilly resigned from the El Paso P.D. a couple of months later and rented an apartment in Houston until he moved in with you.”

Lanie pushed to her feet, pacing to the window. Uncertainty pulsed in her throat. “So maybe there was a relationship beyond the partnership. Obviously it’s over.”

"Obviously," Caitlin agreed, her voice quiet. Lanie spun, glaring at her.

"What does it matter now? John's alive, you have a suspect, and you'll find Beth and Nicole. He can't leave the county if the highways are blocked, so what's the point of all this?"

"I'm not sure he plans to leave at all."

Oh God. Lanie closed her eyes. Caitlin's quiet words conjured awful images. "You think he's going to kill them, don't you?"

"He left John alive for a reason—to punish him, maybe, because Beth preferred him. If he kills Beth, she can't want anyone else. And O'Reilly has to live with the aftermath."

They were already living with the aftermath. She opened her eyes to stare at her cousin and lifted a trembling hand, rubbing at her temple. "Why did Beth lie about being divorced?"

Caitlin shook her head, a frown furrowing her brow. "I don't know. She took back her maiden name, but she wasn't trying to hide her whereabouts."

And John had perpetrated the lie as well. He'd never mentioned a romantic entanglement with his partner, either. Her teeth took hold of her lower lip in a punishing grip, and she rubbed her thumb over the infinity pendant. A shiver traveled down her spine. What else didn't she know?

I've got to find Beth... She needs me... He'll kill her.

John's words rang in her mind. Right now, what she didn't know could wait. Beth and Nicole's safety couldn't. "Cait, we've got to find them before it's too late."

"I know. I'm heading back out in a few minutes. I wanted to check on you, and I'd like to talk to O'Reilly if he's awake. He may be able to give us a focus."

Lanie glanced toward the window, thinking of Beth and Nicole, somewhere out there in the darkness. Nicole's bright smile swam in her memory. Surely he wouldn't hurt his own daughter? Urgency surged through her, and for the first time in eight months, she wished she weren't pregnant. Without the burden of her baby, she could be out there, helping.

She wanted Beth and Nicole safe. Their safety had to be the first priority, but with their safety would come answers to the questions pounding in her brain. The thought filled her with a fascinated dread.

John had never said he loved her. He whispered how much he wanted her, how beautiful she was to him, but never that he loved her.

And you never said you loved him, either, not until tonight. That didn't mean the emotion wasn't there.

Other uncertainties rushed in, filling the void of unanswered questions. His lack of interest in their child. The forgotten doctor's appointments. The nights she woke alone, to find him standing at the window, brooding and staring out at the waves.

Had he been thinking of Beth? Wishing he were free of Lanie and his unborn son?

A sob strangled in her throat. She'd thought she had everything—John, his love, their child. The suspicion that she had nothing crept into her mind.

Stop it. Just stop it. Later, there would be time to sort everything out. Right now, the focus had to be on Beth and her daughter. Dragging in a deep breath, Lanie met Caitlin's gaze and swallowed hard against the lump lodged in her throat. "He was awake just now. He...he was upset. He even ripped out his IV line."

"I'll keep it short." Concern shown in Caitlin's eyes. "Do you want me to take you home?"

To that empty house now filled with doubts? Lanie shook her head. "No. I want to stay here. I'll try to catch a nap later."

Caitlin's gaze flickered to Lanie's rounded stomach and away. "You should think about—"

"I'll be fine." Her voice sounded harsh, and she concentrated on smoothing it out. "I don't sleep well now anyway. Dr. Shaw says that's normal. I'll rest, I promise."

"Do you want to come in while I talk with him?"

Lanie shook her head. "No. I think I'll go find a vending machine and get some juice or something." Food held no appeal, but not taking care of herself wasn't an option.

"Okay." Caitlin smiled in reassurance, her hand rubbing over Lanie's upper arm. "I'll be right out."

Even a slight smile made her face ache. Lanie leaned against the wall, eyes closed. "Take your time," she whispered.

"Lanie?"

Her eyes snapped open at Caitlin's soft question. When she saw the knowing concern in the dark green gaze, her self-protective defenses kicked in. "Don't worry about me. Go talk to John and find out what you need to know."

"I know what you're thinking. It's not true."

She had no doubt Caitlin knew what was in her mind but damned if she'd admit it. Old habits—and old competitions—died hard, and allowing anyone to see her weakness wasn't an option. "Right now, I'm thinking you're wasting precious time."

"You're not your mother."

Why did Caitlin always have to go straight for the jugular? No dancing around a subject, no time to prepare. "I know that."

Who was she kidding? Why bother to lie now? "But I've made the same mistake, haven't I? He loves someone else."

"You don't know that."

"Oh, please. You didn't hear him when he woke up." Bile pushed in her throat as the reality of John's reaction set in. "I'm in love with a man who loves another woman, and I've trapped him with a pregnancy. Oh my God."

"It's not the same. Your mother set out to get pregnant so she could have your father. You didn't get pregnant on purpose—the birth control failed."

What did that matter? Lanie laughed, repulsed by the harsh sound. "Want to hear something ironic, Cait? An hour ago, I was worried this baby wouldn't have a father. Now I wish... God, I wish there wasn't even going to be a baby."

Horror tightened Caitlin's features, the skin around her mouth pale. "Don't say that."

Lanie ran a hand over her burning eyes. "I won't allow this baby to grow up like I did, with a resentful father."

"Lanie, you don't even know that he's resentful. You—"

"He is." Forgotten appointments. A crib he had yet to put together. Cases that came before childbirth classes. Another woman's name on his lips. The defenses crumbled, and she fought back tears. "I thought he was getting used to the idea, that he loved me and would love our baby... God, how could I not have seen this?"

"Because you loved him and you didn't want to." With the soft whisper, Caitlin hugged her. "It's amazing what we can hide from ourselves."

For just a moment, she let go of the need to be invincible and clung. "What am I going to do?"

A light touch brushed over her hair. "You're going to be strong. You're going to be the mother you wanted to have."

Chapter Three

"Detective O'Reilly?" The husky female voice pulled John from the sea of gray again. Surrounded by a cookie-cutter hospital room, he felt more alert, more whole. More pain, he thought, rotating his injured shoulder in gentle circles.

The woman standing over him looked familiar, although he was certain he'd never seen her before. Black hair, green eyes, a determined, pointed chin. Something about the curve of her mouth struck him—he knew that mouth. He swallowed, his throat dry. "Yeah?"

She held up FBI credentials. "I'm with the FBI's Child Abduction and Serial Killer Unit. I need to ask you a few questions."

The letters on the identification swam before his eyes, then solidified into words. Falconetti, Caitlin. He met her cynical gaze, the familiarity explained by the name. Lanie's perfect cousin. Hell, she would turn out to be a Fed. Right now, though, he was glad to see her. Maybe that meant Beth still had a chance. "You want me to help you get into Mitchell's head."

"Anything you can tell me would help."

That meant laying out the entire tangled mess—to Lanie's cousin. Lanie would never understand. Regret rose, replacing for a swift moment his concern for Beth. He shifted, his shoulder and his ribs screaming in protest. "What I say stays in this room."

Her eyes narrowed, and she pulled a small, leather-bound notebook from her jacket pocket. "What you say will be used to help us find your partner and her daughter. Whatever needs to be said between you and my cousin will be your responsibility later."

He attempted to moisten dry lips with an even drier tongue. Caitlin watched him a moment then handed him a small foam cup of ice chips. "That should help. And if you have a reaction to the pain killer, they won't make you throw up."

She sounded as though she relished the prospect. John let an ice chip as cold as her voice melt on his tongue. She didn't like him. That was okay—he didn't like himself much right now, either. "Do you have any leads?"

"Not many. A gas station attendant tentatively identified Mitchell as a man who's bought gas on several occasions over the past few weeks. An agent is reviewing the station's security tapes."

John cursed, dragging his hands over his face. "So he's been here that long, watching her."

"Probably watching all of you." Accusations hovered in her voice. "Why did Beth lie about him, tell everyone he was dead?"

Tension tightened his jaw. "Because that's what she wanted to believe—that he was gone and the past was behind her. She wanted to think she was safe."

"Okay, that I get. You know what I don't understand, O'Reilly? Did you think this guy would just go away? That he'd just forget the whole thing?"

"Why do you think I came down here? To keep her safe."

He'd done a lousy job, too. She didn't say it, but the implication was there in the way she arched one eyebrow at him. "What about Lanie?"

"What about her?" He wanted to call the sarcastic rejoinder back. A CASKU agent, she was probably Beth and Nicole's best chance. Pissing her off wasn't a good idea.

"She didn't need to know there was a possibility this maniac would turn up?"

Uncomfortable heat rose on his neck. "Lanie was never in any danger."

"Really? I don't think Beth Cameron is the only one who wants to deny reality. How long did you say you'd been a detective?"

The insult clenched his jaw, and he forgot about not pissing her off. "Just ask your damn questions, Agent Falconetti."

"Mitchell believes his wife left him for you, doesn't he?"

"Yeah, he does. She left him because he was abusive, but it's easier for him to blame me."

She scratched a note on the pad, and then her gaze flickered to his face. "Were you involved?"

He shifted his gaze away. "That came later. Beth... She was scared and alone."

"And you were her knight in shining armor." Sarcasm clipped the words.

John bristled. "Are you always so antagonistic when questioning a witness?"

"O'Reilly, you haven't seen antagonistic yet." She lowered the notepad, pinning him with a stare. "I'm trying to ignore for the moment that you exposed Lanie to danger."

"Damn it, she's not in danger!"

“This from the guy who let down his guard enough to allow someone to take his service weapon. Mitchell left you alive for a reason—he thinks you’re to blame for the failure of his marriage. He’s been here for God knows how long, obviously surveilling you. He has to know about Lanie and your involvement with her, has to know she’s pregnant, and you don’t think she’s in danger? I figured you for a selfish jerk, but I didn’t think you were stupid. Hell, was I wrong.”

Anger battled against the fear rising in his throat. “Are you done?”

She snapped the notebook closed. “Not really, but this is getting us nowhere.”

“He won’t hurt Lanie.” He wondered if he meant to reassure her or himself.

“That’s right, he won’t. I’ll make sure of it. Martinez is going to stay with her.”

“I wouldn’t have let him near her.”

“You did a really good job of protecting Beth, too.”

“You—”

The door swung inward, and Sheriff Dennis Burnett stepped into the room, his dark hair disheveled. “Cait, we’ve got the little girl.”

Hope surged through John, and he struggled up against the pillows. Agony stabbed at his ribs, and he subsided, gasping. “Is she all right?”

Caitlin ignored him and tucked her notebook back into her pocket. “Where?”

“Couple of teenagers found her wandering the parking lot of the hamburger joint out on Route Six. Right now, she’s downstairs in the ER, being checked out. Other than being cold and scared out of her mind, she seems to be okay.”

She moved toward the door. “We need to spread out a net from that point—”

“Already doing it. Who put you in charge, anyway? Did you forget you were on vacation?”

Ignoring the teasing, Caitlin glanced back at John, her smile cool. “Thank you for your help, detective.”

John matched her stare for icy stare. “Sure. Anytime.”

Once the door closed with a soft click, he dropped his head back against the pillow and stared at the ceiling. He welcomed the pain that shot through his skull. He deserved it. Guilt coiled through him. She was right—he’d let down his guard, let Mitchell catch him unprepared.

Beth was paying for his mistakes.

He couldn’t stay here in this bed while she was out there, somewhere, at Mitchell’s mercy. A grim chuckle escaped him. Mercy. Mitchell didn’t have any, and Beth bore the scars to prove it.

Teeth gritted against the pain, he shoved to a sitting position and swung his legs over the side of the bed. Waves of dizziness attacked his head, and he closed his eyes, swearing. Beads of icy perspiration broke on his upper lip, and he brushed at them, the slight weight of the intravenous line dragging at his arm.

He glanced at his hand, a large purple bruise spreading to his wrist, and memory returned of pulling the needle out earlier. Gritting his teeth, he tugged the line free once more. Stinging hurt shot up his arm. He held on to the discomfort, using it to focus his flagging energy. His feet slid to the floor, and he stood, shaky knees not wanting to bear his weight.

The door opened, and he glanced up, his gaze clashing with Lanie’s. Her full mouth, already bracketed with tension lines, twisted in frustration. “Damn it, John, I warned you.”

"I'm getting out of here." He glanced down at the hospital gown and his bare feet. "Where the hell are my clothes?"

One hand holding the door open, Lanie glanced back over her shoulder. "Steve, I need your cuffs."

"Like hell you do!"

Martinez appeared in the doorway. "Falconetti, you're not really planning to—"

"Watch me."

"Don't touch me," John snarled, pushing her hands away.

"Believe me, right now I'd rather pick up a live rattlesnake." Lanie glanced at him, her hazel gaze far colder than her cousin's had been. Unable to meet her eyes, John glanced away. Damn it, he'd never wanted her hurt. He struggled to stand again. "But you're going to hurt yourself if someone doesn't stop you."

Her fingers slid into the pressure point behind his clavicle, buckling his knees, sending numbness along his arms. "You damned—"

Cold steel closed around his wrist; a metallic ring told him the other cuff had closed around the bed frame. Lanie glared down at him. "Just spit it out, O'Reilly."

He gave a hard, ineffectual tug at the cuff, then matched her glare. Defensiveness tightened his lungs. "I guess you've been talking to your cousin."

Her eyebrows lifted, a cold smile curving her mouth. "I'm just finally seeing what's been right in my face all along. Steve, would you leave us alone?"

"You're not going to hurt him, are you?" The joking didn't cover the concern in Martinez's disembodied voice.

"No." The disdain in her voice matched the emotion that John watched flicker in the golden depths of her eyes where before he'd only seen affection and desire.

"I'll be right outside. Holler if you need me."

Silence followed the click of the door closing. His chest heaving and aching, John stared up at Lanie. Blood dripped down his wrist and pooled at his elbow. "You have to take that cuff off. I've got to get out of here."

Her stony expression didn't change. "I don't *have* to do anything, you lying rat."

"Lanie, please." He rattled the cuff again, hating the hoarse pleading in his voice. "You don't understand."

"I understand plenty. Do you have family I need to contact?"

He frowned. She knew his parents were dead, that he was an only child. "No. You—"

"So at least part of it was the truth. Wait, you didn't really lie, did you, O'Reilly? You just didn't tell the whole truth."

"I know you're angry, but I've got to—"

Her harsh laugh exploded in the quiet room. "Angry? I wouldn't exactly call it anger. And what you're going to do is stay in that bed and recuperate."

Desperation slid under his skin. "He let Nicole go because he won't hurt Beth in front of her. She's in danger, and I—"

"You love her, don't you?"

The quiet, deadly words brought him to a stop. For the first time, he glimpsed agony beneath the ice. Guilt cramped his stomach, and he softened his voice. "Lanie, I didn't mean for this to happen."

"I'm sure you didn't." Her gaze didn't move from his, but the existence of their unborn child hung between them, the double meaning heavy in her words. "Were you sleeping with her, too?"

Anger rocketed through his veins. "No, damn it, I wasn't sleeping with her."

"Of course not." That same harsh laugh escaped her, and she turned away. "If she was sleeping with you, you wouldn't have needed me, would you? So were you thinking of her while you were with me?"

Her voice dropped with the accusation, and he shook his head. He hadn't had to think of Beth because the physical attraction, the pleasure, had always been so strong with Lanie. She'd made him forget anything or anyone else existed. "No."

"Liar."

"Lanie, it's the truth, I swear."

She shot him a glare, sliding the infinity pendant over her head and letting it drop into a silver pool on the bed. "Right."

He watched her move toward the door, and panicked helplessness rose in him. "Where are you going?"

"I'm going to check on Nicole, and then I'm going home."

"Take Martinez with you. Your cousin thinks Mitchell might try to use you to get back at me."

"I can take care of myself. And as good as Cait is, there's only one problem with her scenario—in order for Mitchell to use me against you, you'd have to give a damn about me. Goodbye, John."

"Damn it, Lanie, I do care about you." The words fell in the empty air, the door closing behind her. Dropping against the pillow, he muttered growling curses, jerking at the cuff and sending pain shooting up his arm and through his upper body.

She wasn't going to listen to him. The lump of cold fear in his stomach grew larger. What if Ms. Perfect was right? What if Mitchell decided to go after Lanie?

He tugged at the cuff again. He had to get out of here. He couldn't let another woman die because of him and his failures.

ঙ৪ঌ৯

"Steve, really." Lanie huffed a sigh and pulled the pin from her hair, letting the heavy mass fall about her shoulders. Her spine ached all the way from the base of her skull to her lower back. "I don't need a babysitter."

"What if the FBI chick is right and this nut decides to come after you?" Steve tapped his fingers on the open refrigerator door, examining the contents of her fridge. "Did you know you're out of beer?"

"First, she's not a chick—she's my cousin and she'd kick your ass if she heard you call her that. Second, she's been wrong before, and she's wrong this time. Mitchell wants Beth. Not me. Third, I have a state-of-the-art security system, not to mention a rather large caliber handgun. And yeah, I knew I was out of beer. The rat drank the last one yesterday."

Steve straightened, a soda in hand, and swung the door closed. "You're really ticked at him, aren't you?"

"Ticked doesn't begin to cover it." Lanie moved by her partner to the refrigerator and grabbed the milk, drinking from the carton. Satisfactory spite warmed her veins—John *hated* when she did that.

After taking a swig of soda, Steve shook his head. "Getting involved with your partner is always a bad idea. I don't know why guys do it."

"Well, you don't have to worry about that, do you, Martinez?" Even if she'd ever been remotely attracted to him, she was off men for life. Lord, she should have followed through on that vow the first time she made it. She slumped against the counter, swirling the milk in the carton. "I think I'll become a lesbian."

He brightened. "If you do, can I watch?"

She slugged his shoulder and stuck the milk back in the refrigerator. "No."

He laughed, opening the cabinet and surveying the junk food selection. "Listen, I really don't mind hanging out here. I can crash on the couch, catch the end of the game on the tube—"

"Eat me out of house and home," Lanie finished for him. She resisted the urge to push him toward the door. "I appreciate it, truly I do, but I really just want to be alone right now."

"All right, but let's check and make sure you have everything locked up. Then I'll call dispatch and have them put a car outside, just in case."

The plan sounded like overkill, but Lanie relented, following him from the kitchen. "I'll sleep with my weapon, too. Will that make you feel better?"

Steve grew serious. "Yeah, it will. This whole thing makes me nervous."

They moved through both levels of the house, checking the locks on all of the windows and doors. Lanie endured her partner's safety instructions and breathed a sigh of immense relief when she closed the door behind him.

Solitude.

The quietness wrapped around her, sheltering her from the emotional storm brewing on the horizon. She walked to the bank of floor-to-ceiling windows that lined the living room wall. Rain clouds gathered over the Gulf, wind whipping at the white-capped waves. She wrapped her arms around her stomach and leaned her cheek against the cool window. Tears leapt to her eyes. How could she have been so wrong? The story had been so plausible—a young widow moving to escape the memories, her partner with no family ties seeking the excitement and warm weather of Houston. John's attitude toward Beth had been friendly and warm, never that of a lover, not in Lanie's presence.

And God knew, if anyone could see the signs of infidelity, she could. She'd lived them, had them drummed into her psyche by her mother's litanies.

Lightning streaked across the black-purple sky. Acting on protective instinct, she backed away from the glass, drawing the ivory sheers closed. Picking up the remote, she fired the gas logs in the fireplace, the cheerful flames doing little to elevate her spirits. Everywhere she turned were reminders of the folly that had been her relationship with John O'Reilly.

Relationship. Anything but. She'd been a convenient lay. Scratch that—an eager, ultimately inconvenient lay, she corrected, still hugging the swell of her baby. Could she have made it any easier for him?

Tears dripped down her cheeks, and she let them fall as she gathered emergency candles, matches, blankets and pillows. The electric service was notoriously unstable in windy weather, and she couldn't face sleeping in the bed she'd shared with John. The cold sheets were still rumpled and tossed from their early evening lovemaking, and she would not crawl between them.

This wasn't much better. With a shuddery sigh, she settled onto the couch. How often had they made love in front of the fire, the curtains open so they could look at the water afterward? The images came too easily—firelight on burnished skin, highlighting the ripple and play of muscles as he moved above her, within her.

That hadn't been making love. That was sex, pure and simple. The memory of the desire that had seemed so pure, so strong, pulled at her, and she shuddered with self-disgust.

All he ever had to do was look at her with those dark blue eyes, smile at her a certain way, and she was ready for him. Once upon a time, the reaction thrilled her. Now it damned her, made her feel again like the girl she'd been in high school—the one who had sought with desperation the love and affection so lacking at home, who traded her body and her self-esteem for the illusion that someone cared.

She'd taken years to rebuild that self-respect, and in one night, John O'Reilly had taken it away again. *Hell, be honest, Falconetti. He didn't take anything. You* gave *him everything.*

She pulled the blanket closer to her chin and stared into the leaping flames. The baby stirred, rolling beneath her hand. The tears fell faster. What was she going to do?

Wind gusted, rattling the glass, and the rain began, harsh sheets of water blown against the house. Lanie shivered. Beth was still out there somewhere. Lord, this entire situation was a mess, the emotional equivalent of an atomic bomb waiting to go off, but she wanted the other woman safe.

Repeating prayers for all of them, she drifted into sleep.

ଓଃଛ

"Let me get this straight—your girlfriend's idea of a joke involved handcuffing you to the hospital bed?"

John met the security guard's incredulous gaze and nodded, trying not to look like the worry-crazed maniac he was becoming. The more he'd thought about it, the more Caitlin Falconetti's theory made a sick sort of sense. Mitchell could very well go after Lanie, and John meant to stop him. "We're both cops. She got mad at me and..."

He let the words trail away, lifting his cuffed wrist for illustration.

After radioing the main desk, the security guard shook his head and released John's wrist. "Craziest damn thing I ever heard."

His bladder threatening to burst, John rubbed at his wrist and swung his feet over the side of the bed. "Thanks."

The guard eyed him with lingering suspicion. "Where do you think you're going, young feller?"

One hand keeping the back of the too-small gown closed, John tested weak legs. "To take a leak."

Still muttering, the guard left the room. John eased into the bathroom, trying to get his thoughts in order. He didn't even have his watch. He had no clue what time it was, what was going on with the search for Beth, or how long Lanie had been alone.

Please let Martinez be with her. The wish was pointless, though. Lanie's stubborn independence had been one of the traits that had drawn him to her most strongly. She could stand on her own; she didn't *need* him. Lanie could take care of herself.

That's what you thought, O'Reilly. How do you know what she needs? You never asked. You just took what you wanted and the hell with her feelings.

The memory of the awful hurt in her eyes stabbed him with renewed guilt, but he shook off the emotion. She knew what she was getting into from day one with him. Her eyes were open.

Yeah, sure. But she didn't know everything, did she, O'Reilly?

Guilt grabbed at his gut again. After flushing the toilet, he ran cold water over his hands, splashing his face. He'd worry about blaming himself later. Right now, he had to get to Lanie before Mitchell, and maybe in the process, he could help Beth as well.

First, though, he had to find a way to cover his bare ass.

Chapter Four

Wind shuddered against the glass, and Lanie jerked awake, the remnants of a panicked nightmare still clinging to her throat. Only the fireplace flames lit the room, and she sat up, her lungs fighting for air. Pushing the blanket away, she laughed at herself. Lord, she was letting Caitlin and Steve get to her. Having a nightmare and waking up in the dark weren't reasons for panic.

She reached for the matches and froze at the sticky wetness between her thighs. Hands trembling, she lit a candle, and the leaping flame cast shadows dancing about the room. The material of her leggings clung to her upper thighs, and she touched the dampness, holding her fingers to the light.

Blood.

The crimson stain on her skin sent panic skittering along her nerves. Her hands folded around the stillness of her swollen abdomen. *Move, baby. Please move.*

No response came. No movement, no pain, just the blood. Maybe it wasn't as bad as she thought. Maybe it was just the pre-labor show. Somehow, even weeks-early labor seemed preferable to this painless bleeding.

With shaking hands, she grabbed the candle and the cordless phone and edged her way to the bath off the small foyer. The gush of fluid between her legs took her breath. This wasn't normal. No way was this awful flow of blood normal.

Frightened tears clogging her throat, she sat on the edge of the tub and tried to dial her doctor's number. The only reply was a dead line. Oh God, not the phone lines, too. Not now. A panicked sob tore at her lungs.

Her cell phone would be in the charger next to the refrigerator. Maybe the battery had enough power to let her make a call, and Steve had said he'd have a car posted outside. Help was available.

She wanted John with a breathless urgency, wanted the feel of his strong arms, the security of his deep voice. Lanie forced herself to breathe at a normal rate. She was on her own in this, and she might as well get used to that now. John O'Reilly didn't belong to her. He never had.

When she opened the door, the draft extinguished the flickering candle flame. With a muttered curse, Lanie felt her way along the wall. If only the batteries weren't dead, a flashlight lay in the junk drawer by the stove. As she made each sliding step, more blood pulsed from her body. Weak tears burned her eyes again.

Guilt tore at her. Earlier, glaring at John, she'd wished she weren't bearing his child, and now that wish seemed to be coming to pass.

No. Stop it. The baby will be fine. You'll be fine. You're a Falconetti, and everyone knows a Falconetti never quits.

A few more feet and she would reach the kitchen. A few more seconds and she could call for help. Afraid moving too quickly would accelerate the blood flow, she took slow, easy, sideways steps, her hand sliding along the wall for guidance.

Her fingertips brushed wet, warm human skin, and she jerked away, her heart pounding in a sick, accelerated rhythm.

A flashlight beam flared, blinding her, and a deep, raspy voice reached out for her. “Well, hello, babe.”

Lanie screamed.

Cruel fingers covered her mouth and nose, cutting off the cry. A tall, stocky body pressed hers against the wall, her womb compressed at an uncomfortable, awkward angle. Her lungs begging for oxygen, she clawed at the smothering hand.

“Scream again, and you’re dead.” The whispered promise iced her veins. He removed his hand with slow deliberation, and Lanie drew in a deep breath. The mingled scent of sea air and stale sweat assaulted her nostrils, and she forced her mind to click through her training. Her attacker made himself vulnerable by getting this close—she could take him down, but she assumed he was armed. The certainty he would carry through on his threat settled into her mind.

He’s going to kill you anyway.

The disjointed thought flitted through her mind, along with the knowledge that Caitlin had been right again. “Doug Mitchell?” she whispered.

“At your service.” His ugly laugh sliced at her ear, and he pressed closer. Nausea climbed in her throat. “I see my reputation precedes me.”

Where was Beth? Was she in the house? Already dead? Lanie swallowed. “There’s a deputy en route. My partner—”

“Your partner never had a chance,” Mitchell whispered against her ear, and she gagged. Oh God, not Steve. “No one’s going to interrupt us. No one’s going to save you.”

Her lungs froze, and cold fear trickled down her spine. She was truly alone in this. *Lord, please. Help me. Don’t let me panic. Help me think.*

Her gun. She'd left it on the kitchen counter, next to her cell phone. Her hope lay in that gun, in distracting him. "If you're hoping to get back at John by hurting me, it won't work. He won't care... Our relationship is over. He never loved me."

"He helped take my daughter out of my life." The flat blade of a knife pressed to the swell of her stomach, and Lanie fought down a clenching wave of terror. "We'll see how he feels about having his kid cut out of his life, won't we?"

Lanie forced her muscles into deliberate relaxation. "We can talk about this. My father is very wealthy."

"I don't give a damn about money," he snarled. "Money's no good to me now."

"You think? My father..." She sagged, throwing her entire weight on him. His grip went slack, and Lanie drove her forearm against his throat, followed by blows to his solar plexus and instep, her movements made clumsy by her increased weight. The flashlight fell to the floor, and he doubled over, cursing. She made a break for the kitchen, using the reflected light as a guide.

More blood left her body, and she bit back a terrified sob. Her hands closed on her gun and phone. Mitchell cursed, crashing down the hall, and she chambered a round, sliding the safety off. The phone hit the floor when she dropped it to grip the gun in a two-handed combat grip. His silhouette appeared in the doorway, and she fired, the muzzleflash appearing before the report exploded in the room.

She fired again, but he was on her before she got the third shot off. Her head glancing off the cabinet, she hit the floor, and his knee slammed against her chest. Mitchell's hands gripped her skull, and with a mad growl, he thrust her head into the floor. Lights and agony exploded behind her eyes, and her hands covered her stomach, protecting her child, as blackness descended.

ଔଷଔ

Desperation did crazy things to a man, and John supposed this was as good an example as any. Clad in turquoise surgical scrubs he'd lifted from a supply closet, he lay across the seat of an ancient Ford pickup and twisted ignition wires together. A homicide detective, sworn to protect and serve, escaping from a hospital, wearing stolen clothes and hotwiring a truck.

The engine fired to life, and brief elation shot through him. This time around, things would be different. Mitchell would not win.

Worry and guilt swallowed the elation as he navigated Cutter's rain-drenched streets. Patrol cars from the city and county departments as well as unmarked units filled the roads, and he dodged a couple of roadblocks. This needn't have happened, if he'd refused to let Beth cling to her denial. He'd wanted her to be happy, and he'd been sure he could keep her safe.

He'd failed. Beth's life was in danger once again, but the worst part was that his failure to protect Beth endangered Lanie.

Remembering the angry pain in her golden eyes twisted his gut. *How could you not see how all of this would hurt her, once it came out? You wanted her, and that was all that mattered to you. Did you ever stop to think about what you were doing?*

He was no better than Mitchell. Disgusted fury slammed through him, and he slapped a hand on the steering wheel, welcoming the stabbing pain the sharp movement brought. He'd find a way to make it better. Damp hair fell on his forehead, and he pushed it back. He'd be more supportive of her through the remainder of the pregnancy, and he'd be as active in the baby's life as she would allow him to be.

If she survived.

John shook his head. Her not surviving wasn't an option. The idea of a world without Lanie in it cut his breath short. A world without that sassy sense of humor, that beautiful laugh, and those gorgeous golden eyes? A life without Lanie's touch on his skin?

God, he couldn't let anything happen to her. He wouldn't be able to stand the emptiness.

Blind son of a bitch. You really screwed up this time, didn't you?

His hands trembled on the steering wheel, and he pushed down harder on the accelerator. He couldn't fail again. He had to get to her before Mitchell.

ଔଓଓ

When Lanie's eyelids fluttered open, electric lights blazed around her. Pain thudded through her head with her pulse, her teeth chattering with intense cold. Cool tile pressed against her cheek. Her mind working with dazed lethargy, she rotated her head, watching the room come into focus. White tile, white cabinet, seashell prints on the white wall, a glass hurricane globe holding a collection of multicolored sea glass.

The bathroom. The tiny bathroom off the foyer.

Memory returned in a flood, and she straightened, a groan slipping past her lips as the pain stabbed behind her eyes.

“Don’t move.” Gentle hands gripped her shoulders, pressing her back against the wall, and Lanie met Beth’s haunted blue gaze.

Beth’s spiky copper hair was wet, plastered around her pale face, a fresh bruise standing out along her jaw. Blood congealed at the corner of her split lip. Pain and fear tightened her delicate features.

At least John hadn’t chosen Lanie because she looked like Beth. The bitter thought flitted through Lanie’s confused mind. Beth’s petite, curvy build was nothing like the tall, slender, athletic frame Lanie shared with her Falconetti cousins.

She could feel her pulse under her skin, the rapid beat unnerving. Lanie pushed the jealousy aside. They had other things to worry about. “Nicole’s safe,” she whispered, glancing at the closed door. “She’s at the hospital. And John’s alive.”

“Thank God.” Beth’s eyes closed, tears sparkling along her thick lashes. She opened her eyes, fingers curving along Lanie’s jaw. “I was beginning to think you were out for good.”

Lanie tilted her head away from the touch. “I—”

“Lanie, were you bleeding before Doug and I got here?” Hands shaking, Beth folded a towel into quarters.

Finding it hard to concentrate on the question, Lanie glanced down, staring at the folded towel between her thighs, the white terrycloth turning crimson. Her gaze followed a trail of scarlet drops on the tile, finding a small pile of blood-soaked towels in the corner behind the door. The reality of what she saw slammed through the fuzziness in her brain. “Oh my God.”

Beth’s fingers gripped Lanie’s chin, forcing her gaze up, away from all that blood. “Focus. How long have you been bleeding?”

“I—I don’t know.”

A low, rough curse hung in the air between them. "Do you hurt?"

Her head pounded, and her lungs ached as if she'd been running. But the bleeding brought no discomfort—not the burning contractions her childbirth classes described. She tried to shake her head, her eyes slipping closed as pain exploded with the movement. "No."

"Lanie." Beth tapped her cheek. "Can you feel the baby? Is he moving?"

Lanie flexed her fingers on her stomach. When was the last time he'd kicked or rolled over? "Not right now."

Beth touched her forehead. "We've got to get you out of here."

Disconnected, Lanie watched as Beth pushed to her feet, favoring her left ankle. "He's going to kill us. What is he waiting for?"

Beth glanced over her shoulder. "He's waiting for John."

An image of John's outraged face rose in Lanie's mind, sparking a weak, inappropriate giggle. "He's going to be waiting for a long time. John's cuffed to his bed."

"I'm not even going to ask why." Beth rested her ear against the closed door.

Lanie closed her eyes again. Lord, she was tired. An ache pulsed in the back of her head. Slipping away, into the darkness of slumber, seemed so easy. Slipping away from the reality. "He loves you."

"Did he *say* that to you?" Beth's horrified voice penetrated the fog. "That stupid son of a bitch."

"It's true, isn't it?" Weak tears slipped beneath Lanie's lashes, and her hands rested on her stomach. "I'm losing the baby, aren't I? That's probably for the best—"

"Stop it." Beth's hands closed on her shoulders with bruising force. "Lanie, listen to me. You are not going to lose this baby, and it would not be for the best. You are the best thing to ever happen to John O'Reilly, and he's just too freakin' blind to see it—"

"Isn't this touching?" Mitchell swung the door open, sneering.

"Doug, do what you want with me." Beth's voice trembled over the words, but a note of iron lay beneath them. "But you've got to get her some help. She's bleeding. And her head... Call an ambulance, and we'll leave. I'll go anywhere you want, do whatever you want—"

"Nobody's going anywhere." Pain edged Mitchell's voice, and blood oozed from his shoulder. One of her bullets had found its mark. On a wave of woozy satisfaction, Lanie let her eyes drift closed again. "We're waiting for O'Reilly to join the party. Meanwhile, you'll do whatever I want anyway, won't you, babe?"

"You sick bastard."

The voices wafted away as the darkness swallowed Lanie once more.

ᏋᏋ

Parked up the street, John surveyed the house. Lights blazed in the windows, but the outdoor lights remained dark. The sheer curtains were drawn, and no shapes moved behind them. His gaze zeroed in on the upstairs windows. Even the extra bedrooms were lit.

John's gut clenched. The two guest bedrooms were shut off to save electricity. Lanie had not turned on those lights; he was sure of it. Mitchell was already in the house, possessing all the advantages. John scanned the street, his gaze lighting on Steve Martinez's Honda parked a few vehicles away.

Maybe Martinez was in the house as well. John slipped from the truck and eased toward the car, using shadows as cover. Foreboding gripped his stomach as he approached the car and saw the silhouette slumped in the front seat. Martinez wasn't the type to sleep on surveillance duty.

The streetlight illuminated the front of the car, and John recoiled at the sight of Martinez's staring eyes, blood spilling from the wide gash at his throat. He didn't have to check to know that Lanie's partner was dead or that his weapon was gone.

As badly as he wanted to burst into the house and kill Mitchell with his bare hands, the reality remained that John was barefoot and unarmed. Mitchell wouldn't have any qualms about killing again. John needed backup, someone who wanted Lanie safe as much as he did.

Easing into the shadows, he slipped back up the street. Around the corner was a small convenience store, and once out of sight of the house, John jogged to the payphone against the store's wall, ignoring the slice of gravel and broken glass under his feet and the stabbing pain in his ribs. He punched in nine-one-one and waited.

"Haven County Emergency. How can I help you?" The female voice was pleasant, impersonal.

"This is Detective John O'Reilly, Houston P.D., badge number three-zero-four-seven-nine." His own voice sounded raw, like an open wound. "I need you to patch me through to Agent Caitlin Falconetti."

"Sir, I'm sorry, but—"

Anger spurted through his veins in a hot rush. “Listen, damn it. Your kidnapping suspect is in my house. Now patch me through.”

Silence clicked over the line. “Please hold.”

In the seconds that passed, images of what could be happening to Lanie surged through his mind. John pressed the heels of his hands to his eyes, trying to block the horrific pictures. Nothing would happen to her. He wouldn’t let it.

Wouldn’t let it? He already had. Resting his head against the wall, he swallowed a moan.

“Falconetti.” Even through the static, the ice was apparent.

“Martinez is dead. Mitchell’s in the house,” John grated without preamble. “I think he has Lanie.”

“Where are you?” The ice receded, urgency rising to the foreground.

He rattled off the address. “Don’t bring in the cavalry. I don’t want him tipped off that we’re here.”

“Give me some credit, O’Reilly. I’ll be there in five minutes.”

ଓଃଃ

“Lanie?” Strong fingers gripped her chin, forcing her back to awareness. “Lanie, talk to me.”

She lifted heavy lids, staring into Beth’s desperate blue eyes. “Beth, leave me alone.”

“No. You’ve got to stay with me. You could have a concussion. Talk to me. Baby names. Did you and John ever decide on a name?”

What did she mean, *you and John*? Didn’t Beth know there was no her and John? Lanie attempted to collect her scattered thoughts. Names...somewhere upstairs, in the journal in her nightstand drawer, was a scribbled list of first names she'd thought would pair up well with John as a middle name. She'd wanted their son to carry his father's name.

A sob trembled on her lips, and she fought weak tears again. If they didn't get out of here, there might not be a baby. She pressed a hand to her motionless stomach. If it wasn't already too late.

"Lanie, *please*. What name?"

She shook her head, a slow side-to-side roll against the tile wall. "We... I didn't... He doesn't have one yet."

Beth's hands smoothed Lanie's damp hair from her face. "Just don't name him John, Jr. Everyone will want to call him J.J. or something."

"John is a Jr. He'd be John III if we did that." Lanie stilled, staring at Beth as a horrible possibility occurred to her. "Do you love him, too?"

Crystal tears washed Beth's azure gaze, and her lashes swept down, blinking them away. "He's my partner, my best friend. Of course, I love him. But not the way you mean, no. And he doesn't love me. God, Lanie, haven't you ever seen the way he looks at you?"

No, but she'd never *really* seen the way he looked at Beth, either. She'd looked at them and seen close partners, the camaraderie she shared with Steve. Grief reared its head, and she fought it down, touching her stomach once more. No movement greeted the contact. She'd lost John and Steve, all in one night. Would she lose her baby, too?

Gripped by an intense weariness, she leaned her head back, aware of the maddening sensation of her pulse thudding under her skin. "He looks at me like he's thinking about—"

"No." Beth tilted Lanie's chin up with a gentle finger. "Not like that. I'm talking about how he looks at you when he thinks no one is watching."

A desperate need to ask about that expression tickled her throat, but Lanie swallowed the question. How he looked at her really didn't matter—what mattered was his expression when he'd awakened and whispered Beth's name. He hadn't looked like a worried partner. The agony in his navy blue eyes had belonged to a man facing the loss of the woman he loved.

And that woman wasn't Lanie.

Chapter Five

Hunched in a shadow behind the stolen Ford, John stared at the front windows of the house. His eyes strained with the effort of detecting motion that just wasn't there. Beside him, Caitlin Falconetti whispered into a handheld radio, communicating with the cavalry, waiting one street away.

John pushed a hand through his hair, tension gripping his body, his torso aching with each agonized breath. Not all of the pain was physical. In that too quiet house were the most important people in his life, and God only knew what was happening to them. The only thing worse than not knowing was the awareness that the situation was his fault.

Caitlin tapped his arm, and he glanced over his injured shoulder. Her eyes glittered at him in the dark. "Mitchell called dispatch. He's asking to talk to you. They bought us some time by saying you were still unconscious."

His gaze slid back to those bright, empty windows. "Did he say anything about them?"

"No. Listen, I'm not sure letting him talk to you is a good idea. I think we should set up a mobile command center, get an entry team in place."

He hated to admit she was right. Any conversation between him and Mitchell was hell-bent for disaster. "I guess you want to play hostage negotiator."

"Me? Hardly. No, I had someone else in mind."

The events of the next few minutes transpired with smooth, secretive ease. A nondescript van appeared at the end of the street, and dark shadows moved into position around the house. John, relegated to waiting in the back of the van, chafed while the minutes stretched.

Sheriff Dennis Burnett adjusted the radio's channels, making sure a tape would record all transmissions. He fitted a pair of headphones with an attached mike, then handed John a pair with no microphone. "Thought you might want to listen in."

While putting on the earphones, John shot him a glance. So Caitlin trusted him enough to put Lanie's life in his hands. "Are you experienced with hostage negotiations?"

The other man shook his head. "I've done it once or twice, though, and completed the FBI's basic training in handling hostage-takers. The Bureau's negotiator team from the Houston office is unavailable since they're at a training seminar. Houston P.D.'s team is already out on a call; they said they'd be glad to assist when they finished that one."

He'd done it once or twice? Basic training? John didn't find the thought reassuring. Burnett frowned at Caitlin when she appeared at the van's open door. The sheriff adjusted another knob and glanced sideways at Caitlin. "I know you don't think you're going in on that entry team."

She smiled a cool, little smile. "I know you don't think you're going to try to tell me I can't."

"What if I said please?"

"She's family."

Burnett sighed, but the sound held more resignation than exasperation. "Which is exactly why you shouldn't go."

"Give it up. I'm going." With one last smile in his direction, she disappeared around the corner of the van.

"I don't know why I even try to argue with her." Burnett plugged a phone line into the recorder.

John grabbed the conversation as a way to keep the worry at bay. He pressed a hand against his aching ribs. "How long have you known her?"

A grin quirked at the other man's mouth. "Since she was ten. Heck, I was engaged to her once. You just have to know how to take her."

How to take the quintessential arrogant Fed? Falconetti didn't seem like the easiest person to deal with, but maybe she was different with Burnett. Lanie could be prickly as hell, and John knew she had colleagues who weren't fond of her. He liked the sharp edges of her honesty, though—a guy always knew where he stood with her. Underneath the razor-sharp exterior lay softer layers, the ones only a privileged few got to see.

An image rose in his mind—Lanie in the small bedroom she'd painted a deep blue for their son, her hands smoothing over a stack of tiny T-shirts and fleecy blankets, her face alight with a joy that had taken his breath. Remorse tightened his throat. She deserved someone to share that joy with, someone better than him. She deserved someone whole.

"So what's the story with Mitchell, anyway?" Burnett's quiet question dragged John from his reverie. "Is he a couple of bales short of a full hay loft or just plain mean?"

"He's not crazy." John wished the situation was that simple. Obsessed was the only word he could think of to describe Mitchell's desire to control Beth's life, to *be* her life. "He wants to own her, and if he can't have her—"

“Then he’ll fix it so no one else can.” A sickened expression twisted Burnett’s face for a moment. “Where do you fit into the whole mess?”

Mess pretty much covered it. “She… I helped her get away from him.”

Burnett’s hazel gaze flickered in his direction. “So the way he sees it, you took his wife and his family away from him.”

As he remembered Falconetti’s suspicions, foreboding shivered over John’s skin. “Yeah,” he said, the words hurting his throat, “that’s the way he sees it.”

Arms crossed over his chest, Burnett settled deeper into his seat. “That’s not good. He doesn’t have anything else to lose.”

Anger born of fear curled low in John’s stomach. “Your positive outlook is inspiring, Sheriff.”

Burnett reached out to fiddle with the squelch knob. “And I’m not going to blow sunshine up your rear end, buddy. In that house is a desperate, obsessed man with a freaking vendetta against you, and he has a couple of human bargaining chips. Make that three human bargaining chips. Compared to that, we have squat."

John latched onto his description of Lanie, Beth and the baby. Slight hope rose. “Bargaining chips? You think he’s going to want to bargain?”

“You could say that. Cait thinks he’s going to try to use the women.”

The newborn hope died under Burnett’s ominous tone. “Use them how?”

Burnett fixed him with a look. “She thinks Mitchell will try to force you to choose.”

At the bald statement, John’s stomach churned, bile forcing into his throat. Mitchell would love possessing that power over him, and John knew there wasn't a real choice to make. Falconetti was right—his own stupidity had thrown Lanie into danger. He couldn't allow anything to happen to her.

If it hadn't already happened. He glanced through the windshield at the still, quiet house. Falconetti's theory remained mere speculation. For all any of them knew, Mitchell may have already taken his revenge. He'd killed once. What was another death if it struck back at John? Lanie could already be dead or dying behind those bright windows.

His fault.

John closed his eyes. Not again. Not Lanie. He'd sworn a long time ago that no other woman would die because of his failures. He hadn't been able to protect his mother. Even though he'd thought he'd protected Beth, he hadn't, not really. All he'd accomplished was making everything too easy for Mitchell. He cursed himself in a shaky whisper.

"You don't look so well. We can handle this. Maybe you should let someone take you back to the hospital." Genuine concern lingered in Burnett's voice.

John's eyes snapped open, and he stared at the house again. "I'm not going anywhere."

"Your shoulder wound is seeping."

He gave his shoulder a cursory glance. Spots of red dotted the turquoise cotton. "I'm fine. I'm not leaving her."

"Which her?" The question came in a casual drawl but didn't fool John for a second. The guy might talk slow, but a quick intelligence lay behind that sharp, hazel gaze. "Which one will Mitchell expect you to choose?"

A pent-up breath escaped John's burning lungs on a trembling sigh. Agony stabbed at him, and a moment passed while he struggled for breath. "Beth. He thinks I'll choose Beth, and then he can kill her in front of me."

"And if you choose Lanie?"

Eyes clenched shut against the images beating in his brain, John swore. "Same thing. Hell, Falconetti's right. Mitchell wants to take what matters most from me."

Denim rustled against the tweed seat cover. "I think the real question might be who matters more—your partner or the mother of your child?"

The phone rang, and John jerked in his seat, ignoring the pain that rocketed through him with the action. His gaze locked on the attached caller identification unit. The call came from inside the house, and Burnett drew in an audible breath before picking up the call. "Hello?"

"I want to talk to O'Reilly." Mitchell's malevolence crawled through the headphones like a living thing. A chill crept over John's skin, even as anger heated his gut.

"Detective O'Reilly is still hospitalized." Burnett's low voice was even. "Talk to me."

"You're one of them. I want O'Reilly." Chimes rang in the background behind Mitchell's voice.

Burnett rubbed his palms over his denim-clad knees, the only sign of nervousness John could see. "Then just talk to me until they can get O'Reilly for you."

"Until I can talk to O'Reilly, I got nothing to say." The line went dead, the dial tone echoing through John's head. He wanted to scream, to remove the headset and throw it across the van, to smash something, anything.

He wanted Lanie out of that house. He wanted her safe, with him.

Shoulders slumped, Burnett passed a hand over his eyes. "Well, that was productive."

John glanced at his watch. Ten to three. "He's in the foyer."

Burnett lifted his head. "What?"

"The chimes. The foyer clock runs fast. It was chiming three o'clock. He's in the foyer."

"Are you sure?" The other man was already reaching for the handheld radio.

"As sure as I can be." John let Burnett's conversation with Falconetti wash over him, his eyes trained on the front of the house.

The pattern repeated through more conversations, but each one was a few minutes longer than the last. Exhaustion and pain tightened Mitchell's voice, and as the tension grew, Burnett's patient demeanor deepened.

John was glad one of them could be patient. The forced waiting and not knowing what went on in the house drove him crazy. He wanted to be out of the van and doing something; he wanted to be on the entry team, first in the house, first to see if Lanie was all right.

The hints of light at the horizon added to the stretching of his taut nerves. Instinct whispered that dawn would not only reveal their presence to Mitchell, but would also be his breaking point. The approaching dawn heralded disaster—John was sure of it.

"Cait." Burnett picked up the handheld once more, and the note of unease in his voice dragged John back to reality.

Her husky voice blended with the static. "What?"

"He's slowing down. The calls were getting closer together, coming about every five minutes. It's been twelve since the last one."

"Sunrise is going to be the crisis point." Resignation hung in her words. "We can't wait for that. Is O'Reilly sure he's in the foyer?"

Burnett glanced his way, and John nodded. "Sure as he can be."

"It's all that glass. He'll see us coming, from the front or the back."

The phone's shrill ring cut through the van once more. Without a goodbye, Burnett killed the connection on the handheld. Silence thrummed over the phone line. Burnett rubbed at the back of his neck. "Doug?"

"I want O'Reilly. Now."

"The man's been shot. He's—"

"He's in the van with you, isn't he?"

John watched Burnett's body jerk with surprise before he spoke again. "Yes, Doug, he is. He's here, like you asked. Now I need something in return."

"Like what?" Mitchell sounded smug, as if he were finally winning an extended game of Monopoly.

"Let the women go."

"You know I can't do that."

"Then one, Doug. Give us one. I got you O'Reilly, now you return the favor."

"Fine. I'll let one of them go." Taunting satisfaction curled through Mitchell's voice.

Burnett glanced over his shoulder, and John read the nonverbal message in his sharp gaze. *That was too easy.*

The knowledge lay heavy in the air. Mitchell would release one of the women. The other would die. John closed his eyes—this scenario was worse than any nightmare his mind could devise.

"Just one thing." Mitchell's voice snapped John's eyes open, his entire body back to alertness. "O'Reilly chooses."

No surprise in that. Body singing with tension, John sat forward, waiting to see how Burnett would handle this turn. "No can do. We're not letting him call the shots. You choose, Doug."

Mitchell hadn't expected that. Silence stretched over the line, and when Mitchell spoke again, anger curdled his voice. "Now, listen to me, you son of a bitch. I said O'Reilly chooses—"

Over the line came the sounds of breaking glass, splintering wood, and multiple shouts. An authoritative male voice barked commands for Mitchell to drop his weapon and surrender. Curses hung in the air, but John didn't wait to hear more. A hand pressed to his ribs, he bolted from the van and made for the house in a painful, limping run.

His lungs burned, and it took him a moment to realize Burnett was at his side. Still clumsy from the painkillers, John stumbled on the front steps, and Burnett reached out to steady him. The front door stood open, the frame splintered, and light and personnel spilled onto the porch.

Mitchell's muffled curses rent the air, and John pushed past a couple of black-clad deputies. A deputy knelt in the foyer with one knee on Mitchell's back and recited the Miranda warnings while another snapped cuffs on Mitchell's straining wrists. Beth sagged against the wall, blood-spattered hands pressed to her wet cheeks.

"Oh my God, John!" She threw herself at him, her arms clenched around his neck. "I'm so glad you're here."

"You okay?" His hand pressed against her spine for a moment, his gaze searching beyond the chaos, seeking Lanie. Where was she? The thick, heavy scent of blood hung in the air. He pulled back, his heart thudding against the wall of his chest. "Where's Lanie? Is she—"

"Get the EMTs in here!" Falconetti's panicked voice carried from the small bath off the foyer, and that note of alarm sent terror racing over his skin.

John put Beth away from him, and she reached for his arm, a beseeching note in her voice. "John, wait, she's—"

He ignored her and steeled himself for what lay on the other side of that door. Blood, the bright crimson startling against the snowy tile. Falconetti knelt by Lanie, fingers that visibly trembled brushing over her throat, seeking a pulse. Her pallor terrified John—the only color in Lanie's face was the dark slash of her eyebrows and the feathery shadow of her lashes. Even her lips lacked color. His lungs constricted.

She looked dead.

Aware of the paramedics clambering up the steps, John crossed the room to Lanie's side, the blood-spattered tile cold and slick under his bare feet. Her limp hand lay on the mound of their baby. He dropped to his knees, and the impact sent pain jarring through his torso. He touched her cheek, the skin cold under his touch. "Lanie?"

"Good God." The paramedic swore under his breath. "I need you out of the way. Now."

Falconetti moved immediately, but John faltered until she leaned down and jerked him to his feet. The harsh move rocketed pain along his nerves, and he backed up a step, watching as the medics cut away clothing, checked Lanie's airway and vitals and inserted an IV line. "What's wrong?"

The medic didn't look at him. "She's got a head injury, and she's going into shock from the vaginal bleeding. How advanced is her pregnancy?"

The question threw him, and he counted back, trying to come up with an accurate number. "Thirty-five weeks. Maybe thirty-six."

"Any bleeding before this?"

"No."

A second medic appeared with a stretcher. "Clear the room, please."

John backed out of the room, his gaze never leaving her face. She was so still, as still as his mother had been... No. God, please, she couldn't die.

A soft touch fluttered over his shoulder. "John? You're bleeding."

He grabbed Beth's hand, her fingers cold in his. "I'm fine. How long has she been bleeding?"

Beth's teeth chattered, blurring her words. "Since we got here. She—she hit her head when Doug... John!"

Rage burst into flame in John's soul. Ignoring the pain clutching his chest, he moved toward the door where Burnett and a deputy were escorting a strangely subdued Mitchell from the house. He'd kill him. "Mitchell, you bastard, I'll—"

Burnett caught him up before he made contact, and John fought against the other man's hold. With ridiculous ease, Burnett pushed him against the wall, holding him with one arm. "Stop."

Dragging his gaze from Mitchell's retreating form, John glared at Burnett. "He—"

Sympathy glinted in Burnett's hazel eyes. "This isn't going to help her. Get yourself together, O'Reilly. Stop thinking about what you want and think about what she needs."

The words quieted the clamoring vengeance. The stretcher rattled as the medics carried it from the bath. Caitlin brushed her hair away from her face and glanced in John's direction. "You should go in the ambulance with her and let them take a look at your shoulder."

Burnett nodded. “We’ll meet you at the hospital.”

Chapter Six

With impatience burning under his skin, John submitted to having the pulled stitches in his shoulder repaired. Lanie lay in the ER room next to his, but with the plaid privacy curtains pulled, he couldn't see what was going on. The level of activity scared the crap out of him—a doctor ordered a CT scan and mentioned coma scale scores, another voice called out blood pressure numbers that seemed way too low and offered the chilling information that the fetal heart rate seemed unstable.

John closed his eyes, his throat tight. *God, please. She wants that baby. Don't. Please don't.*

The young physician's assistant pulled the last stitch taut. "Do you want something else for pain? That local's going to wear off in an hour or so."

"No." He deserved the pain, and he'd take it.

After handing John a sheaf of discharge papers, the PA rattled off wound care instructions that John only half-heard. He shoved the papers in the chest pocket of the ruined scrubs he still wore. Outside the cubicle, he hovered and peered into Lanie's room. Twin IV bags hung above her sheet-draped body, pushing blood and fluids back into her system. A harried nurse glanced up and hurried in his direction, attempting to push him down the hall. "Sir, you can't be here. You'll have to go to the waiting area."

John dug in. "How is she? What about the baby?"

For a second, her face softened. "She's stable. Dr. Lott will be out in a few moments. Now, please, go to the waiting area."

With one more long look, he went. Guilt crushed his throat. If not for him, she wouldn't be in this damned, sorry situation. If he'd ignored the attraction and kept it in his pants, there wouldn't be a baby to risk losing. Mitchell wouldn't have seen her as a target. And she wouldn't be lying there, with doctors struggling to save her life.

Even at this early morning hour, the waiting room was crowded. Haven County deputies formed a sea of green uniforms, and John ignored the baleful looks sent his way. They blamed him, and that was okay. He blamed himself.

A long bank of windows comprised the room's eastern wall. Caitlin Falconetti stood in front of those windows, arms wrapped around her midriff. Burnett stood behind her. The other man bent his head, lips moving in a whisper. Eyes closed, Caitlin nodded, tired worry etched into every line of her face. Burnett wrapped her in a quick embrace, and she leaned on him, the bond of a strong friendship obvious between them.

Had Lanie ever wanted to lean on him that way?

The idle thought brought a fresh wave of guilt. She was eight months pregnant, for God's sake, with a baby that had been a complete surprise to both of them. But if there had been times when she'd wanted reassurance, he hadn't known. She'd said everything was fine, and he'd taken the words at face value, relieved at not having to delve deeper. Shame burned along his skin. He'd failed her in so many ways, starting with the first time he touched her while still believing he loved another woman.

He walked toward Burnett and Falconetti. She looked up, and her gaze bored into John. "What's going on?"

John jerked a hand through his hair. "I don't know. They wouldn't let me in. She's stable, though. The nurse said the doctor would be out soon."

Caitlin tucked her hands in her pockets, her gaze straying to the window again. "Not soon enough. Lord, I don't believe this is happening."

"John?" Beth's soft voice slid over his jangling nerves. The blood was gone from her face, but rusty stains still marred her ivory sweater. Her blood or Lanie's? He shuddered at the memory of all that blood, red splotches against white tile, a small pool beneath Lanie's still body. "I'm going upstairs to Nicole's room. Is there any news?"

He shook his head. "Not yet."

Beth glanced sideways at Burnett and Falconetti. Resentment at Beth's presence radiated from Falconetti's stiff posture. Beth touched his forearm, a quick, light brush of her hand. "Do you need anything?"

"No." He forced a smile for her benefit. "Go see about Nicole. I'll come find you once I know something."

A weary smile flitted across her face, and her fingers tightened for just a moment on his arm. "She's going to be just fine. You know how strong she is."

"Yeah." He cleared his throat of clogging emotion. From the corner of his eye, John caught that odd resentment flashing through Falconetti's eyes again. He watched Beth walk away and rubbed a hand over his nape.

"You know, you don't have to stay if you'd rather be somewhere else." Falconetti's cold voice jerked his attention away from Beth, and John glanced around to find her watching him with narrowed eyes.

"What the hell is that supposed to mean?"

"Cait." Burnett reached out for her arm, and she shrugged him off. "This isn't—"

"Caitlin?" The double doors to the ER unit swung open, and Sheila Dolciani strode into the waiting area, accompanied by the tall, balding man John had glimpsed in the ER with Lanie earlier. "This is Dr. Lott. He's been Lanie's physician tonight. Doctor, this is John O'Reilly, the baby's father."

Lott gave him a curt nod and turned his attention to Caitlin. "I understand you hold a medical power of attorney for Ms. Falconetti?"

Caitlin darted a startled look at Sheila. "I do. We had them written up years ago, when we first went into law enforcement. But—"

Sheila smiled, a strained expression that didn't last long. "She's going up to surgery in a few minutes. We need you to sign the consent forms."

Foreboding slithered down John's spine. "Surgery for what?"

Lott and Sheila exchanged a glance, and she drew a deep, visible breath before speaking. "There's intracranial bleeding from the head injury. A craniotomy will be performed to suction out the blood and relieve the pressure on her brain—"

"Oh God," Caitlin whispered, a hand over her mouth. John shuddered. The idea of someone cutting into Lanie at all made him want to throw up. The idea of someone cutting open her skull was worse.

Sheila's dark gaze flicked in his direction. "And then there's the baby."

She'd lost the baby. The knowledge slammed into John's chest, his heart jerking. He ran a hand over his face, swearing beneath his breath.

Sympathy glowed briefly in Sheila's eyes. "She lost a lot of blood. We've had her hooked up to a fetal monitor, watching the baby's vitals, and they're not evening out like they should. The attending OB/GYN thinks the best route is to deliver him. He may be a little underweight, and his lungs will need to be monitored. But he stands a better chance if we deliver him."

His head snapped up, relieved disbelief surging in him. "She didn't lose the baby?"

"No." Sheila shook her head and glanced at Caitlin. "But his heart rate is slower than it should be, and it's not climbing. We need to get her into surgery."

Caitlin ran a hand through her hair. "Two surgeries? Is she stable enough for that?"

An uneasy look flashed between the two doctors before Sheila spoke again. "We don't have any other viable choices. We've got to stop the bleeding on the brain, and we have to deliver that baby, not only to save him but to save her. We haven't been able to stop the vaginal bleeding."

"Are you saying she could still die?" Fear made John's voice hoarse.

"Without the surgery, yes."

"My God." Caitlin closed her eyes. "Get me the forms."

Sheila held out a clipboard, and John watched Caitlin peruse the papers. Tears shimmered on her lashes, and a couple escaped to trickle over her cheeks. With shaking hands, she signed each copy and shoved the clipboard back.

Sheila tucked the board under her elbow. "We'll get her up to the surgical unit to be prepped."

Caitlin wiped her eyes. "May I see her first? Please?"

Dr. Lott's nod was curt. "Two minutes. We don't have time to lose."

Sheila slanted a reassuring smile in John's direction. "Would you like to come?"

He nodded and followed them beyond the doors marked *No Admittance.* A nurse hovered in Lanie's cubicle, monitoring her vital signs. The stretched skin of her exposed abdomen, circled by a wired belt, glowed white under the bright lights. Her eyes remained closed, her face pale, but some color had returned to her lips. John advanced as far as the bed, hesitant to touch her. His touch had placed her in this situation.

Caitlin showed no such hesitation. She curled her fingers around Lanie's hand and leaned close to her ear. "Lanie? It's Cait."

If she'd expected a reaction, none came, just the steady blip of the heart monitor. John watched her thumb stroke over the back of Lanie's limp hand in a light caress. Her low whisper seemed loud in the eerie quiet of the cubicle. "You've got to get better, Lane. You just have to. I love you."

She straightened and brushed at her wet cheeks, not looking at John. "I'm going to leave you alone with her."

"Thanks." His throat closed. A draft rippled the privacy curtain with her exit. He stared down at Lanie's still form, her chest rising and falling in shallow breaths. On the nights when he couldn't sleep, the nights that had come more and more often in recent weeks, he'd often watched her while she slept. The abandoned way she lay, the soft sighs she sometimes made, her warmth next to him had soothed the tight knot that held permanent residence in his gut.

Nothing about her unnatural sleep soothed him now.

Still afraid to touch her, he leaned close. Her long lashes cast smudges of shadow on her cheekbones, and he remembered the way that dark fringe felt brushing his skin. An unfamiliar dampness burned his eyes. "Lanie?"

Her name left his lips on a rough, hoarse whisper. He brushed a finger over her jaw, let his hand settle for just a second on the swell of her stomach. The faint scent of mingled cinnamon and vanilla tickled his nostrils. A harsh, dry sob dragged at his chest. “Oh God, Lanie, I’m sorry.”

ભ※ဆ

Surrounded by the utilitarian white walls of the surgical unit waiting area, John stared at the television, the twenty-four hour news channel unable to hold his attention. His shoulder and side ached, and a dull pain throbbed through his head with his pulse. His tongue, coated with two cups of vending machine coffee, was a thick, dead thing in his mouth.

The occasional Haven County deputy wandered in to ask if there was news, then wandered out again. Some of Lanie’s friends came and went. Across from John, Burnett sat on the low vinyl couch, one ankle crossed over his knee, an outdated fishing magazine balanced on his lap. Caitlin leaned against the other end of the couch, eyes closed, seemingly asleep, but the tense awareness in her posture indicated otherwise.

Time crawled. John tried not to think about what was happening behind those imposing doors. Tried not to think about what could go wrong.

Elbows on his knees, he dropped his head into his hands and stared at the speckled pattern in the linoleum. *All you had to do was walk away, O’Reilly. Leave her alone. Ignore the attraction and what you wanted to do the first time you saw her. Well, you really screwed up this time, didn’t you?*

He’d been weak, and he’d failed. A shudder traveled through him, and he dragged trembling hands over his face. Another life ruined, maybe even lost, because of him. Somehow, he'd make it up to her. He would. He didn't know how, but one way or the other, he'd make everything up to her.

If he got the chance.

With a deep breath that pulsed agony through his chest, he pushed up from the chair and stalked to the bank of windows on the east wall. Late morning sunlight sparkled off the distant waters of the Gulf. On a normal Saturday morning at this time, they'd be together—walking on the beach, getting housework out of the way, playing a set of tennis, making love.

Damn it, he wanted to hear her fuss at him about not folding the towels the right way. He wanted her bitching at him to get the damned crib put together before the kid learned to drive. He wanted to see the way her eyes lit up when he handed her another shell or piece of polished sea glass to add to the glass bowls that held their collection. He wanted to dodge those wicked serves she had when she was pissed off at him for some stupid, inconsequential reason. He wanted her taking charge in the bedroom, holding his wrists so he couldn't touch her while she rode him and pleasured them both.

He wanted their life back.

The reality of the thought skittered through his brain. *Their life.* Not Lanie's life or the baby's life. Their life.

A nasty voice whispered at the back of his mind. *And what about Beth? The love of your life? You can't have them both.*

He passed a hand over his eyes again. The point was moot anyway. Lanie wouldn't want him now, and there was Beth. They didn't have to worry about Mitchell anymore. What would that mean to her? Would it change her mind?

The thought didn't bring the spurt of anticipation he expected. Instead, weary depression tugged at him. He didn't see how anything good could come out of this mess. No matter what, someone stood to get hurt.

He'd come full circle, and there was still no place to go.

The whoosh of the doors had him spinning around, his heart a dull thud against his ribs. Caitlin was on her feet, piercing gaze alert, confirming his suspicion she hadn't been asleep at all. Sheila, who'd gone to observe Lanie's surgical procedures, removed her surgical cap. "Dr. Haynes, her surgeon, is closing up now. She'll be in recovery in a few minutes."

Caitlin's fingers covered her lips briefly. "So she's—"

"Doing as well as can be expected. Once she's out of recovery, we'll perform a CT scan and bring in a neurological consult if needed." Sheila slid a tired smile in John's direction. "John? You have a son. A little small—five pounds, three ounces, but his Apgar scores are good, his breathing is strong, and his lungs are clear. He's gone to get cleaned up, and you should be able to see him in a few minutes."

A son. The words he hadn't been able to get his mind around last night didn't seem any more real now. Panic curled in his throat. He didn't know the first thing about being a father. How could he? He didn't remember his own father, the man whose name he carried, the young stern face in the photo hidden in his mother's bottom drawer. His stepfather? Everything a father shouldn't be, including the man who'd killed John's mother.

And John had started out his son's life by putting him and his mother in danger. He was off to a great start.

"John?" Sheila's tone made him suspect she'd called his name more than once. He shook the panic away, pain shooting through his skull. "Do you want to see him? I can take you up to the nursery."

He wasn't ready. Seeing him meant he was real. If he was real, avoidance was no longer an option. John tugged a hand through his hair and over his nape. "I...I'll go up in a little while. I'm going to check in on Nicole and Beth."

Wrong answer. Caitlin glanced away with a whispered curse. John ignored her and focused on Sheila. "Can I see Lanie when she's out of recovery?"

Discomfort passed over Sheila's face. "She'll go into the surgical ICU. I'm sorry, but there's a family-only rule on visitors. If things go well, she shouldn't be there more than a couple of days, and then you can see her."

A couple of days? He was supposed to wait a couple of days to see for himself that she was all right? He opened his mouth to argue, but snapped it shut. He'd see what he could do about that later. Right now, he wanted to make sure Beth and Nicole were okay. Then he'd go meet his son.

യ്യ

Beth wasn't in Nicole's room. The little girl slept, her hand tucked under her cheek. John knew his partner wouldn't be far away, and he thought he knew where to find her. Stress always made her nicotine jones stronger. At the end of the pediatric hall, a door opened onto a sheltered balcony that offered refuge for the hospital's smokers.

Sure enough, Beth leaned on the railing, a cigarette burning to ashes between her fingers while she stared out at the waves. She glanced up when John joined her. "How's Lanie?"

He let his breath go in a long, shuddery sigh. "In recovery. They took the baby up to the nursery."

A spark lit in her dull blue eyes. "That's wonderful! Oh, John, I'm so glad for you. I bet he's beautiful. Does he look like you or Lanie? What about hair? Nicole was bald."

At her enthusiasm, a reluctant smile quirked at his mouth. "I haven't seen him yet."

Her smile faltered. "What? Why not?"

"I just...needed a minute first."

"Bull. You're scared."

He leaned his elbows on the railing. "Yeah."

"John. You're going to make a great dad. Go see him."

He shrugged. "Want to go with me?"

Her body stiffened, and the smile disappeared altogether. "No. I'm not the person who should be there."

"Damn it, Beth, it's not a proposal—"

"Thank God for that." Anger twisted her features. "Why the *hell* did you tell Lanie you still loved me? Are you stupid?"

Outrage traveled under his skin. "I never told her that."

She pulled another cigarette from the pack and lit it with shaking hands. "What is with you, O'Reilly? What we had... It wasn't real. You swore it was behind you. Why are you still hanging on to it?"

He wanted to shake her. "Not real? That's funny. I could have sworn that was you with me that night in Atlantic City, screaming you loved me while we made love."

If he wanted to shake her, the desire to slap him was plain in her eyes. "I'd just gotten out of a hellish marriage. You were my partner. I knew I could trust you. You were strong and there for me, and you're good in bed. But that's all. I never loved you. Not really. Not that way."

His hands tightened on the railing until his bloodless knuckles glowed. "Thanks a lot."

A harsh laugh cut between them. "I don't think you know what love really is. It's all mixed up in your head with your protective instincts. You don't know love from duty and obligation. I was someone who needed a knight, and that shining armor was a perfect fit for you. But it wasn't *real.*"

"Yeah." Bitterness dripped from the word.

With a frustrated growl, Beth ground the cigarette out and threw up her hands. "Fine. I love you. Is that what you want to hear? Nicole needs a daddy, and it's been a while since I had a really good lay. The doctor says she can go home this afternoon, and I'm planning to catch a flight back to El Paso as soon as humanly possible. I can't stay here. Want to come with us? We'll set up house."

Anger curled up in his gut and licked at his nerves. "You know I can't go now."

She leaned in, her expression intent. "Why not? I'm offering you what you said you wanted. Me, Nicole, us. The whole shebang—a brownstone, a minivan, trips to Disney World. Hell, we can get a dog."

He jerked a hand through his hair. "You think I'd leave Lanie now? And what about the baby? I can't just abandon him."

"The reality is you left her as soon as she told you she was pregnant, if you were ever there to start with. Write her a child support check every month and get out of her life. You'll be doing her a favor."

Chapter Seven

John stared through the nursery door's glass insert. Plastic bassinets filled the cheerful yellow room, and he counted seven tiny occupants. One of them was his son. He glanced down at the plastic hospital bracelet inscribed with Lanie's name, the word *boy*, and the time of birth. 9:43 A.M. This bracelet was his ticket into his son's life.

No more avoidance. He couldn't turn away. Right now, the kid didn't have anyone else. With a deep breath that set his chest aching again, John pulled the door open. The taller of the two nurses working the room approached, a wary smile on her face. "May I help you?"

John could only imagine the picture he presented—still clad in the bloody scrubs, his nose swollen and bruised. Without venturing further into the room, he held out his arm. "I'm John O'Reilly. I'd like to see my son."

She checked the bracelet and nodded. "If you'd go back to the mother's room—"

"She's in the surgical ICU." Unintentional curtness colored his voice.

"Oh." She looked taken aback for a moment, then glanced at his clothing. "Let's get you a sterile gown and you can scrub up. You can visit with him here, or we can find you a room."

The idea of being alone with the baby scared him worse than facing down a crackhead with a gun. “Here is fine.”

He wished the act of preparing took longer. Within minutes, he faced one of those plastic bassinets containing a small, still bundle. His chest heavy, John stared down at the infant swaddled in the white blanket with wide blue and pink stripes. Wisps of black hair graced a head smaller than John’s hand. One tiny hand had escaped the blanket and lay against his cheek. The long slender fingers flexed, and the minuscule mouth pursed and relaxed in a suckling motion.

His mouth looked like Lanie’s.

The thought slammed into John, and reality crashed home. The baby was here; he was real. Lanie’s child.

And his.

The tall, blonde nurse smiled. “You can touch him, you know.”

He nodded, making no move to do so. The fear was unbelievable. Before him was the smallest person he’d ever seen, and he was responsible for him, for his safety. The future stretched before him, fraught with unseen dangers John had never considered.

God, one day he’d have to hand this kid the keys to a car.

With a slight mocking glint in her eyes, the blonde indicated two Windsor rockers in the far corner. “Why don’t you sit down and you can hold him?”

John darted a glance at her. Hold him? Hell, what if he dropped the kid? She smiled, and he had the distinct feeling she was tamping down a laugh. He gave a slow nod. “Okay.”

Careful of his ribs, he eased into a chair and eyed the deft way she handled his son. With another smile, she settled the warm bundle into the crook of his left arm. "I'll just leave you two big guys to get acquainted."

He wanted to call her back, but pride wouldn't let him. Big guys? He had shoes bigger than this. With the baby's head nestled at his elbow, the other end of the blanket barely reached his palm. John forced himself to relax into the chair. This was almost like cradling a football. He shifted his arm closer to his chest, and the baby stirred against him, an eerie echo of him moving within Lanie's stomach. Dark lashes lifted, and murky blue eyes looked up in an unfocused stare.

A tired smile quirked at John's mouth. The Gerber baby, he wasn't. With the almost-crossed eyes, red skin, wrinkles and nearly-bald head, he looked like a miniature old man with a bad comb-over and an even worse attitude.

That gaze remained locked on his face. John tried to remember anything Lanie had read aloud from the baby books stashed all over the house. Were you supposed to talk to them? Did they understand? Could talking to him make John feel any more foolish than engaging in a staring contest with a baby not two hours old?

"Hi." The word came out froggy, and John cleared his throat. "I…I'm your dad. Is this as weird for you as it is for me?"

The baby watched him with an unblinking stare. Encouraged, John tried again. "I bet you're wondering where your mom is. I know her voice is a lot more familiar than mine is. She's, well, she's sick right now. But she'll get better because she knows how much you need her. She, um, she's really something special… You couldn't ask for a better mom, kid. You know, the kind that cuts your PBJ into shapes and helps you with your homework. Shows up for your school plays."

Everything John's own mother hadn't done. He cleared his throat again. "I'll give you fair warning, though. I'll probably suck at being your dad. Patience isn't one of my virtues, but maybe I can fake it. See, I never really had a dad, so I'm not sure what one is supposed to do. We'll figure it out. But I promise you one thing—you will never see me raise a hand to your mom or say anything bad about her."

Five pounds was heavier than it sounded. His arm ached, the bruise at his wrist stinging. With great care, he shifted the baby to his right arm. A frown appeared between those blue eyes, drawing the thin dark brows together.

"He's about to start squalling." Burnett's voice cut through John's musings. John looked up, heat touching his neck, hoping Burnett hadn't heard him conversing with someone who couldn't talk back. Burnett hefted a small stack of clothing—what looked like jeans and a sweatshirt. "Cait thought you might want a change of clothes. Your house is still closed off while the crime scene crew finishes up, so you're stuck with a pair of Levis and my UT sweatshirt."

"Thanks." John dropped his gaze back to the baby, whose face reddened with each second. His mouth opened, and a series of small coughing cries emerged. Panic bloomed in John's chest. "Oh, crap. Now what do I do?"

"Well, you might try lowering your hand," Burnett offered, wry laughter lurking in his drawl. "You've got his butt higher than his head."

Desperate, John complied, but the crying continued. He glared at Burnett as the baby's sobs intensified, the small face scrunched into an expression of utter outrage. "Now what, genius?"

The blonde nurse approached, a small bottle in hand. She held it out as John prepared to hand over the baby. "Nope, sorry, Dad. You'd better get used to this now."

John took the bottle, glanced at it then down at his son. How hard could this be? He brushed the nipple against the tiny mouth, and the crying ceased. Amazed, he watched the baby suckle with comical eagerness.

"Tilt the bottle up a little," Burnett instructed, dropping into the other rocker. "He's swallowing air."

John slid him a glance. That sounded like the voice of experience. "You have kids?"

"Two. Had 'em young, and we grew up together after my wife took off. Man, look at him eat. He won't be a lightweight long."

Pride struggled to life deep in John's chest. "I guess not." He looked at Burnett again. "Is she out of recovery?"

Burnett nodded, sympathy plain on his face. "A few minutes ago. She's in the surgical ICU. Cait and Sheila went in to see her. She hasn't woken up yet, but Sheila says that's pretty normal. They'll do another CT scan this afternoon, maybe run an EEG—you know, measure her brain waves."

An unseen fist squeezed John's heart. God, he wanted to see her. He glanced down at the baby, wishing she were here to see their son, to hold him.

Burnett cleared his throat, drawing John's attention. The other man leaned forward, elbows on his thighs, hands between his knees. "Does he have a name?"

John shook his head. "We hadn't decided on one yet." Guilt cramped his stomach. Hell, he hadn't even discussed names with Lanie. He'd done his best to pretend this baby didn't exist. Now he had to find a way to make up for that. "Guess he'll have to wait until his mom wakes up."

ଓଃଡଃ

But Lanie didn't wake up. For two days, John haunted the hospital, dividing his time between the sterile waiting area outside the surgical ICU and the cheerful yellow walls of the nursery. With each moment, his apprehension and guilt grew. Not being able to see her only made the waiting worse.

The only consolation in his day was his son. In the waiting area, he listened with Caitlin to doctors explain about states of consciousness and arousal and talk about coma scales. In the nursery, he held and fed his son, learned to bathe him, watched him sleep. And through it all, he prayed as he'd never prayed before and wondered if God really listened to the prayers of someone like him.

The fear didn't go away. Coiled in his chest, it reared a hideous head with every medical conversation. It haunted his dreams when he managed to doze off in one of the uncomfortable waiting area chairs.

Embroiled in another nightmare that was all too real, he gasped awake to find Sheila shaking his knee with a gentle hand. He straightened, his ribs catching with the abrupt motion. "Is she awake?"

Sheila smiled, a genuine expression completely unlike the cold, feral things Caitlin always sent in his direction. "No, but she's off the ventilator. We moved her down the hall to a private room."

Hope stirred and for a swift moment blotted out the fear. "Does that mean I can see her?"

Her smile widened. "It does, but visits are time-limited. No more than ten minutes. And I want you to be prepared. Even with the ventilator gone, you'll see lots of tubing and monitors. Her face is bruised, and the incision area on her head has been shaved."

He didn't care. All he wanted was to see her, touch her, tell her about their son.

"Dr. Ridley is looking for you." At the mention of his son's pediatrician, the fear quirked awake. "He wants to talk to you about discharging the baby."

"Discharging him? I thought... I assumed he wouldn't go home until Lanie did."

Sheila covered his bruised hand with hers. "John, we don't know when that will be. Everything depends on when she comes out of the coma. The baby is gaining weight, he's not experiencing any pulmonary difficulties, and there's no reason why you can't take him home."

Other than the fact that he just wasn't ready. Feeding and bathing and changing diapers with a watchful nurse nearby was one thing. Being totally alone with him was another. "I haven't even been home yet. How can I take him home and still be here—"

"That's another thing. You need some rest and some real food. Trust me, one of us is here all the time. I had to throw Cait out this morning and make her go get some rest. Vince, Cait's brother, was here this morning. I'm here. If anything changes—anything—we'll call you."

John dragged a hand over his face. "I just... I don't want to leave her. And I'm not sure I'm ready to take care of him full time. Isn't there another option?"

Sheila lifted an eyebrow at him. "A couple. One is foster care until Lanie's better."

John shuddered. "Like hell. What's the other?"

"You take him home and hire a part-time nurse. Your insurance plan is more likely to agree to that than more days in the hospital. I can recommend some, but your best bet is

Tristan Ransome. She does a lot of private care so she can pay off her student loans more quickly."

John nodded. Tristan was the tall, blonde nurse who had introduced him to his son. He liked her no-nonsense manner; he could handle leaving the baby with her. "I'll talk to Dr. Ridley later. Right now, I'd really like to see Lanie."

She rose. "Come on."

The room was dim, the sole illumination from the fluorescent light over the bed. The bluish glow cast shadows on Lanie's bruised face. His throat tight, John approached the bed. Her dark hair, swept to one side, highlighted the pale scalp and bandage where her head had been shaved. Tubing snaked under her gown; an IV was taped to her left hand. Monitors beeped in time with her heart and breathing. Without the swell of pregnancy, her body looked small and frail in the bed.

He pulled the chair up to the bed and tucked her right hand carefully in both of his. "Lanie?"

His whisper echoed in the quiet room. Could she hear and understand, or was she too far away? The sensation was much like talking to his son. He cleared his throat, his thumb brushing over her limp hand. "Honey, I hope you can hear me. We have a son, baby. He's real, and he's incredible. He's a little small, but he's a fighter, like you. You've got to fight. He needs you."

She lay, still as an open grave, and his throat tightened. "You hear me, Lanie? You've got to keep fighting, baby, because he's not the only one who needs you. I want our life back. Do you hear me, Lanie? *I* need you."

ଓଃ୫ଠ

John arrived home to find an unmarked Haven County patrol car parked in the drive. He moved up the front steps as quickly as his aching ribs would allow. The heavy aroma of bleach permeated the air and burned his nostrils when he stepped into the foyer. The bathroom door stood partway open, and he pushed it inward to find Burnett scrubbing at the white tile.

With a grin, Burnett rocked back on his heels and wrung out a sponge into a nearby bucket. "Hey. I hear they moved Lanie out of ICU."

"Yeah." The pink-tinged water in the bucket turned John's stomach. "What are you doing?"

Burnett shrugged. "Cait didn't want you to have to clean this up, and the one crime scene clean-up company in the area is booked for weeks. I sure as hell didn't want her to do it, either. I, uh, already cleaned up the kitchen floor."

Burying the images Burnett's words invoked, John tugged a hand through his hair. "Thanks." He plucked at the front of the sweatshirt he wore. "I'm going to change then I'll toss this in the washer for you."

"No problem." Burnett swept the sponge over the tile again, eradicating the last traces of the blood trail. Another grin quirked at his mouth. "Sheila said something about you bringing the baby home, too. You ready for that?"

An answering grin, an unfamiliar sensation these days, pulled at his own mouth. "Hell, no, but I didn't have much of a choice. I've still got to put that damned crib together."

Laughing, Burnett dropped the sponge in the bucket. "Have you ever put one together before?"

"No." John frowned at the knowing glint in Burnett's dark gaze. "Why?"

"Because it's definitely a two-man job." Burnett rose and stripped off the yellow latex gloves he wore. "Want some help?"

Forty-five minutes later, John tossed the screwdriver on the floor and glared at the white-washed pine crib, listing to one side. "I refuse to be defeated by a bad set of directions."

Burnett, sitting against the wall with his hands dangling between his knees, laughed. "You'd think it would get easier with experience. Kids, too."

Retrieving the screwdriver, John glanced at him. "What? That it gets easier with experience?"

"That it *doesn't* get easier with experience. My youngest son was a terror, and all the stuff that worked with my oldest just didn't with him."

"You have no idea how much better that makes me feel." John unscrewed the last plate they'd put on and shifted its position, bringing the crib into alignment.

"Let me tell you, a kid changes everything. Your career, your life, the way you think."

"Yeah." John stared at the caster in his hand and ran his fingers over the smooth surface. One more thing he hadn't considered—how their son would affect Lanie's career. And his. He knew all about killer hours—twenty hour days, calls in the middle of the night. From the beginning, he'd thrived on the uncertainty, the wildness of law enforcement. Somehow he doubted he'd feel the same now, knowing that if he got himself killed, his son would grow up without a father, the way he had. He couldn't do that to the boy.

Burnett gathered the other casters, and they turned the crib on its side to screw on the wheels. Once they were done, Burnett rose and shoved the packing material into the empty box. "Well, I'm out of here. I'll drop this in the trash can out front."

"Thanks."

After Burnett left, John spent a few moments putting the bedding and bumper pad on the crib. Bright-colored fish swam across the blue sheets, matching the ones that dangled from the mobile Lanie had purchased. After attaching it to the crib rail, John touched a silver and blue fish with one finger, setting the fish and starfish to dancing. He glanced around the room, at the way Lanie had stamped her love of the ocean here. More than love for the ocean—love for her baby as well.

He walked out of the room and down the hall with heavy steps. Their bedroom door stood open, and John paused in the doorway. Vanilla and cinnamon lingered in the room, the rumpled sheets mocking him. Their tennis rackets leaned against the wall in one corner. The novel Lanie was reading lay face down on her bedside table. He had the eerie sensation she was just downstairs and would walk up behind him any second now, wrap her arms around his waist and press her cheek to his back.

He ached for her presence in a way he had never ached for Beth's. Reaching into his pocket, he pulled out the infinity pendant and chain. He turned it in his hand, watching the afternoon light play over the stylized swirl. She'd been so pleased with the gift Christmas morning—she'd dashed away tears from her shining eyes and wrapped her arms around his neck, kissing him hard on the mouth.

The memory burned him with shame. She'd loved him, and he'd been too blind to see it. He crossed to her side of the bed and sat, letting his hand drift over the indentation in her pillow. Vanilla and cinnamon enveloped him. He closed burning eyes and swore, the harsh words of self-recrimination hanging in the air with the scent that was so uniquely Lanie's.

How had he not seen it? How could he not have realized that she loved him?

You were too busy thinking with your crotch, too busy feeling sorry for yourself because Beth didn't want you anymore. So busy that you didn't see what was right in front of you all along.

With the slow movements of an old man, he placed the pendant on the bedside table, the chain a silver pool. When she came home, it would be here, waiting for her.

And so would he.

Chapter Eight

An incensed wail mingled with the rising steam in the bathroom. John peered around the shower curtain to make sure the baby hadn't somehow managed to tumble out of the carrier. He didn't think four-day-old babies could do that, but you never could tell. Still strapped in, his son squalled, face twisted into a dried-apple expression.

Shampoo dripped into John's eyes, and he brushed the wet hair back from his forehead. "Sonny, come on. Give your old man five minutes to finish showering."

As he expected, Sonny didn't seem inclined to agree. The howl intensified. How much would it hurt to let him cry a few minutes? John stuck his head under the spray, the sound of rushing water not drowning out Sonny's cries. Then again, maybe being left to cry made him feel abandoned. Neglected. A shiver traveled the length of John's spine. Not his son. With a sigh, he shut off the water and reached for a towel. While drying off, he studied his enraged son. "You know, kid, just because you don't like a bath doesn't mean other people don't."

With the towel wrapped around his waist, he leaned down and lifted Sonny from the carrier. The baby tucked against his uninjured shoulder, he lifted the carrier and took it through with him to the bedroom. Sonny screeched, his entire body scrunched up. Like always, the level of need in that cry unnerved him. How could he ever be what Sonny needed? He'd let Lanie down. What would keep him from failing his son?

After depositing the carrier on the bed, John headed for the kitchen, talking to the baby all the way down the stairs. He brushed his mouth against the wispy hair on the tiny head. Warmth flooded his chest. He wouldn't fail with Sonny. He'd make sure of it. No matter what else happened, this kid would always have a dad who cared about him, who put him first.

"All right, what's the matter? Hungry?" The heartbroken wails subsided a little. John didn't glance at the unpainted drywall patch in the hallway. He'd had someone in yesterday, filling in the hole left by Lanie's shot that didn't find its target. The memories the patch aroused turned his stomach—he didn't need to see it to be reminded how close Lanie and Sonny had come to dying or how close to death Lanie remained.

The rich aroma of fresh-brewed coffee permeated the kitchen, and as he pulled one of Sonny's bottles from the fridge, he sent a yearning look at the coffee maker. He couldn't bring himself to risk trying to juggle a mug of hot coffee, the baby and a bottle. Coffee would have to wait since Sonny had no intention of doing so.

"Just a second." He dropped the bottle in the warmer and rubbed Sonny's back in light circles. He disentangled the baby's clutching fingers from his chest hair. "Guess what we're doing today? We're going to see your mom. She's not awake yet, but I'll bet she'll know you're there, Sonny Buck."

The nickname sent a grin quirking at his mouth, as it always did. Out of desperation, he'd started calling the baby Sonny, as in *my son*, not wanting to officially name him until Lanie awakened. Somehow, Buck had ended up attached to the Sonny and seemed a natural addition.

The act of getting out of the house took much longer than John was used to. No more tossing on jeans and a sweater and heading for the car. He was still trying to master the art of dressing his son—just keeping socks on his tiny feet was a major feat. He lived in fear of snapping a fragile arm or leg while easing it into a garment. Once he had Sonny dressed, the formula bottles, diaper bag and car seat remained to be tackled.

The absolute worst was driving with the baby in the back seat. John found himself driving ten miles per hour slower than he ever had before, watching each intersection for crazed, drunken drivers.

When he finally reached the hospital parking lot, he released a relieved sigh. The exhalation resulted in a wave of pain across his still-healing ribs. Waiting for the soreness to recede, he watched his fingers tremble on the steering wheel, a trembling that had nothing to do with physical pain and everything with fear.

He remembered this helpless apprehension from childhood, born from long hours of gauging his stepfather's moods and later from those two short days spent praying with the fervency of a child that his mother would live. Only waiting for Lanie to wake up clenched his gut with two warring fears—panic that she wouldn't, dread that everything was over when she did.

When he stepped out of the car, a cold, salty breeze tickled his ears and nose. He lifted Sonny's car seat from the back and made sure the blanket protected him from the wind. With his collar flipped up against the chill, he jogged across the parking lot as fast as his ribs would allow.

At the front desk, John picked up a visitor's pass, glad he'd cleared this visit with Sheila. Early in the morning, few people walked the halls, and the waiting room area on Lanie's wing was empty. Eerie silence hung in the disinfectant-laden air.

John pushed Lanie's door open and stepped into her room, greeted by the steady pulse of her heart monitor. The puffiness under her eyes had receded, the bruising fading from red to purple with tinges of yellow at the edges. He eased Sonny's carrier to the floor and sank into the chair by the bed. "Lanie? It's me."

As always, he waited for a response that didn't come. He touched her hand, a careful caress designed to avoid the IV tube. He glanced up at the bag of fluids and antibiotics. "Honey? I brought Sonny with me. I thought if he was close...maybe it would help. You've got to wake up, Lanie. He needs a name, and I...I don't deserve to be the one to name him. Sheila helped me get around that for now, but he can't be Baby Boy Falconetti forever, hon. We're getting on okay, I think. I haven't dropped him yet, but he needs his mom. He needs you."

With cautious movements, he leaned over and lifted Sonny from the car seat. The baby made a hiccuping sound in his sleep, and John smiled, turning his head to look at Lanie's still form. "He doesn't like to be picked up when he's asleep."

He settled the baby in the curve of Lanie's right arm, away from the IV tubing and monitor cords. His hand cupping his son's head, he stroked Lanie's face with his other. Guilt raked at him. It shouldn't be this way. She should be awake, enjoying the first days of her son's life, falling in love with him the way John had.

He didn't deserve to be falling in love with Sonny. He deserved to be the one lying in that bed, adrift. Eyes clenched shut, he leaned close. His lips feathered across her cheek, the skin warm under his mouth. His nose brushed her temple. The sharp, stinging aroma of Betadine had replaced the sweet scents of vanilla and cinnamon. "I'm sorry, Lanie. For everything. I know I keep saying that, but I am. More than you'll ever know."

Before when he'd been this close to her, the sexual need had always blindsided him. Now, he still yearned, but the wanting was different. He wanted her awake, with him. He wanted her to look at him the way she had before, with love in her eyes. Again, he cursed himself for being too blind to see what had been right in front of him all along. What he felt for Beth—that hadn't been love.

The attraction, the overwhelming need he felt for Lanie—they had nothing to do with sexual fulfillment. He hadn't been able to get enough of her because she'd filled the holes in his soul that being with Beth never had. Clinging to his hopeless infatuation for Beth had been a futile effort at self-protection, keeping him from seeing how empty his life would be without Lanie.

Now he couldn't miss it. He lived it, every second. The house echoed with her absence. At night, he woke and reached for her, his hand closing on vacant air. The heaviest emptiness lay in his heart.

Sonny stirred, his tiny face scrunched in a grimace of displeasure. John lifted him before the cry started. With his son cradled against his shoulder, he took the chair by the bed again, the warm weight of Sonny's small body his only real comfort.

ঙ৪৯৪

Bright morning sunlight bounced off the hospital's wide, white steps. John squinted, glad the outside air had warmed while he'd been with Lanie. He glanced down at Sonny, who blinked at the brightness like Mr. Magoo. A rusty laugh rumbled through John's chest, and he winced, regretting the lapse.

"Didn't anyone tell you not to laugh with broken ribs?" Burnett asked from John's left. "It hurts."

"No kidding." John wasn't surprised to see him since he'd met Caitlin in the hall on his way out. She'd been chillier than the weather outside. He joined the other man against the railing and set the carrier on the low brick wall that ran the length of the steps. John tucked one of Sonny's hands back under the blanket and quirked an eyebrow in Burnett's direction. "What are you doing here?"

"Cait's car wouldn't start. Gave her a ride over. Hey, have you eaten yet? I skipped breakfast, and I'm starved."

During the conversation, Sonny's eyes had drifted shut. John watched his son's mouth purse in a suckling motion and remembered that cup of coffee he'd never gotten. He shrugged. "I could eat."

Within minutes, they settled at a sunny corner table near the windows in the hospital's cafeteria, but when John looked at his plate, his appetite vanished. How the hell could he eat when Lanie still hovered where no one could reach her? He laid his fork down and took a long sip of coffee.

"You know, your guilt isn't doing any of you any good."

At Burnett's matter of fact words, John's head jerked up. Coffee sloshed over the rim of his cup, scalding his fingers. Anger sizzled along his nerves. "What the hell do you know about it?"

Burnett picked up his own cup. "Probably more than you think."

"Sure you do." John reached for his jacket. He didn't need this.

"I know it eats you up inside until there isn't anything left for you to give to someone else." Burnett indicated the baby with a glance. "I know you're not responsible for Mitchell's actions."

The words slammed against his chest. John closed his eyes. "Yeah, right. I put her in that situation just as surely as I did Beth. I *am* responsible for what happened to her. I should have—"

"What? Kept Mitchell from getting to her? The way you did Cameron?" The questions hit John like punches to the gut, and he glared at the other man. He wanted to get up and leave, tell Burnett to go to hell, but something held him glued to the chair. "Come on, O'Reilly. Think like the cop you are. What could you have done?"

"I don't know." John pushed out the words between clenched teeth.

"The fact is, some people are just plain evil." Burnett stabbed the tabletop with his index finger. "Mitchell is one of them. The question is this—how long are you going to let that evil run your life?" He tilted his head towards Sonny, still sleeping. "His life? Lanie's?"

John continued to glare at him, but the awful weight around his heart lifted, just slightly. "Are you done, Burnett?"

"Yeah." Burnett grinned and pointed his fork at John's plate. "Now eat your breakfast."

ଓଛ୍ଡଓ

Vanilla and cinnamon wrapped around him; hot fingers skimmed over his stomach. John reached for the hand, encircling the wrist and pulling those teasing fingers to his lips.

Desire rippled through his abdomen, but he wanted more than physical release. “Lanie.”

“What?” Her teasing laugh warmed his skin, her lips feathering along the edge of his ribcage.

“Come here.” He tried to pull her up, into his embrace, but his leaden arms refused to work. “I need to tell you—”

His eyes jerked open, and he stared at the living room ceiling. Nerves quivered under his skin, and he sat up, rubbing a hand over his face. On the television, Jay Leno poked fun at a politician embroiled in a scandal. John shot a glance at the baby monitor on the coffee table. The absence of lights and sound told him Sonny still slept.

God, that dream had been so real. He could still feel her touch on his skin, still smell her. Head thrown back, John rested an arm over his eyes. The urge to shout pushed against the lump in his throat.

The phone’s shrill chirp shot through the room, and John startled, pain freezing his chest for a moment. The phone was on its fourth ring before he was able to grab it. “Hello?”

“John, it’s Sheila.” Elation bubbled in her voice, and hope lifted in his chest. “She’s waking up.”

An unfamiliar prayer of thanks flitted through his mind, and he reached for his discarded shoes. “How is she?”

“She isn’t fully conscious yet. Cait’s with her now.”

“I’m on my way.” He cradled the phone between chin and shoulder, tying his shoes with clumsy fingers. The awkward position compressed his screaming ribs, but he didn’t care. She was awake.

“Would you like Tristan to stay with the baby? She’s getting ready to go off duty and said she wouldn’t mind staying the night over there so you could be here.”

He was on his feet, searching for his car keys. "That would be great."

Impatience crawling under his skin, he met Tristan at the front door ten minutes later. When he paused to give her instructions, she laughed and pushed him toward the car. "I know what to do with a baby, John. Just go see about Lanie."

Doubt shadowed him during the drive to the hospital and along the quiet corridors. The memory of the angry hurt in her eyes rose to taunt him. What made him think she'd want to see him? He'd screwed up, destroyed everything. An icy lump of dread settled in his stomach, warring with the warmth of hope around his heart.

Sheila met him in the waiting area. A hopeful smile lightened the tired lines of her face, but she shook her head at him when he entered the room. "She's sleeping. She came around for a couple of minutes, but she wasn't very coherent."

John jerked a hand through his hair. "I want to see her."

Her smile widened. "I thought you would. You can go in. I sent Cait home. She needs to get some sleep before she falls out from exhaustion."

Nerves holding his stomach in a vice grip, he eased into Lanie's room. She lay with her eyes closed, one hand resting on her stomach, but there was a difference to this unconscious state. John couldn't explain it, but he could feel it, could feel Lanie in the room with him again.

Taking the chair by the bed, he folded his hands around hers and settled in to wait.

Lanie drifted into awareness. Pain came first, a dull thud in her brain and a stinging in her arm. The detestable scent of hospital disinfectant followed, with an odd, rhythmic beeping noise trailing behind. A shiver sent fiery discomfort slicing through her abdomen. An urgent question nudged at her mind, but she was too tired to put the disjointed words together. Her teeth chattered, elevating the thud to a sharp roar.

Warmth. The one warm spot on her body was her hand, and she focused on that sense of comfort.

She opened heavy eyes to find John slumped in a chair by the bed, her hand in his loose grip. She blinked. What had happened to put that lost, tense expression on his face?

His presence made her uncomfortable, sadness squeezing her heart. She tried to think past the pain and fuzziness, the fingers of her free hand tangling in the sheet. What happened to his nose?

Her fingers moved in slow motion, brushing her thigh before resting against her lower stomach. The slight pressure increased the burning tenderness. Under her questing fingers, her stomach was soft and rounded, nothing like the hard bulge she knew should be there. *The baby.*

A deluge of memories rushed in—blood, pain, a madman's voice. *What had happened to her baby?*

She moved her hand, trying to pull away. The only sound her raw throat produced was a weak mew. The effort drained her strength, and black dots hovered in front of her eyes. Weary, she let her lids drift shut. The darkness offered forgetfulness, and she reached out for it, let it take her.

Fingers shifted, pushed at his grasp. That was enough to bring John to screaming awareness. He lifted his head. Lanie's eyes were open. His fingers tightened around hers, and he rose to lean over her. "Lanie?"

Her eyes widened, and her lips trembled. "Go..."

Tears made her eyes glitter, and her fingers moved again. He stroked her forehead, a gentle caress. Joy tightened his chest, and his own eyes burned. "Hush. Don't try to talk."

The tip of her tongue touched her chapped lips. "Baby?"

Pride and love curled through him. A wide grin tugged at his mouth. He wished Sonny were here, that she could see the boy they'd made together. "He's fine. The most incredible thing I've ever seen, next to you. Lanie, baby, I need to tell you—"

"Cait." Panic colored the word, and dread settled in his gut.

He glanced at his watch. "It's almost eight. She'll probably be here soon." He smiled at her, his fingers touching her cheek in a tentative caress. Her eyes narrowed. Foreboding shivered over his nerves, and he swallowed hard. He recognized that look. The same expression had iced her eyes when she'd cuffed him to his hospital bed. "I've missed you."

"Get...out."

He stilled, the smile wiped from his face. Desperation rushed through him in a sickening rush. "Lanie, baby, please. Don't-"

"Beth." She spat the name at him, the heart rate monitor jerking to a higher speed. The single syllable said everything.

John pulled his hand from her face. Was this it? How everything between them was going to end? Damn it, he wouldn't let her go this easily. He had to find a way to make her listen, make her see how wrong he'd been to think he still loved Beth, had ever loved her. "Baby, I know I screwed up—"

"Don't...want you...here." Her lashes dipped, and a pair of tears shimmered across her cheek.

"Lanie." He took her hand again and felt the tension singing in her body. This couldn't be good for her, but he had to try one last time. "Listen to me. Please."

Her wet, spiky lashes lifted. The florescent light glinted off her wet cheeks. John stared into golden eyes that before had always held warm desire for him. This time he saw nothing but ice—a cold, dark lack of emotion. She was lost to him. Her lips moved, and he leaned closer to catch the raspy word.

"Out."

Chapter Nine

"I can't believe you're defending him." Lanie wrapped her fingers around the foam cup, willing them to work. She lifted the cup, and the weak trembling attacked her hand. Rivulets of icy water sloshed into her lap, and she winced. The urge to cry tickled at her throat. She hated being weak, so the last few hours had proved torturous. At least she could sit up, if resting against the elevated bed counted.

Caitlin reached out to help her steady the cup. "I'm not defending him. All I've said is that he's haunted the hospital the whole time you've been here."

"And I'm supposed to be impressed by that?" She took a couple of sips and set the cup down. Weakened by the effort of sitting up to drink, she subsided against the pillow and stared up at the ceiling. The incision on her lower abdomen burned, matching the resentful anger roiling in her chest. "Award him brownie points for hanging around to make sure I didn't die?"

A wry smile curved Caitlin's mouth. "He doesn't strike me as the kind of guy who worries about scoring points."

Lanie shook her head and glanced away. She didn't feel like talking anymore, didn't want to think about John. Tears pushed at her eyes, and she squeezed them shut. She wished she could just blot him out, like smearing correction fluid over a mistake, like having a coma erase days of your life.

Blotting him out wasn't an option, though. Her fingers lingered over her oddly flat stomach again. She would be tied to him the rest of her life now. They had a child, a baby she hadn't even seen yet.

The weak tears were stronger than she was. They pushed between her lids and trickled down her face. "Cait," she whispered, weariness tugging at her body. "I want to see my baby."

"I know." Caitlin's warm fingers covered hers. "Sheila's working on it."

"What is there to work on? Just bring him down from the nursery." Was that thready, plaintive voice really hers?

Caitlin's fingers tightened in a calming gesture. "He's not in the nursery, Lane. They could only keep him two days. He went home with John."

Shock skittered through her, and she opened her eyes. "What?"

Discomfort fluttered across Caitlin's face. "He's a healthy newborn. Without a reason for him to stay, John had to take him home. It was that or foster care."

Feeling out of control, Lanie stared at her cousin. Panic rose in her throat. "He took him home. He has my baby."

"His baby, too, Lane, even if you don't want to face that right now."

John didn't know anything about taking care of a baby. He couldn't do it alone. An ugly suspicion crept through her mind. "What do you mean by home? Beth's?"

Caitlin shot her a level look. "Your home. From what I understand, Cameron went to El Paso a couple of days ago."

Lanie fought down rising fear. Beth had gone to El Paso? Oh God, what would keep John from taking the baby and following her? Nothing. Caitlin was right—he had as much right to their son as she did. Eyes closed, she stifled a raw moan with her fingers. Her life had turned into a waking nightmare that got worse with each second.

Gentle fingers brushed her hair away from her face. "You need to rest," Caitlin whispered, her voice somewhere over Lanie's head.

Sleep. The darkness beckoned, promising shelter from the pain and fear.

☙❧

A soft sucking noise penetrated Lanie's consciousness, layers of sleep falling away. From a distance, a deep male voice murmured, and she flinched from the emotions it evoked—anger, betrayal, pain. *John.* Her eyelids lifted, and she blinked at the brightness.

She turned toward his voice and found him sitting in the chair by the bed. In his arms was an incredibly small infant, taking a bottle with comical eagerness. *Her baby.*

The unreal thought took her breath. The pride and love warming John's bruised face kept it from returning. A sob strangled in her throat. She didn't want him to feel that way about the baby, not now. She needed him to be uncaring and uninvolved, the way he had been during the pregnancy.

He looked up, his navy gaze clashing with hers. He didn't smile. "Hey. How do you feel?"

She felt like running as far from him as she could. Swallowing hard, she brushed her hair from her face. "Okay."

His hand shifted under the baby's head, and he returned his attention to their son. "Sheila said you were asking to see him."

Mesmerized by his gentleness with the baby, Lanie feathered her hand across her stomach. "It doesn't seem real yet."

His jaw tightened, and when he looked up, remorse darkened his eyes. "I know. I felt the same way."

She glanced away, not knowing what to say. She didn't know how to handle this John, and she couldn't allow her defenses to weaken. No one ever got the opportunity to hurt her twice.

"Do you think you could hold him?"

The soft words jerked her attention back to him. He cradled the baby against his shoulder, rubbing the tiny back until a soft belch emerged. Fear and the urge to cry jumped into her throat. "I…I don't know."

He rose and used the remote to lift the head of the bed a couple of inches. As he leaned over to settle the baby in her arms, his clean, woodsy scent filled her nostrils. His throat was at her eye level, so close she could see his pulse throb under his skin. Unwelcome warmth curled along her nerves.

She focused on the slight weight in her arms. John didn't move away, his hand cupping the baby's head. His fingers brushed her upper arm, close to the curve of her breast. The intimacy unnerved her, and she stared down at the baby.

His skin held a reddish tinge, and dark lashes fringed navy blue eyes. Already, his chin showed the Falconetti point and stubbornness. He was hers.

She just didn't feel like he was. He'd been alive, a whole person, for almost six days, and she'd missed all of it. Loss gripped her throat, and she brushed the edge of the blue receiving blanket back, looking at his hands. Ten long fingers, miniature replicas of John's.

Oh dear God, she was never going to be free of him.

"He needs a name." John's voice broke into her panicked reverie. "The records clerk keeps accosting me in the hall."

Desperate, Lanie tried to focus on the topic. She lifted a tiny finger with her own. "What have you been calling him? Kid?"

An affectionate grin quirked at his mouth. "Actually, we've been calling him Sonny Buck."

Sonny Buck? We? She shot a sharp look at him. "We? You and Beth?"

Anger tightened his face, the grin wiped away. "No. Your cousins and me."

Her head pounded, a sickening thud along the row of stitches. "So did Beth have any suggestions?"

"I didn't ask her. I haven't seen her since the day before she left for El Paso. Damn it, Lanie, I tried to tell you—"

"Here. Take him." She tried to lift the baby towards him, but her leaden arms refused to work. He shifted their son into the cradle of his arms, leaving her embrace curiously empty. "You have to go. I'm tired."

"You're not going to let me explain, are you?" Frustration vibrated in his voice.

She closed her eyes, listening to the rustle of fabric and the click of a latch. "What is there to say?"

"A lot." His breath caressed her cheek with the words, and her eyes shot open. He leaned over her, his arms empty, hands gripping the bedrails, navy eyes intense.

"I want you to leave." She turned her face away.

He sighed. “What about his name? Do you have a preference?”

“No. Just go. Leave me alone.”

“Lanie, damn it. Please.”

“Go! Now.”

He went. Her hands covering her face in a futile attempt to muffle her sobs, Lanie cried.

Once the tears started, they wouldn’t stop. She wanted to curl into herself and disappear, wanted the pain and disappointment and anguish to go away. The sobs made her stomach hurt, and her head ached. When she put her hand to her scalp, the feel of the bare skin, returning stubble and rough line of stitches brought more tears, harsher sobs. She buried her face in her hands once more.

“Hey, look what was at the nurse’s station.” Caitlin’s cheerful voice coincided with the whoosh of the door being pushed inward. “Oh, Lanie.”

Lanie hunched inward as much as she was able. Caitlin’s hand soothed over her back in gentle circles until the sobs abated. Lanie straightened and brushed at her damp cheeks. “I’m sorry.”

Caitlin held out a box of tissue. “For what? I think you deserve a good cry.”

“Easy for you to say.” Lanie blew her nose. “Ms. Self-Control.”

Perched on the edge of the bed, Caitlin pinned her with a look. “That’s what you think. Sometimes it helps.”

With a glance upward, Lanie blinked back fresh tears. “Actually, it made my head hurt worse.”

“Sheila says the neurologist will be in later to talk with you.” Caitlin pleated the blanket between her fingers, surprising

Lanie with what appeared to be a nervous gesture. "I ran into O'Reilly in the hall. So you saw the baby?"

A fist closed around Lanie's throat, and she swallowed hard. "Yes. It seems...so unreal, Cait. Like he's not really mine. I thought... I don't know. That I'd see him and there would be this huge rush of love, bonding, *something.* All I felt was panic that because of this baby I'll never be able to put John out of my life. Not really."

Caitlin's fingers covered hers. "Give it time. Once you're home, taking care of him, everything will fall into place."

"Yeah, and when will that be?" Before she remembered the stitches, she shoved her fingers through what was left of her hair and winced at the raking pain. "I can't even hold a freakin' cup of water. Someone has to walk into the bathroom with me. How am I going to take care of him?"

"With help. From Sheila, from me and whoever else we can enlist. But you'll do it, Lanie, and everything will be fine. You'll see."

No, she didn't think she would, and just talking about it exhausted her. Her gaze fell on the small blue and white bouquet Caitlin had placed on the bedside table, and she latched on it as a way to escape the conversation. "Who sent those?"

"I don't know." Caitlin reached for the card. She stilled. "Marie Martinez."

Lanie took the small piece of white vellum. Steve's mother sending her congratulations and wishes for a quick recovery. Oh God. The tears rose again, and she clenched the card in one hand. "I can't believe she did this. She just buried Steve, because of me."

"No." Firmness coated Caitlin's voice. "Not because of you. Because of Doug Mitchell. You and Steve just got caught in the crossfire."

Lanie recalled Steve's good humor and his concern for her that night. He'd been her *partner*, and now he was gone. She hadn't been able to say goodbye, had been unconscious when he was buried. Tendrils of anger slid through her, looking for someone to blame. She didn't have to look far.

John. Everything traced back to him. If he'd told her about Mitchell, that he might be a threat one day. If he'd been honest about his feelings for Beth. If he'd done the honorable thing and not pursued her while he still loved another woman. Hatred and resentment coiled in her stomach, joining with the panic and grief to make her nauseous. "Cait, I need to talk to Troupe."

At the mention of her grandfather, also a local judge, Caitlin lifted an eyebrow. "Why?"

"I want to make sure he can't take the baby and leave. What's stopping him from taking off?"

"I honestly don't think you have to worry about that—"

"I don't trust him!" Her voice rose, and Lanie cringed from the note of hysteria she heard. "Don't you see? I can't ever trust him again."

"All right." Caitlin smiled, her voice soothing. "I'll call Troupe and ask him to come by on his way home. Will that make you feel better?"

Not really, but she didn't know what would. Somehow, she knew things would never be right again.

☙❧

"What the hell?" John stared at the paper Burnett had laid in his hand moments before. The words swam together in an angry haze. "An injunction?"

Face set in an uncomfortable expression, Burnett hooked his thumbs in his belt loops. "She's upset and worried that you'll hightail it somewhere, taking Sonny Buck with you."

"I don't believe this." John crumpled the paper and crammed it into his pocket. Jerking a hand through his hair, he paced across the living room. "Freaking hell."

She thought he'd take their baby. She actually believed he would leave her now, and she'd taken legal action against him. An indefinite court order barred him from taking Sonny Buck out of the state of Texas. Anger burned in his chest, but beneath the fury was a tearing hurt that had nothing to do with his broken ribs.

A harsh chuckle escaped him. "I guess I'm lucky she's not having me evicted, too."

Burnett scratched his temple. "You know, I think that came up, but Cait talked her out of it."

Thank God for small favors. John sank into the leather chair by the fireplace, his head in his hands. He'd been so focused on Lanie waking up that he hadn't thought ahead. For the first time, the enormity of the situation sank in. Her trust in him was demolished. Talking to her, making explanations about his confused feelings for Beth and for her, wasn't going to fix that.

"She's asked that you not come to the hospital again."

John lifted his head and stared at him. "What?"

"She doesn't want you there, and Sheila says being upset isn't going to help her get well."

He pushed to his feet, pacing again. “What about Sonny Buck? Does she want to see him?”

Burnett’s shrug reeked of discomfort. “She didn’t say.”

John threw up his hands. “So I’m not supposed to take him anywhere, but she doesn’t want to see him, is that it? She’s his *mother.* Hell.”

“Look, give her some time. She’s been awake, what? Thirty-six hours? She’s got a baby she doesn’t remember giving birth to, a neurosurgeon telling her everything that could still go wrong, and you’re pissed off because she doesn’t want to see you? You royally screwed up, O’Reilly. You’re lucky she didn’t dispatch Cait to kill you in your sleep and hide the body.”

An unwilling laugh started in John’s throat, but he stopped it before it took hold of his chest. “What did the neurosurgeon say?”

Burnett shrugged again. “I wasn’t there. All I can tell you is what Cait told me. Basically, with a head injury, there can be a lot of aftereffects. Loss of impulse control, headaches, stuff like that. Lanie’s having trouble with numbers.”

John shook off a chill. “Numbers?”

“Transposing numbers in birthdays and phone numbers. Problems with figuring time and some math items they tested her with. The doctor said there may be other issues that turn up over the next few days.”

His anger had cooled into a lump of ice low in his abdomen. Shamed by that earlier anger, he rubbed a hand over his face. Burnett was right—he’d screwed up, and Lanie was paying for his mistakes. He had no right to anger. He had no right to anything except the scourging remorse that did neither of them any good.

He moved through the next few minutes in a daze, not able to remember afterward what he and Burnett talked about on the way to the door. He checked the locks and turned off all the downstairs lights except the small lamp on the end table. On that table lay a photo album, one Lanie had catalogued with painstaking care. He tucked it under his arm and headed upstairs.

In his crib, Sonny slept on his back, one hand curling and uncurling. John made sure he was covered and warm, his hand lingering over the baby's head. "I'm sorry," he whispered, throat tight. "You deserved to come into something better than this mess I made."

When he entered the bedroom, he sank into the chair by the window and stared at what had been his and Lanie's bed. The album on his lap, he flipped the cover open. Lanie's neat handwriting captioned a photo chronicle of their relationship. Tennis tournaments, lazy days on a chartered sailboat, a snazzy New Year's Eve party. In all of them, Lanie smiled, her golden eyes bright with love and laughter. Why hadn't he seen it? Or had he simply not wanted to?

He pulled a photo from its sleeve and stared at it. He couldn't remember where they'd been or who with, but Lanie wore the little black dress with spaghetti straps and sequins that always took his breath. Her hair was up, and diamonds glittered at her ears. With his arms wrapped around her waist, she smiled at the camera, an affectionate hand on his wrist.

But it wasn't the emotion on her face that stopped him. His nose rested against her temple, his eyes were closed, but written all over his face was the same emotion that glowed in Lanie's eyes. He looked like a man in love, like a man who held what mattered most in his arms.

God, it had been right there in front of him, all along. He'd had everything, and he'd blown it. His eyes burned. He'd hurt

Lanie, almost gotten her and their baby killed, destroyed her trust in him.

A droplet splashed on the photo, and he brushed it away, returning the picture to its protective sleeve. Leaning his head back, he closed his eyes and let the tears have their way.

Chapter Ten

"So basically you're telling me I'm screwed." John stopped in front of the window and glared out at the busy Houston street. Behind him, Sonny slept, his carrier on the floor in front of Jeff Reinholdt's desk. In the glass, John could see Jeff's reflection—tilted back in his chair, reading glasses perched on the end of his nose, his gaze on Lanie's injunction.

"I did not say you were screwed," Jeff said, laying the paper down on the desk. "I said, right now I have as much right to that child as you do."

John ran his hands through his hair and paced back to the worn leather chair facing the desk. "So what do I do?"

Removing his glasses, Jeff set them aside and folded his hands on the blotter. "The first thing you do is get a DNA test to prove your paternity."

"I know I'm his father."

Jeff waved a hand in a dismissive gesture. "I'm not implying you're not. You need the DNA results to establish legal paternity. From there, we ask for joint managing conservatorship, or if you want, under the circumstances, you could probably go for sole managing conservatorship. That would give Lanie specific visitation rights—"

"I'm not taking him away from her. That's not why I'm here." John paused a moment and rubbed a hand over his jaw. "What does that mean, joint managing conservatorship?"

"Basically, you make decisions about the child together. One of you would be granted possession of the child, the other visitation. The law specifies every first, third and fifth weekend, plus extended visitation during school holidays."

Sonny sighed in his sleep, and John stared down at him, trying to imagine only seeing him a couple of days every other week. The baby grew and changed daily. Loss squeezed his chest. He didn't want to miss anything, not one second of Sonny's life. In one short week, his son had gained a stronger hold on him than any other person ever had, with one possible exception—Lanie.

Jeff cleared his throat, drawing John's attention. "Are you sure there's no hope for reconciliation?"

John shook his head. He'd spent half the night looking for that hope and hadn't found it. "She won't even see me."

"Well, I called Troupe Cavanaugh's office this morning. You know he's the cousin's grandfather—the FBI agent. Besides being one of the area's most politically connected judges, he's a damn good lawyer. I clerked for him one summer. At this point, it would seem that Lanie's only concern is that you not remove the child from the jurisdiction. She's not seeking possession. The fact that she hasn't asked you to leave the house is good, too. But, John?"

"Yeah?"

"Get the damn DNA test done. Today."

ଓଃ୧ଚ

The hallway looked like ten miles instead of fifty feet. The half Lanie had already walked felt like a hundred miles. With a hand on the wheeled IV stand, she put one foot in front of the other and told herself to stop feeling sorry for herself. She could still walk. Others in her situation couldn't.

"You're doing great," Caitlin said, hands tucked in the back pockets of her jeans.

"Oh, screw you, Cait." Lanie wished the words back as soon as they were out, but Caitlin only laughed her rare, rich chuckle.

"Lanie?" John's quiet voice sent shock slithering over her nerves. She didn't want to him to see her so weak.

With Caitlin's hand steadying her, Lanie turned her head in his direction. He stood a few feet away, his dark hair windblown, the baby carrier in one hand and a small diaper bag slung over his injured shoulder. "What do you want, John? I told you I didn't want you here."

"I know." His navy gaze flickered over her face and away. He swallowed, and she watched the muscles move in his throat. "I had to bring Sonny in to see Dr. Ridley, and I thought you might want to see him."

His voice trailed away, and he shifted his weight. Lanie narrowed her eyes, not wanting to notice how awful he looked. Exhaustion shadowed his eyes, and although the swelling around his nose had disappeared, the bruising remained, a dull purple mixed with yellow. He'd lost weight, his low slung jeans hanging at his hip bones.

She glared at him, glad he looked miserable. "Heard from Beth lately?"

"No. I told you—" He bit off the words, and his shoulders slumped. "Do you want me to leave him with you or not? If you do, I can go grab a cup of coffee."

"That would be great." Making the decision for her, Caitlin stepped forward and took the carrier from him. He handed her the bag as well.

He jerked a hand through his hair. "I'll be back in a little while, then."

One hand wrapped around the metal stand until her knuckles ached, Lanie watched him walk away. She wanted anger and hatred, wanted to feel satisfaction at his dejected demeanor. Instead, despondency weighted her chest.

"Come on." Caitlin smiled and nudged her toward the room. "Let's get you two settled."

The slow walk back to the room depleted Lanie's flagging strength. Once back in bed, she watched Caitlin lift the baby from the carrier and snuggle him under her chin. A wistful expression flitted across Caitlin's face, replaced in an instant with a bright, too cheerful smile. "He's grown."

Caitlin settled the tiny stranger in Lanie's embrace. He was awake and stared up at her with dark blue eyes surrounded by a fringe of dark lashes. She waited for the rush of emotion, the connection she'd heard so much about. Nothing stirred within her, and guilt clogged her throat. This was *her* baby, the one person she was supposed to love most in the world, and she didn't even feel like he was hers.

Oh God, it was worse than she'd thought. She wasn't like her mother. At least she'd never doubted her mother's love. Instead, she'd turned into her father—incapable of loving her own child.

"Lanie?"

At the soft concern in Caitlin's voice, tears swam in Lanie's eyes. She shook her head, blinked them back, and glanced up to meet her cousin's insightful gaze. "I don't think walking was such a great idea. I'm tired."

Caitlin rested her head on her hand. “You know that whole business about instant bonding between mother and child is a lot of hype, right?”

Lanie shot her a glare. “How would you know?”

The baby yawned, his mouth open so wide Lanie could see his tongue, toothless gums, and the back of his throat. The tiny hand lying against his cheek flexed, fingers opening and closing. The weight of him in her arms dragged at her heart. “I wanted him so much.”

The raw whisper hung in the air. Caitlin leaned forward and rubbed at Lanie’s arm, a comforting gesture. “Of course you did. You still do, Lane, but look what you’ve gone through in the last week. Give yourself some time to heal.”

Lanie rubbed a finger down his cheek, lost in the sensation of the impossible softness. Wispy dark hair stuck out on his head and brushed her arm. “He’s so perfect.”

“Look at that Falconetti chin. You’ll have your hands full in a couple of years if he’s as stubborn as the rest of us.”

That seemed impossibly far in the future. She didn’t know what would happen tomorrow or next week, and sometimes couldn’t remember what she’d done an hour ago. The chill of worry stabbed through her stomach again. With a small sigh, he closed his eyes. Lashes fanned over his cheeks. “He has John’s eyes. And his hands.”

The words caught in her throat. She burst into tears, and Caitlin’s fingers tightened on her arm in silent comfort. The baby startled in Lanie’s hold, and his eyes opened. He blinked a couple of times, scrunched his face up, and howled. While sobs and panic racked her body, Lanie shifted him into Caitlin’s surprised hold. “Take him back to John. Please. I can’t do this right now.”

Hands wrapped around an untouched cup of coffee, John stared out the cafeteria window. People streamed in and out of the hospital parking lot, in pairs or small groups, some carrying flowers, holding hands, leaning on each other for support. He watched them, trying to remember a time when he felt more alone.

This is what it would be like, those days when Sonny Buck was with Lanie. Just him. The idea scared him. How was it possible to get so attached to someone in seven short days?

Even worse was the prospect that he'd lost Lanie for good. He had no one to blame but himself. His lack of honesty had destroyed her trust, and he had to find a way to rebuild it. On the drive back from Houston, he'd been able to think of nothing else. The first step, the one that scared the living hell out of him, had sneaked into his mind while he crossed the Wesley Parker Memorial Bridge coming into Cutter.

"Hi." Caitlin's husky voice jerked him out of the reverie. She set the carrier with the diaper bag balanced in it on the table. Cuddled in the curve of her arm, Sonny Buck grumbled. "I think someone's hungry."

The cold lump in his stomach lightened somewhat. He grinned, taking his son from her. "Hey, big guy. Did you miss your old man? I bet you had a good visit with your mom."

He quirked an inquiring brow at Caitlin and frowned at her uncomfortable expression. She sighed and shook her head, pulling out the empty chair at the table. "Her emotions are really close to the surface right now."

With Sonny in one arm, he reached for the diaper bag and the bottle he'd prepared earlier. He glanced at Caitlin from the corner of his eye. "I don't want her worried that I'm going to try to take off with him or anything, but I, um, I did talk to my lawyer this morning."

Caitlin's only reply was a short, cool nod.

John cleared his throat. "I had the blood test done to establish my paternity, but that's it. I'm not doing anything else right now. I don't want her to think I'm going to fight her for custody or anything. I just needed to make sure everything was legal."

She lifted one shoulder in an off-hand shrug. "So you're not going to sue her for custody while she's recovering from major surgery. What do you want from me, O'Reilly, kudos for your sensitivity?"

Dealing with this woman required the patience of a damned saint. John bit back the first words that sprang to mind, the ones that definitely wouldn't earn him any kudos. He shifted his gaze to Sonny Buck's face. Eyes closed, the baby suckled the bottle with single-minded bliss. She was right, though. With Lanie, his track record sucked.

He glanced up at her to find her watching him with a narrow-eyed glare that reminded him of Lanie. His throat ached. "No. I wanted you to make sure she knew that. I didn't want her to worry."

Her harsh laugh grated on his jangling nerves. "You don't want her to worry. That's nice, considering she might not even be here if it weren't for you."

"Don't you think I know that? Don't you think I live with that every second of every day?" His voice cracked, and Caitlin lifted one elegant eyebrow.

"Good," she said. "Maybe now you'll be thinking of her before yourself."

She walked away. John rubbed a hand over his eyes. Despite what Caitlin believed, he was trying to put Lanie's needs first.

"She's worth it though, isn't she, Sonny Buck?" he whispered, feathering a finger over the baby's cheek. Sonny turned in his direction and smiled. John laughed, but a chill stripped some of the proud warmth from around his heart. What if his risk didn't pay off? He'd not only lose Lanie, but Sonny Buck, too. He had to make this work because if he didn't, he stood to lose everything that mattered.

Chapter Eleven

"What do you mean, no?" Lanie pleated the blanket between her fingers in an effort to stave off the panic curling in her throat. The early morning quiet of the hospital pushed in on her nerves. If she never had before, she *needed* Caitlin now.

Caitlin pulled the dry cleaner's plastic from Lanie's white sweater and hung it up on the back of the bathroom door. "Just what I said. No."

"Cait, please." She hated the pleading note in her voice, almost hated Caitlin for making her ask again. "I can't do this by myself."

With a sigh, Caitlin perched on the foot of the bed. "Lanie, you're the closest thing I ever had to a sister, and despite the crap there's been between us over the years, I love you. But I can't do this for you."

"You mean you won't."

"That, too. Damn it, I can't, okay?" Distress crackled along Caitlin's voice for a moment, then disappeared under her customary control again. "I have to get back to Virginia. Tristan will be there when you need her, and O'Reilly seems to be making out okay with the baby. You'll be fine."

Trapped in the house with John, surrounded by memories of the way it had been, the way she'd wanted it to be. Trapped in the house where a madman had brought all her dreams to a crashing end. Oh, yeah, she'd be just dandy. Lanie blew out a shaky breath. She wasn't ready for this. She'd been trying to tell her doctors for two days that she wasn't ready to go home yet. They weren't listening, so she was headed home today.

Home to her baby, and that meant home to John. She wasn't sure what frightened her more—the thought of not having enough emotion where the baby was concerned or too much where John was.

"Lanie?" Caitlin's concerned voice cut across her musings, and Lanie looked up to find her cousin's intense green gaze on her. "You don't have to have him in the house. You can ask him to leave."

"I know." Didn't Caitlin realize she'd agonized over that? While stoking her resentful anger against him, she'd indulged in fantastic scenarios of throwing him out of the house and her life, throwing him out of the baby's life. Only the remembered loneliness of her own childhood stopped her. According to all accounts, John had turned into a devoted father. She couldn't deprive her baby of that.

"Do you need any help?"

Lanie gathered her scattered thoughts and swung her legs off the bed in a slow, cautious motion. "I can do it."

"Are you sure?"

"I said I can do it." The words came out sharper than she intended. Getting dressed was something she had to do on her own. If not, what would she do once she returned home? Ask John? Hardly. Besides the fact that she never intended to get naked with the deceitful bastard again, the idea of baring her post-pregnancy body to him or anyone else bothered her. The Cesarean scar didn't bother her. The stomach bulge and stretch marks were a different matter.

In the bathroom, with Caitlin standing watch outside the door, Lanie slipped the hospital gown over her head. The abdominal incision was on its way to healing, but she touched her stomach with ginger movements. Having him see her when she'd been large with pregnancy hadn't bothered her. The urgency of his desire had made her feel beautiful and sexy.

Sex, she reminded herself. That's all. To keep his mind off Beth. Anyone would have done. With painstaking care, she pulled on the sweater and loose, flowing black slacks. Even the simple act of dressing exhausted her. Hands clenched on the cool porcelain sink, she blew out shaky breaths between parted lips. Her arms trembled from supporting her weight, and she lifted her head, staring into the mirror.

Pulling on the sweater had shifted the camouflaging layer of hair from the incision area. The pale skin of her scalp glowed, a blue-white color. The black stubble of her returning hair fuzzed around the row of angry stitches. She averted her gaze and blinked away an assault of tears. With a slow, shaky breath, she knuckled the tears away. Stupid to be upset about her looks when she was lucky to be alive.

"Hey," Caitlin called with a soft rap on the door. "Okay in there?"

"I'm fine." Lanie pushed down the unreasonable anger that lay banked in her stomach all the time, waiting for the slightest provocation. The effort required to contain the emotion frightened her. She'd always had a quick temper, but had learned to smother it with a self-control that rivaled Caitlin's. This anger seemed to be a separate entity, not a part of her personality.

Eyes closed, she took several deep breaths and hoped her nerves would calm. Sucking up her resolve, she opened the door, ready to face Caitlin, far from ready to face what awaited her at home.

ଔଓ

The coastal drive didn't take long enough. Fiddling with her seatbelt, Lanie stared out the window. Where before the sight of the ocean, the boardwalk and the colorful homes had been her favorite part of the drive home, the familiar landmarks only heightened her anxiety. Her stomach tightened, and her heart thudded against her ribs in a rough, uncomfortable rhythm. The ache in her head intensified.

The driveway was empty—only her car sat under the carport. Lanie took a deep breath and stared at her house, the memories skittering through her mind, pinching her with sharp claws. She pushed the car door open and sat a moment, trying to gather her strength. Caitlin appeared at the side of the car with a smile of encouragement on her face.

Climbing the long front steps took forever and left her feeling wrung out. Blinking back tears, she tried not to remember that climbing them while pregnant had been easier.

The house smelled different, and she paused in the foyer, leaning on Caitlin's supportive arm, attempting to decipher the difference. Cinnamon and vanilla mingled with something cleaner, softer. Baby powder. The weak tears threatened again.

The sheer drapes in the living room, thrown wide, let the weak winter sunlight fill the room. John's leather chair had been pushed to one side to make room for a battery-operated baby swing. A couple of tiny diapers, a bottle of baby powder, and a box of wipes shared the coffee table with the newspaper and a sports magazine. The portable bassinet sat at the end of the couch, empty.

Unease stirred in her stomach. The house was too quiet, too empty. The last time it had been this quiet, it had been far from empty. Remembered fear sent bile pushing up her throat.

"O'Reilly left you a note." Caitlin's voice pulled her back from the abyss. Lanie released her fingers from their death grip on the couch's back and glanced at her cousin. Eyes narrowed in concern, Caitlin handed her the piece of paper.

Ran out of formula. Went to store. Be back soon.

She crumpled the note and John's typical telegraphic words. Panic washed through her in waves. She couldn't do this—couldn't live in this house with him under these circumstances. He had to go. If Caitlin wouldn't stay, she could hire someone. Her lungs closed, refusing to allow air in.

"Lanie." Caitlin's cool fingers caught her wrist. "Breathe. Slowly. In and out. Come on—that's it."

The rush of emotion subsided but left her knees weak. Agony pounded behind her eyes. She rubbed a hand over her face and blew out a shaky sigh.

"We're getting you into bed." Caitlin's voice brooked no arguments. "Can you manage the stairs or do you want—"

"I can make it."

Again, the climb was arduous. If the effort hadn't taken her breath, the sight of her bedroom would have. The stamp of John's personality was gone from the room. The bare top of his bureau glared at her. The closet door stood open, revealing his half to be empty.

Alarm exploded in her head. The note had been a ruse. He hadn't gone to the store, but had ignored the court order, taken her baby and disappeared. Sagging, she groped for Caitlin's hand. "Cait...he...he's gone."

Caitlin's sharp gaze darted around the room, but her voice remained soothing. "We don't know that—"

"Check the baby's room." She envisioned it in her mind, the bureau drawers open, the tiny T-shirts and blankets gone. The panic in her voice frightened her. Caitlin made no effort to move, and the fearful anger flashed through her again. "Now! Please!"

Eyes closed, Lanie slumped against the door frame. Why had she trusted him? She should have known he'd do something like this—hadn't he shown her he couldn't be counted on? Tears slipped down her face and clogged her throat. He could be anywhere.

"Lanie, calm down." Caitlin's hand smoothed the tears from her cheeks. "His clothes are in the baby's closet, and it looks like he's been sleeping on the daybed in there. He just moved out of your room."

Her eyes snapped open. "Are you sure?"

"As sure as I can be. Want me to check the bathroom?" Wry patience colored the words.

Lanie nodded. Caitlin disappeared into the Jack-and-Jill bathroom between the two bedrooms and returned moments later. "All his toiletries are still here. Looks like he went to the store. I tell you what. You get into bed and give me his cell phone number. I'll call and find out exactly where he is."

Exhausted, Lanie let Caitlin put her to bed. The smooth sheets smelled clean and fresh, with no trace of John's scent. Lanie drew the covers to her chin. Caitlin picked up the pad and pen from the nightstand. "What's his cell number?"

Eyes closed, Lanie searched her memory for the familiar number. The digits didn't come. She reached out for them, and nothing happened. A void answered her. Tears slipped between her lashes, and she lifted them to stare up at Caitlin. "I can't remember."

"Okay." Caitlin brushed the damp hair away from Lanie's face. "You don't worry. I'll handle it."

Don't worry? She couldn't remember a phone number she knew by heart. What else had she lost? She clutched the pillow, the fear growing until it pulsed in the room, an entity unto itself.

ଔଔ

When Lanie woke, darkness lay outside the window. The bedside light glowed, casting shadows in the empty closet. She lay on her side, staring at the bare hangers on the rod. A cold lump settled in her stomach.

Delicious aromas hung in the air—the scent of sizzling steak and spicy peppers. The lump grew. John was cooking. Male voices drifted up the stairs, and Lanie recognized Dennis Burnett's deep drawl. She forced her muscles into relaxation. If Dennis were here, Caitlin hadn't abandoned her yet. She wasn't alone with John.

She closed her eyes, shutting out the sight of that empty closet. With a deep breath, she shifted her thoughts to the doctor's discharge instructions. Rest, limited physical activity, keep her stitches—both sets—clean and dry. Nothing but sponge baths until the incisions healed. She shuddered, wanting nothing more right now than a long soak in the oversized tub.

Unbidden, the memory rose of the last time she'd soaked in that tub. John shucking his shirt and pants so that the candlelight gleamed along the taut muscles of his arms, stomach, thighs. His deep voice rumbling along her nerves as he climbed into the tub with her, water sloshing onto the floor. Warmth flashed through her, followed by the unrelenting anger. That was not what she needed to remember—she needed to remember his deceit, what his wide grin kept hidden from her.

Clinging to the anger, she opened her eyes and stared at the ceiling. She just had to keep reminding herself of the way he'd pretended with her, and while he played daddy with the baby, she would count all those missed doctor's appointments.

"Hey, you're awake."

With cautious movements, she shifted to sit against the pillows and met Caitlin's affectionate gaze. "How long have I been asleep?"

"A couple of hours." Caitlin came into the room and sat on the foot of the bed, feet tucked under her. Her linked hands hugged her knees in a loose hold. "Feel better?"

"I guess." Lanie's gaze strayed to that empty closet again. She pulled it back with an effort but avoided the knowing expression in Caitlin's green eyes. "Did you book a flight?"

Caitlin nodded. "I'm staying a couple more days, just until you get settled in. Dennis is here to see how you're doing."

Male laughter rumbled up the stairs, and Caitlin shot a cynical glance at the door. Lanie pulled her knees up as far as her sore stomach would allow. "Sounds like male bonding."

Caitlin brushed her hair back. "Seems O'Reilly shares my ex's obsession with old cars. They've been discussing their dream rides for the last hour. That, and swapping cop stories. Are you hungry? If you don't feel like coming downstairs, I'll bring something up and hang out with you."

"No." Lanie shook her head and immediately regretted the movement. She might as well remind him right now that he only remained in the house because she allowed him to.

Recuperating or not, she had no intention of being a prisoner in her own bedroom. "I'll come downstairs."

The whitewashed pine table held the bright Mexican pottery plates they'd found at a junk shop in Corpus Christi. A platter of steaming stuffed tomatoes sat next to a large bowl of mixed greens. Ice water sparkled in swirled painted goblets, and fury sizzled along her nerves. Beth had given her those goblets for her last birthday. Was he that insensitive?

Dumb question, Falconetti. The man is oblivious to everything but his own wants and needs. Don't forget that.

She dug her fingers into the hard wooden chair back. In the kitchen, John transferred shrimp skewers from the stovetop grill to another platter, and Dennis arranged strip steaks next to the seafood. Hurt seared through her. When Caitlin had called and said she was visiting for a couple of days, this was what Lanie wanted—dinner, laughter, happiness. Only this wasn't that—this was a travesty of that vision.

Like having a baby with a man who didn't love her.

Glad her white-knuckled grip on the chair hid her trembling hands, she watched Caitlin bend over the bassinet. "He's sound asleep."

Lanie looked at the baby and wondered if her face showed as much wistful hunger as Caitlin's. Head covered by a fuzzy blue hat with embroidered ducks, he lay on his back, arms on either side of his head. An impulse to pick him up and hold him close surged through her, but the unrelenting fear kept her still.

"Wait until two in the morning." John's dry voice near her ear sent a startled quiver over Lanie's skin. He leaned around her to set the platter of steak and shrimp on the table. His clean, spicy scent filled her nose. "He'll be wide awake and ready to tank up."

His hand rested on the chair back next to hers, and she could feel the warmth his skin radiated. She stepped back and glared at him, but without a word, he pulled out the chair for her and walked back to the kitchen.

After a brief hesitation, she sat, hoping Caitlin would take the seat next to hers. Instead, her cousin sat across the table, so when the men joined them, John sat inches away from Lanie. With him so close she could feel the warmth of his body, she was glad for the activity of passing platters, filling plates and eating. Lost in the effort of ignoring him, she took several minutes to catch the direction of Dennis and John's conversation.

"So the desk work doesn't bother you?" John stabbed a shrimp with his fork.

Dennis lifted his water goblet. "Only at budget time. I still get out on the road every so often, and that relieves the monotony."

"But your hours are regular?"

"Pretty much. So you're seriously considering this?" Dennis stretched his arm along the back of Caitlin's chair, his fingers brushing her upper arm.

John shrugged. "I've got a couple of months of leave left, so I don't have to rush into a decision. But, yeah, I'm looking at it. I passed my sergeant's exam—"

"You passed your exam?" The words slipped out before Lanie could stop them. He'd been waiting on those results forever.

With a quick glance at her, John nodded. "Yeah. I tried to tell you, but it was the same day the baby furniture was delivered. You weren't real focused on what I was saying... It doesn't matter."

She ran her fingertip around the rim of her goblet, trying to suppress the tiny spurt of guilt. Had she been so focused on the nursery furniture that she'd misread his excitement? "So you'll advance to sergeant detective, right?"

He chuckled, a low, self-deprecating sound. "Or desk sergeant in the records division."

Desk sergeant? During the last year, she'd watched him thrive on the challenges of working homicide, and he was talking about a desk job? Who was this man, and what had he done with the real John O'Reilly?

She looked for answers during the remainder of dinner, but didn't find any. Listening to the men talk about hot rods, she poked at her food. She wanted the evening over, but didn't want Caitlin to go either.

The inevitable couldn't be postponed, though. Finally, with Dennis claiming exhaustion, Caitlin stood to hug Lanie. "You don't have to walk us out. I'll see you tomorrow, okay?"

"Sure." Unease gathered in her stomach, but Lanie forced a smile. As John walked them to the door, she rose and began stacking plates.

"I'll get those." Laughter tinged John's voice, and she startled, unaware until he spoke that he'd returned to the room. She was suddenly, achingly aware of being alone with him.

"What is so funny?" she snapped.

He set the plates on the counter and returned for a pair of goblets. "Your cousin and your boss. He's still hot for her, and she has no clue."

"What are you talking about?"

"You didn't catch it?" He shot a glance over his shoulder at her, a grin quirking at his mouth. "Hell, Lanie, she accidentally nudged his leg under the table. I thought he'd come out of his skin."

"And *you* would notice that."

He lifted the platters. "Actually, I was thinking how much I missed having you tease me under the table. How much I miss you, period."

His words left her speechless. In the bassinet, the baby stirred with a soft cough. Lanie watched John lean over him, adjusting the blanket. The affection on his face was all too real, everything she'd dreamed of seeing on his face when he looked at their son. The emotion, the conversation, the enforced closeness was all too much.

The anger snapped to life. "What are you doing?"

He straightened to look at her. Wariness took over his navy gaze. "What do you mean?"

Lanie waved a hand at the table, the living room, the bassinet. "This. Cooking. The whole perfect-daddy thing. The desk sergeant's job. What are you doing?"

He swallowed, the muscles in his throat moving in a convulsive thrust. "Honey, I—"

"Don't you dare call me that." When he reached for her, she shoved him away, the exhausting effort barely moving him. She flung out her hands again, and the jerky motion toppled a goblet. Water flowed across the table, but neither of them moved. "Do you think my letting you stay changes anything?"

He stared at her, his face pale and gaunt, and she hated him for staying, for not leaving when he'd had the chance to go with Beth. She leaned closer, teeth clenched to prevent her from screaming at him, her voice a raw whisper instead. "It doesn't matter what you do. Nothing changes what you did."

Water dribbled onto the floor, a muffled splatter rising as it hit the carpet. He shook his head. "Don't you think I know that? I'm trying to show you—"

"No." She shook her head, pain shooting along the incision, digging deep into her senses.

"I know I hurt you. I'm sorry."

"Hurt me?" The anger flared, drowning the pain, drowning everything but the overwhelming urge to strike back. "You ruined my life. You ruined everything! I wish I'd never met you, that I'd never gotten..."

The awful words died in her throat, and she stared at him, his blue eyes blazing in his pale face. He swallowed again. "I'm sorry for a lot of things, Lanie, but I can't be sorry about that baby. Not about having him."

She backed away, shaking her head. Why was he saying this now? Why not when it would have mattered? She forced a whisper past numb lips. "I hate you, O'Reilly."

Instead of fleeing as she wanted, she took the stairs with maddening slowness, feeling his gaze on her the whole way. In the bedroom, she remembered the sleeping baby and restrained the urge to slam the door. The empty closet mocked her, and she fought the racking sobs attacking her body. Curled up on the bed, she wrapped her arms around a pillow and stared out at the waves.

Light glittered along a silver pool on her nightstand. Reaching out, she tangled her fingers in the silver chain and lifted the infinity pendant. It dangled from her hand, light reflecting along the links and the stylized swoop. She wrapped her hand around the pendant and drew it close, the edges cutting into her palm.

Chapter Twelve

Lanie's eyes flickered open. The harsh cries of a demanding newborn filtered through the wall. The wails built to a crescendo as Brannigan McCall O'Reilly, finally named for his grandmothers' maiden names during an uneasy truce between his parents, let everyone know he was awake and not happy about it. Lanie waited for the sound of John's sleep-roughened voice as he soothed the baby.

No deep voice rumbled, and the crying continued. She sat up, straining her ears. Where was John? Pushing back the covers, she slid from the bed and padded through the bathroom to the nursery. She stopped in the doorway, transfixed.

Clad only in boxer briefs, John sat in the Windsor rocker by the window, Sonny Buck cradled against his shoulder. Eyes closed, he moved the chair in a slow motion with one foot and rubbed his son's tiny back in circles. His demeanor spoke of the infinite patience Lanie had seen in all of his interactions with Sonny.

John hummed, his stroking fingers moving in a similar rhythm. Eric Clapton. "Wonderful Tonight." She wanted to laugh at his choice of lullabies, but a rapid crush of memories took her breath. John owned every Clapton CD in existence, and how often had they danced to that very song, her arms around his neck, his hands urging her closer?

Those same long-fingered hands cradled her baby with strength and tenderness. A lump settled in her throat. As hard as she'd tried over the five days she'd been home to harden her heart and cling to her hatred, this John kept slipping under her defenses. The discrepancy kept her caught between anger and wanting. How could he be the father she'd wanted him to be, but not the man she wanted in her life?

More and more she had to remind herself of all the reasons why she couldn't forgive him. More and more, as watching him with Sonny Buck forced her to see the changes in his personality, the arguments rang hollow. More and more, she wanted to be drawn into that circle of love and affection.

But the baby is different. John didn't love you before. What makes you think he would now?

Sonny Buck's cries drifted into snuffles, and his small body grew still under John's touch. "Wonderful Tonight" faded to silence, and Lanie tensed, not wanting John to find her watching him but unable to turn away. His long lashes lifted, and she stared into the intensity of his dark blue gaze.

The rocker stilled. John didn't smile. "Sorry if we woke you. He's having a rough night. I think his stomach hurts."

She fingered the edges of her hair. "That's okay. I heard him crying and just wanted to check..."

Her voice died away. The dim light glinted off John's bare skin. John pushed out of the chair and crossed to the crib to lay Sonny Buck down. Lanie watched the ripple of muscle under his skin and averted her eyes from the narrow line of dark hair that arrowed beneath his boxer briefs.

"I think he's down this time." John's gaze flickered her way. He glanced down the line of her body then back up to her face, holding her gaze with his.

Her pajama pants and cami top covered everything, but she felt naked and exposed under that look. Too aware of the quiet surrounding them, she dropped her gaze. "I'll just go back to bed, then. Goodnight."

His quiet voice shivered over her raw nerves. "Goodnight."

Hands pillowed beneath his head, John stared up at the blue and silver fish stenciled on the ceiling. Exhaustion gripped his body, giving him the sensation of moving in thick mud, but sleep wouldn't come. Etched into his mind was that image of Lanie, clad in the too-cute pink polka dot pajamas he'd bought last Valentine's and looking at him with soft, hot eyes. His body stirred, and he gritted his teeth.

Several times over the past few days, he'd caught that same look in her eyes when she thought he wasn't looking at her. Fighting down hope, he wondered if she saw the same hunger on his face. Not that it mattered. He wanted her, but he wanted more. He wanted everything. With that goal uppermost in his mind, he wouldn't settle for just the physical with her.

Mentally, he ticked off the number of leave days he had left. Lanie regained physical strength every day, and soon she wouldn't need him in the house. He had no doubt what would happen then, unless he could convince her first that he could be trusted, could be worthy of her and Sonny Buck. He needed time, and time was the one thing he didn't have.

ଔଷ

With Cary Grant on television and Sonny Buck in his bassinet, Lanie lay on the couch. Half asleep, she listened to John move around upstairs while he put laundry away. Her head ached despite the prescribed pain relievers and the healing scalp incision felt tight and itchy. Edgy and miserable, she pondered a walk on the beach, but her flagging energy made the idea unattractive.

The doorbell rang, and she moved from the couch with a quick glance at Sonny Buck. He slept on, and she went to the door, the now-familiar revulsion shivering over her skin as she passed the foyer bath. She couldn't even walk into that room yet.

A peek through the security hole sent the memories into oblivion and settled old stresses and uncertainties back into place. Her father stood on the steps. She wondered for one wild, brief moment if she could get away with not opening the door. For a second, even wilder moment, she considered retreating upstairs and letting John handle everything.

She drew herself up and took a deep breath. Leaning on John wasn't in her plans anymore. Her damp palms slid on the doorknob, but she managed to open the door. Without smiling, she regarded her father. "Hello."

"Elana." He smiled, but his eyes, the same golden shade as her own, remained cold. Her stomach clenched. Why did looking at him always send her back to that desperate, insecure girl she'd been? "You're looking well."

Was he on drugs? Her face remained drawn with huge dark bags beneath her eyes, and she was sure her hair exposed her lovely new bald spot, complete with Frankenstein stitches. Even John wasn't deceitful enough to say she looked good right now. "Thank you. Would you like to come in?"

He stepped into the house, his sharp gaze darting around the foyer. Eyeing his custom suit and Italian shoes, she wished she'd bothered to get dressed. Almost twelve o'clock, and she still wore pajamas. The impulse to please him, to impress him, angered her. She indicated the living room with a curt gesture. "Please, sit down."

Adjusting the razor-sharp pleat on his trousers, he took John's leather chair and darted a glance at the bassinet. Well, that explained a lot. An icy lump dropped into her stomach. Of course he wasn't here for her.

She returned to the couch, wishing Caitlin hadn't gone back to Virginia. Caitlin's icy disdain always matched up better against Lucas Falconetti's glacial emotions than Lanie's spitfire temper. She picked at a stray thread on the hem of her pajama pants. "You didn't have to come all this way."

Not three weeks after she'd almost died, anyway. At least she had to give John credit for hanging out at the hospital during those first few days.

Her father's easy shrug reminded her of Caitlin's. "I had a meeting in Houston. An hour or so more didn't seem too far."

John's bare feet thudded on the stairs, forestalling the need for her reply. "Lanie, who was at the door?"

He appeared at the bottom of the stairs, and she saw him through her father's eyes—mussed dark hair, a shadow of stubble on his jaw, oft-washed Springsteen T-shirt, faded jeans with a hole in one pocket. A working-class Irish cop who knocked up the disappointing daughter and didn't even bother to marry her.

John paused, and she could see him measuring her father as well. "John," she said, rising to her feet, "this is my father, Lucas Falconetti. John O'Reilly."

Her father stood, and the two men exchanged a brief handshake. Her legs trembling, Lanie sat again and tucked her feet under her. John joined her on the couch, and Lanie resisted the urge to move closer to him.

Silence settled over the room. Lanie had never figured out the right things to say to the man who wished she'd never existed. During her teen years, she'd perfected the art of saying the wrong thing or refusing to speak at all. The familiar rebellious urge to stretch the silence sprang to life.

Lucas crossed one ankle over his knee. "You're feeling better, Elana?"

Her fingernails cut into her palms. "I'm fine."

"Good, good." Her father nodded. "Sheila has been good enough to keep me updated on your condition."

She supposed being able to say that made him feel better. From the corner of her eye, Lanie saw John's hands clench on his knees. She shrugged. "You know Sheila. She likes to be helpful."

He nodded again, adjusting the cuff link at his left wrist. "She says the baby is healthy as well."

Maybe he reserved the famous subtlety for his business dealings. Aware of John's increasing tension, Lanie eyed her father. "Yes."

"Does he have a name yet?" The first hint of real emotion flickered over Lucas's face. Pride, Lanie thought. Resentful anger licked at her stomach.

She tilted up her chin. "Brannigan McCall O'Reilly."

"I see." Distaste curled Lucas's full lower lip. The use of her mother's maiden name hit home, she thought. What had he expected? Lucas Giovanni Falconetti II? For the first time, she was glad the baby bore John's surname.

"But we call him Sonny Buck." A grin tugged at her mouth.

Lucas's mouth thinned. "I see you share your mother's fondness for common nicknames."

Lanie narrowed her eyes at him, her temper sparking. "I always thought nicknames were a Falconetti tradition as well. When was the last time anyone referred to Vince as Vincent or Tony as Anthony?"

"The boy deserves a name he can be proud of," Lucas snapped.

"Like yours?"

"He has one." John's simultaneous words were quiet, cold, deadly. Palpable anger emanated from his tense body.

With a deliberate gesture, Lucas straightened his tie. "I wouldn't have been disappointed to have my first grandson named for me. I'm also more than willing to offer assistance while you get back on your feet, so to speak."

Suspicion nudged at Lanie. She crossed her arms over her chest. "Assistance?"

"With your physical limitations, the demands of a newborn must be overwhelming. Carol and I would be more than happy to look after him during your recuperation."

They could kiss her sweet ass, too. Lanie bit back the words. Her baby in Carol's clutches? Her stepmother made Caitlin at her coldest seem like tropical St. Tropez. She gritted her teeth. "John's here to help me. We're getting along fine, even with my *limitations*."

Irritation tightened Lucas's face. "Elana, I can give him the best of everything—schools, opportunities, connections."

He still didn't see. He thought money and all it provided was enough. When she spoke, her voice shook. "He has everything he needs right here."

Her father's cold gaze flickered to John. "What kind of life can the two of you offer him? You couldn't even be bothered to make him legitimate."

Hands clenched, John was on his feet before Lanie sensed him moving. "You need to leave."

Lucas didn't move, a slight smile playing over his mouth. "This is my daughter's house. I don't believe you have the right to ask me to do anything."

John took a step forward, and Lanie scrambled to her feet. A hand on John's arm, she glared at her father. "Well, your daughter is telling you to get the hell out. And don't bother to come back."

He rose, cold anger glinting in his eyes. "You'll regret this, Elana."

She laughed, feeling free of him for the first time ever. "Oh, sure I will. What are you going to do, shut me out of your life?"

"Do not think you'll be able to come to me for help later."

"I won't. I don't *need* you." One hand still on John's taut arm, she pointed to the foyer with the other. "You remember the way out, right?"

With one last glare, he strode from the room, and moments later, the door clapped shut. Lanie darted a glance at Sonny Buck, but he slept on. Under her fingers, anger vibrated through John's muscles. The same anger tightened his voice. "Is he always like that?"

Her shaky laugh matched her suddenly weak legs. She clutched his arm for support. "Usually, he's worse. You should have heard him when I told him I was becoming a cop and not going for a law degree."

"My God, what a bastard." John jerked a hand through his tousled hair and smiled down at her. "You're incredible, did you know that?"

The affection glowing in his navy gaze set her nerves jangling. She dropped her hand from his arm, her fingertips still tingling from the contact. "He may be a bastard, but my mother loved him. God, did he make her pay for that. I don't think he ever forgave me, either."

"Lanie, what are you talking about?"

The surge of adrenaline faded. She moved closer to the bassinet, sadness clutching at her heart. In his sleep, Sonny Buck's mouth moved in a suckling motion. She closed her eyes. "He was right, you know."

"What do you—"

"He deserves better than us." The yawning void of her childhood opened before her. She shuddered at the thought of her baby enduring that.

"God, Lanie, don't. Money isn't everything. You know that."

"I'm not talking about money." She sighed and opened her eyes, staring out at the glassy Gulf. With a shrug, she turned to face him. "He deserved to come into something better than us. He deserved a real family."

"It's not too late. We could make it better." The naked pleading in his eyes made her stomach jump. "Lanie, I—"

"No." She shook her head, sadness curling around her heart. How could anything be salvaged from nothing? "I'm tired, and my head is killing me. I'm going to lie down for a while."

He didn't reply, and she walked away. At the foot of the stairs, she turned and looked back. "John?"

When he didn't turn, she sighed. "For what it's worth, you're already a better father than he ever was."

ଔଓ

A quiet, dismal air hung over the dinner table. Lanie picked at her food, pushing a green bean around her plate with her fork. Two months remained of John's leave. She darted a glance at him. "When are you going to start looking for a new place?"

His head jerked up, and the look he shot her bordered on a glare. "I don't know. Soon."

She stabbed a tine through the hapless vegetable. "I just know rentals can be tough to find sometimes. It might take a while."

"Tomorrow soon enough for you?" He lifted his glass in her direction.

Sadness flowed through her. "John, I'm not trying to—"

The doorbell pealed, cutting off her words. John pushed away from the table and tossed his napkin by his plate. "Can't wait to see who that is."

Her appetite gone, Lanie laid her fork across her plate. She covered her face with her hands. They weren't going to be able to do this. All they succeeded in doing was hurting each other.

"Hey, gorgeous, how are you feeling?" A familiar male voice brought her head up. Casey McInvale, another detective from John's precinct, grinned at her. She liked Casey, always had. He and his girlfriend had often joined her and John for Saturday morning tennis games.

"I'm fine. How about you?" She rose as he came around the table to give her a swift hug. He pulled back, concern glinting in his brown eyes. "And how's Lisa?"

"She's good. She wants to come see you, but didn't want to wear you out with visitors just yet. She's dying to see the baby."

Lanie smiled, the expression feeling tight and fake. "Tell her to come. I'd love to see her."

His grin widened. "I'll do that."

Indicating the folders he held, Lanie stepped away. "Well, I know you didn't come just to see me. I'll leave you two alone."

"I was just dropping these off," Casey explained. He jerked a thumb over his shoulder at John. "John-boy's got to be in court in a couple of weeks on the Vansant case. The DA wanted Beth to testify, but says he can settle for O'Reilly."

At the mention of Beth's name, Lanie darted a glance at John's face. She wondered how much of the whole sordid mess his colleagues knew. He met her gaze, his expression unreadable. Casey turned. "Have you heard from her? The guys have asked about her."

John shrugged, his gaze not leaving Lanie's. "She's settled in with her aunt in El Paso. Nicole's having some trouble getting adjusted to school. That's about it."

Everything inside Lanie shut down, and she averted her gaze. Why was she surprised he'd been in contact with Beth? Hell, nothing should surprise her anymore where he was concerned. The rest of Casey and John's conversation went over her head, lost in the buzzing of her jumbled thoughts.

The warmth of Casey's quick embrace jerked her to awareness. "Take care," he said. "I'll tell Lisa to call before she comes."

While John walked his colleague to the door, she stood frozen, anger and hurt and betrayal rolling through her. Oh, yeah, it wasn't too late. They could make things better. Deceitful rat. How stupid was she? She'd let his relationship with the baby blind her, let him begin worming his way under her defenses again.

"Lanie." The quiet firmness of his voice raised her anger to fury. "Stop it. It's not like it sounds."

"Really?" She narrowed her eyes at him. "How does it sound, John?"

"We've talked twice. Both times it was because of work, straightening out open and pending cases."

She stacked their plates and took them into the kitchen. "You don't have to explain anything to me, remember? I don't care what you do."

He followed. "Damn it, would you stop? It was two phone calls that didn't mean anything."

A small, derisive snort escaped her. "Yeah, kind of like us having sex."

A hand on her shoulder, he pulled her around to face him. He lowered his head. "You think that? You think making love to you didn't mean anything to me?"

"I think I was an easy lay, a substitute for what you really wanted, and you got caught by a bad condom." She dropped the words between them with deadly precision and watched him flinch. "Are you going to try to make me think differently?"

"Maybe at first it was like that. But not later."

Her harsh laugh exploded between them. "And when did you figure that out? While you were asking for her when you woke up?"

"No," he snapped, his fingers a cruel clamp on her arms. "When I had to face the fact that you might die and I saw what I stood to lose."

She pushed down on the bend of his elbows, breaking his hold. Her fingers rubbed the aching skin where his fingers had been. "That's the thing, O'Reilly. You can't lose what you never really had. We didn't have anything but sex and lust."

"Is that all you felt for me?" Quiet resignation lingered in his voice.

"Yes," she lied. His face paled, but her urge for self-preservation was strong. Having her father in her home had only underscored how close she came to treading her mother's path.

"I don't believe you." The words emerged on a raw whisper.

"Well, that makes us even." Her trembling hands clenched into fists, she walked away, leaving him standing in the kitchen, alone.

Chapter Thirteen

Silence reigned in the house. Lanie lay in bed, watching the early morning sunlight play off the waves. None of them had slept much the night before. Although exhausted from wrestling with her emotions, Lanie found sleep elusive, and she heard John every time he got up with a fussy Sonny Buck. An hour before, she'd heard the rustle of sheets as he went back to bed after settling the baby.

Hope wanted to spring eternal, but she insisted on squashing it. It whispered to her, telling her to remember the intensity in his voice when he'd talked about being afraid she'd die. It curled up in her, warming her, wanting her to see what the future would hold if she'd give him another chance.

Reality said something different. Joined with anger and self-preservation, it cynically insisted that he couldn't be trusted. Whenever hope dared to speak, reality laughed and told her to remember the desperation in his voice when he asked for Beth, not her.

After a sleepless night, Lanie had dry, gritty eyes and the desire to be devoid of emotions. She wanted nothing—to feel nothing, to have a vast Arctic tundra where her heart lay.

Her stomach rumbled, and she pushed away the covers. Physical needs she could handle. Coffee, a pain reliever for her aching head, and food. Barefoot, she padded down the hall, unable to resist a quick glance into the nursery. John slept on his side, back to the door.

The polished wood floor was cool under her feet, and the aroma of coffee filled the downstairs. A cup and spoon sat in the kitchen sink beside one of Sonny Buck's empty bottles. Lanie pulled down another mug. The morning paper lay in sections on the breakfast bar, and sipping her coffee, she climbed onto a stool.

The folded classified rested on top. When she reached to push them aside, her hand stilled. Slashing red circles surrounded several ads for house and apartment rentals. The tiny newsprint blurred, and she blinked. What was wrong with her? She *wanted* him to move out.

Footsteps on the stairs kicked her pulse up a notch. John strolled into the kitchen and poured a fresh cup of coffee. He didn't speak, but leaned around her to pick up the discarded classifieds. The faded scent of his soap, mingled with baby powder, invaded her senses. He dropped bread in the toaster and opened the newspaper with a snap.

Silence and tension hovered in the room until Lanie couldn't stand it any longer. "John, I—"

"I don't want to talk about it, Lanie." The toast popped up, and she watched the play of muscles in his arms as he buttered it. "I'm looking for another place like you wanted, all right?"

She wrapped her hands around her mug. "I think it's for the best."

"Yeah." He slid the toast in front of her and dropped two more slices of bread in the toaster. "We need to make arrangements for custody and visitation."

Her stomach dropped. She'd dreaded this conversation. "You know I wouldn't ever keep him from you. He needs you."

He finally looked at her, and the dead expression in his navy gaze startled her. "Right now, I think he's better off with me."

"Have you lost your mind?" she whispered. Suddenly, she was thirteen again, listening to her father's cold voice telling her mother she was unfit. "No."

"I said right now. Not forever. I spent half the night thinking about this, Lanie. You can't take care of him—"

"Oh my God! You sound just like my father." Anger washed through her in a wave, followed by guilt. God, even he saw what she lacked as a mother. "I can care for him. I may have to hire someone—"

"I'm not having him shoved on strangers who don't give a damn about him." John's jaw clenched in a stubborn line.

Her harsh laugh exploded in the small room. "Listen to you. Three weeks ago, you didn't give a damn about him."

"At least I give a damn now, which is more than you can say," he snapped.

The words hung between them, and she stared at him, her heart thudding. "What?"

His face pale, he shook his head. Mug in hand, he made to walk out of the kitchen. "I'm sorry. I shouldn't have—"

"No. What the hell did you mean by that?" Grabbing his arm, she pulled him around. Coffee sloshed over the side of his mug, splattering her feet. She ignored the pinpricks of pain and stared up him, breathing hard. "Answer me."

He swallowed, throat working in a convulsive motion. "You're not connected to him, are you? You're stronger, better, but when was the last time you held him?"

She didn't want to think about his words, acknowledge he might be right. Her anger prompted an offensive attack. "So the key to getting me connected to him is taking him away?"

"I never wanted to take him away." The torn whisper mirrored the anguish on his face. He shook his head. "You want me out, but I have to think about what's best for him."

"And that's not me." Bitterness curled around each word. He thought she was a failure as a mother. Maybe, but she knew enough not to deprive her son of a father who loved him. Weary, she passed a hand over her eyes, her fingertips still warm from the contact with his bare skin. "Don't go yet."

"What?"

She looked up to meet his gaze. "Don't look for another place yet. We've managed this long; we can make it work a little longer. At least until your leave is up."

ઉ§ⓑ§ಬ

Hot water cascaded over John's neck and shoulders, doing little to relieve the knots of exhausted tension there. He'd been granted a reprieve, but there was still too much to lose.

He stuck his head under the water, remembering the feel of Lanie's hand on his arm earlier. She'd touched him out of anger, but the brief contact had taken his breath. Deprived of her touch, he'd grown hungry for it over the weeks. When her fingertips slid over his arm, he'd wanted nothing more than to pull her into his arms and feel her next to him.

More than anything, he wanted her touching him, kissing him, the way she'd done before he'd screwed everything to hell. No, not like before. He wanted her caressing him with love and forgiveness. He wanted her whispering the words against his skin. He wanted her crying them out while he came inside her.

A shudder worked its way over his skin, and heavy arousal settled in his groin. He groaned. Not likely he'd ever hear those words on her lips. The same words trembled constantly on his tongue, but he couldn't say them. She wouldn't believe him, and he couldn't blame her. Judging from her reaction to just his talking to Beth, he didn't think his campaign to prove himself trustworthy and steadfast showed much success.

Implying she doesn't care about her baby was a damn stroke of genius, O'Reilly.

He didn't get it, though. Once she'd gotten over the initial shock of finding herself pregnant despite their best precautions, she'd been excited about becoming a mother. For months, their conversations—mostly one-sided—had revolved around the baby. She'd wanted that baby with a desperation that bordered on the obsessive.

And now she hardly looked at him. Hardly touched him. What was she afraid of?

Slicking his hair back, he shut off the water and stepped out, no closer to an answer or a solution. A towel wrapped around his waist, he strode into the nursery. The grumbling from the crib told him Sonny was awake—not happy, but not yet squalling.

He dressed quickly and lifted the baby from the crib. "Hey, big guy. Hungry?"

The irritable fussing stopped, and Sonny graced him with a rare smile. John grinned back. He lifted the baby, found a sodden diaper and headed for the changing table. Sonny stretched and kicked while John removed the wet diaper. After seeing the suggestion in one of Lanie's myriad baby books, John had propped an unbreakable mirror on the table, and

Sonny turned his head, staring at his own reflection. His legs pumped faster.

Chuckling, John wiped, powdered and lifted tiny legs to slide a clean diaper under an equally clean bottom. "Kid, you have one serious case of bedhead."

He smoothed the dark wisps down the best he could. Sonny turned toward his voice, and John rested his arms on the railing, bringing his face closer to his son's. "So, what are we going to do about your mom, Sonny Buck?"

Sonny's gaze locked on his face, and John rubbed his palm over the tiny head. His thumb traced a minuscule ear. "Maybe she just needs more one-on-one time with you, an opportunity to get to know you. I mean, you're kind of intimidating at first."

The only reply he received was another wide, toothless grin. With another chuckle, John lifted him against his shoulder and headed downstairs, already feeling better. If time and proximity had worked on him, it had to work on Lanie as well.

Cursing, Lanie ripped another voided check in half. The slips of colorful paper joined the small pile of confetti already on the table. She'd transposed the amounts twice, and once she'd finally gotten the digits correct, she'd screwed up the number words. Math had always been her strong point, and now she couldn't even write a check. Frustrated tears burned her eyes, and she dropped her head in her hands.

"Want some help?" Above her head, John's voice was sympathetic.

The urge to tell him what he could do with his help almost choked her, but she pushed the words down. She lifted her head, brushing her hair back. "All I'm trying to do is pay the mortgage, and I can't even do that."

Horrified, she heard the crack in her voice. John chuckled. “I think I can handle that for you. Here, take him.”

He deposited Sonny Buck in her uneasy hold and pulled the checkbook in front of him. She hated him for the ease with which he scribbled the information. Tired of feeling inadequate, she turned her attention to the baby in her arms. His wide navy eyes were alert and watchful, his gaze locked on her face. She couldn’t remember seeing him this awake before. He blinked, thick, dark lashes fanning over his cheeks.

John tore the check from the pad and stuffed it in the envelope. “You know they’d set this up on automatic deduction for you.”

“I know.” She stared at her son, not wanting to talk about the daily tasks she couldn’t do anymore. Phone numbers she knew by heart she had to look up now, and half the time she still dialed them wrong. The coffee she’d run earlier would choke a camel because she’d added the wrong number of scoops. God knows how her mind would mangle the radio ten codes if she ever got back to work. A shiver tingled over her spine.

Road duty was out of the question. Hell, she couldn’t even dispatch. She couldn’t afford a mistake in the radio room, where minutes and correct codes were a literal matter of life or death. Her throat closed, and she leaned forward, lips pressed to Sonny’s forehead.

“Lanie? You all right?”

She shifted, lifting the baby against her shoulder. His downy head brushed her neck. She didn’t look up at John. “I’m fine.”

“He’s due for a feeding, so don’t be surprised if he starts bawling. I’ll go warm a bottle.”

"What are we going to do, baby?" she whispered once she was sure John had gone. How was she going to provide for him? Sonny Buck lifted his wobbly head from her shoulder for a second and bumped his nose when he couldn't hold it up anymore. He let out an outraged wail.

Lanie clutched him tighter, patting his back. She wanted to howl with him.

"Here you go."

She glanced up, blinking back tears. John held out the bottle, and she stared at it. He wasn't going to feed the baby? Hesitating, she shifted Sonny into the curve of her arm and accepted the bottle, its comforting warmth seeping into her palm. "Thank you."

"I already tested it." John laid a burping cloth over the baby's chest and knelt beside her chair. Sliding his hand behind Sonny's head, he shifted their son's position in her arms. "Hold him up a little, and he doesn't swallow as much air."

His proximity increased her nervousness, and she waited for him to move away. With his hand still cupping the baby's head, his fingertips lay a breath away from the curve of her breast. How many times had she imagined this scenario during her pregnancy? The only difference was, that in her fantasies, their son suckled at her breast. Sadness shivered through her.

"What are you thinking?" John's soft whisper brought her gaze up to his. The jumble of naked emotions in his navy eyes closed her throat and brought a tingling warmth to her lower abdomen.

She dropped her gaze and watched Sonny, his eyes closed in bliss. John's finger stroked over the baby's forehead. Hugging his precious weight against her, she shook her head. "Just that I'm sorry I didn't get to nurse him."

"So am I." His voice remained soft, and she felt the heaviness of his gaze on her again. She refused to look up, but instead watched the rhythmic stroke of his fingers on the baby's head. "Maybe next time."

"You must be kidding." Her heart jerked. She couldn't imagine having another man's baby, but didn't intend to have another with him, either. "Do you want another?"

"I'm still getting used to him." He was so close she felt his easy shrug. "But, yeah, I might like one more."

The idea of another woman bearing his child scalded her with jealousy. She covered it with a harsh laugh. "Shouldn't you talk to Beth about that?"

One of his long fingers tilted her chin up, forcing her to meet his gaze. "Let's get this straight—I have no intention of giving Beth or any other woman a baby. And you're not going to be able to hide behind her forever, Lanie."

She shook her head, and he lowered his hand. "I don't know what you're talking about."

He rubbed his hands over his jeans-clad thighs. "I don't have to be here. I could've walked off, hired a nurse to help you, written you a child support check and gone after Beth. But I didn't. I'm in this for the long haul, honey."

The words and the single-minded intent behind them frightened her. The weak part of her that still remembered the way it had been wanted to trust him, to believe in him. The stronger, self-sufficient part smothered the weakness. He could still walk away. This time, her laugh bordered on a disgusted snort. "Yeah. You're the stand-up, trustworthy type, O'Reilly. I can't tell you how secure that makes me feel."

He looked away with a muttered profanity, and Lanie resisted the urge to cover Sonny's ears.

The phone rang. John pushed to his feet and stalked into the kitchen to answer. Lanie blew out a shaky breath, feeling as though she'd just gone rounds with a recalcitrant suspect. The nipple popped free from Sonny's relaxed mouth, air gurgling into the remaining formula. She set the bottle on the table, watching her shaking hand with detachment. He could be so persuasive and convincing when he wanted to be. She almost believed him.

Almost.

He walked back into the room, hand covering the mouthpiece on the cordless phone. "Lisa wants to know if it's all right if she comes to see you this afternoon."

Lifting the baby to her shoulder, Lanie hesitated. She wasn't sure she was really up for visitors yet, but the day stretched before her—trapped in the house with John. She swallowed and forced a smile. "Sure. I'd love to see her."

�&ಖ

"Lanie?" John's voice drifted through her consciousness. She smiled and reached for him. Her hands brushed the reality of warm skin and brought her awake in an instant.

John leaned over the bed, his face close to hers. Her hands, wrapped around his forearms, tingled with the contact. She jerked away and sat up. "I'm awake."

Strands of her hair clung to her face, and he brushed them behind her ear. "Lisa's downstairs. Do you want me to ask her to come back?"

She shook her head, ignoring the slight ache along her incision. "No. I'll be right down. I just need a couple minutes to freshen up."

He nodded, straightening, his face mask devoid of expression. "Okay. She's oohing over Sonny Buck anyway. I'll let her know you'll be down in a little while."

"Thanks." She waited until he left to leave the bed. In the bathroom, she avoided looking at her reflection. There was little she could do to improve her appearance at this point. After brushing her teeth, she exchanged her pajamas for a velour track suit. The pain at her Cesarean scar had faded to a weird numbness, but she still couldn't zip up any of her jeans.

Barefoot, she went downstairs. The soft sounds of John and Lisa's conversation drifted from the living room. John had the baby in his arms, and he rose when she entered the room. Smiling, Lisa jumped to her feet and ran to hug her. "Oh, Lanie! It's so good to see you."

Uncomfortable with the physical contact, Lanie pulled back. She smiled to cover her discomfort. "You, too. You look wonderful."

"So do you," Lisa said, holding Lanie's hand.

Liar. That was one thing she swore she'd never do again—lie to a recuperating person about their looks. She let Lisa lead her to the couch. Lisa swept her long blonde hair over one shoulder. "The baby is beautiful. You must be so thrilled."

"Of course." Her gaze met John's. He watched with cynical eyes before rising to his feet.

"I'm going to check the mail, so you two can do the girltalk thing." He settled Sonny into her arms. "I'll be back in a few minutes."

Lisa's bright green gaze followed him from the room. "Oh my God, he's different."

Lanie frowned and shifted the drowsy baby to a more comfortable angle. "What do you mean?"

Lisa shrugged, an expression of mild discomfort crossing her face. "Well, before, he was like 'what baby?' You wouldn't have thought he knew you were pregnant. Now, it's all the man talks about. Casey called him the other night about a case and got a play-by-play of the kid's sleeping habits."

Imagining Casey's glazed expression, Lanie giggled. "He did not. When it comes to the job, John's the most focused guy I know."

"I didn't believe it, either." Shaking her head, Lisa laughed. "Until I walked in here and couldn't get him to shut up about the baby. Obviously, you've birthed a prodigy, girl."

"He's just...a proud father." The reality of the words made her heart kick. There were no other words to describe John's attitude toward their child. He was proud. Loving. Involved. The father she'd hoped he would be.

"Hey." Lisa waved a hand in front of Lanie's eyes. "Where'd you go?"

Lanie smiled, trying to collect her scattered thoughts and deal with the implications. "Sorry. I was thinking."

"Ready for that six weeks' exam, aren't you?"

"What are you talking about?"

Lisa nudged her arm. "You know. The one where the doctor clears you to have sex again."

Flustered, Lanie slid her hair behind her ear. "Lisa, believe me, sex is the farthest thing from my mind."

"Yeah, right." Her friend looked less than convinced. "I've seen y'all when it looked like you wouldn't even make it off the dance floor."

Heat burned along Lanie's cheekbones. Unwilling, she remembered a few of the nights Lisa alluded to. The baby in her arms had been conceived after one of those nights. They'd made it off the dance floor, but not past their foyer. She swallowed hard. "Things are different now."

Lisa sighed. "I gathered that from the way John looked at you."

Lanie shot a quick glance in her direction. "What do you mean?"

"Listen, the way he looked at you before was hot, like he was always planning your next lovemaking session. Now...it's still hot, but it's different. I guess it's that whole 'mother of his child' thing."

"Yeah, I guess so." A curious sense of despondency settled over her.

Lisa didn't seem to notice. "I mean, before you could tell by the way he watched you that he lusted after you. Now, you can tell by the way he looks at you that he loves you."

Chapter Fourteen

Lanie held her breath and forced her muscles into relaxation. Dr. Shaw removed the speculum and rolled the stool back before rising to her feet. "Okay, Lanie, you can sit up now."

When Lanie reached a seated position at the foot of the exam table, Alexandra Shaw smiled. "Everything looks great. Your recovery is textbook perfect, which I think is wonderful, considering the circumstances."

Hands clenched in her sheet-draped lap, Lanie forced a smile. "Great."

"According to your neurologist, your scans look good, too. Still having trouble with numbers?" Alexandra looked up from scribbling on Lanie's chart.

Lanie nodded. "Yes, and some short-term memory issues. I walk into a room and can't remember why. Put things down and forget them. The therapist tells me I can relearn the math and that the memory problems usually correct themselves in a few months." She hoped so anyway. She hated the forgetfulness, the struggles with numbers.

"Would it help to tell you I do the same thing sometimes?" Alexandra placed the chart on the counter. "The memory issues bother you, don't they?"

"Well, yeah." Lanie's laugh was harsh. "What if I go to the grocery story and forget to take the baby out of the basket? Or put his car seat on top of the car and forget to put him in the backseat?"

A wry smile curved Alexandra's mouth. "You wouldn't believe how often I hear the same thing from new mothers who haven't been through what you have. Those are really normal worries, you know."

Sure they were, but how many new mothers had to have someone else prepare bottles because she couldn't keep the measurements straight? John never said a word, just prepared twenty-four hours' worth of bottles every morning. Over the last three weeks, she'd slowly taken on more of the baby's care, spent more time with him, surrendered more of her heart to him. Maybe that explained why her fears and insecurities had increased.

"Do you have any other questions?" Alexandra made another note in the file.

"No." Lanie twisted her fingers together.

"Well, you're clear to resume all of your regular activities. I think you're wise to take the extended leave from work, but around the house, as long as you're careful, nothing is off limits." She smiled. "And that includes intercourse. What method of birth control are you interested in?"

Lanie swallowed. "That's really not an issue. Sex is the last thing on my mind, believe me."

Alexandra laughed. "Now where have I heard that before? Yes, taking care of a newborn is exhausting, but you will want to have sex again one day. Make sure you use some type of birth control, Lanie. A lot of women experience an increase in fertility following the birth of a baby."

And she'd gotten pregnant this time despite the extreme care she and John had taken. Good thing she had no plans to sleep with him again. Alexandra didn't need to know that, though. She murmured some reply that seemed to placate the doctor, and finally she was free to go.

She paused in the doorway to the waiting room. John, his long frame folded into a chair, garnered more than his share of attention. Although she'd been forced to have him drive her to the appointment, she'd drawn the line at having him in the exam room. Now he flipped through an outdated Cosmo magazine, Sonny Buck asleep in the carrier at his feet. Aware of the envious looks the other women in the room sent her way, Lanie crossed to stand before him. She wanted to tell them they had no reason to envy her. "Ready to go?"

He glanced up, a ready smile on his face as he put the magazine aside. "Everything okay?"

Under his white buttondown, the muscles in his back rippled when he bent to pick up the baby. Lanie averted her gaze, focusing on her son's sleeping face. "Perfect. I have a clean bill of health."

"That's great." He held the office door for her with his spare hand. "You have anything else you want to do before we head home? Shopping? Lunch?"

The simple domesticity of the conversation clutched at her heart, and she covered the yearning with cool irritation. "Just take me home."

His mouth tightened. "Whatever you want."

What she wanted was the six feet three inches of pure male sliding into the driver's seat. Damn it, she wasn't supposed to think about sex, and she sure wasn't supposed to think about sex with him. She was a new mother, one who'd gone through two major surgeries—she should be too weak and exhausted to remember what being with him was like. If she had to forget things, why couldn't she forget that?

Instead memories sprang to life at the oddest times. She watched him lift Sonny Buck with those long-fingered hands and remembered his touch on her skin. He smiled at the baby, and her body tingled with the recollection of his kisses. He napped with his son on his chest, skin to skin, and she recalled sprawling on his chest after they'd exhausted themselves making love.

She stared out the window, the Gulf shore whizzing by. Everyday, with the baby sleeping and the two of them alone in the house, the lingering attraction grew harder to ignore. Forgetting Lisa's words, her implication that John loved her, was impossible, as was resisting the man who cared for her and her child with such tender dependability. Did she really want to resist him any longer? More important, could she handle the repercussions if she didn't?

John slowed to pull into the parking lot of the convenience store around the corner from the house. "We're out of milk. You want anything?"

"No, thanks." She watched him saunter into the store, jeans hugging his lean hips. A frisson of awareness slid over her nerves. She wanted him, and he'd always wanted her. Lanie rested her cheek on her hand and eyed him through the window. He pulled his wallet from his pocket, flashed the clerk a smile and handed over a bill. She shivered.

A transaction. That's what their affair had always been. Each had something the other wanted. He lived with her for mutual convenience. Other than the baby, they had no strings between them. No real emotion until she'd gotten pregnant and stupidly allowed herself to fall in love with him. Even dumber was believing he loved her, too. If she'd followed her own rules about not getting emotionally involved, his feelings for Beth wouldn't have seemed like such a betrayal.

But now her eyes were open. Wanting him was one thing—letting herself have him was quite another. If she took him now, knowing how he felt about the other woman, she had no one else to blame when she got hurt again.

The wind rippled his hair as he walked back to the car. That little curl of desire sent tentacles through her stomach again, but she ignored it. When he smiled at her, she turned her head. She couldn't break the rules again. The risk was too great.

Once home, she took the sleeping baby from him. With his easy-going nature, Sonny Buck maintained a predictable routine. He woke early, wanting to be fed and changed. He took a long morning nap, woke for lunch, took a second nap, then was alert and playful most of the afternoon and evening. His nighttime feedings had gone from four to two. Soon, Lanie thought, placing the baby in his crib. Soon, she wouldn't need John in the house anymore. The torment of his presence would be gone.

She'd be safe.

Fidgety, she wandered downstairs and found John in the kitchen, putting away clean dishes. The drapes were open, sunlight bouncing off the waves and into the living areas. She paused, staring at the hallway wall. In the intense light, the paint color seemed off, the texture different. She ran her hand over the wall. "John? Did you repaint this?"

He turned, his brows jerking together. Anguish darkened his eyes. "I had it done. I guess the guy didn't get an exact match on the paint. It's where your other bullet went wild and hit the wall."

"Oh." Her fingertips slid over the surface, feeling the invisible bumps and ridges of the drywall patch. The horrible sensation of touching wet human skin in the dark rose in her memory, remembered panic choking her.

"Don't." John's hand covered hers, pulling her fingers from the wall. "Don't think about it."

Surprised by the strain in his voice, she glanced up at him. He stared at her, his jaw tight, tormented guilt etched into the lines of his face. She'd wanted him to hurt, wanted him to suffer for betraying her, but seeing the raw emotion in his eyes brought no satisfaction. Lanie shook her head. "I have to face it sometime. I'm not going to be a prisoner in my own home. I can't walk into that bathroom, but I will someday. He took enough from me. I'm not letting him take my home, too."

Face pale, John flinched. "I'm sorry I put you in that situation. Falconetti was right. I should have known sooner or later he'd come back, that he'd want to get back at me. Touching you was the worst thing I could have done."

The words stung, and she backed up a step. Her anger directed at Mitchell for the first time, she didn't quite understand the urge to offer John absolution. "You couldn't have known—"

"Couldn't I?" he snarled. "Don't men like him always end up destroying someone? I saw it happen with my mother. I should have known what Mitchell would do."

His mother? Struck by how little she really knew of this man, the father of her child, she reached for his arm. "John, what do you mean—"

"I've got to get out of here for a while." He stepped away, her hand falling between them. "I'm going for a walk on the beach. Will you be all right?"

"Yes, but—"

"I won't be long." Moving as though pursued by Furies, he left, the glass door sliding closed behind him with a soft hiss.

True to his promise, he stayed gone less than fifteen minutes. Lanie, drawn to the bedroom window, watched him walk back up the beach. His head bent, shoulders hunched, his posture screamed of dejection and pain.

Mitchell had hurt him, too.

She didn't want to admit it, but John had suffered at Mitchell's hands, been a victim as well. He'd been placed in the untenable position of choosing between the woman he loved and the woman he felt responsible for, the one carrying his child. Lanie closed her eyes against a spurt of agony. At least the entry team had spared him actually making that decision and spared her the knowledge that he would have chosen Beth over her.

God, she was tired. In the nursery, the baby still slept. She opened her eyes. Outside the glass doors, John climbed the stairs to the deck, moving like an elderly man. He was home, so she could rest without worry. If Sonny needed anything, John would be there.

ଓଃଋଌ

From the dark, terror reached out for her with long, wet tentacles. Lanie tried to scream, but the tentacles covered her mouth and nose. Pressed into the darkness, she couldn't breathe, couldn't get away.

"Lanie! Wake up!"

Jerked into awareness, she stared into John's pale face, his navy eyes burning with fear and concern. Sobs shook her body, and he brushed her hair away from her face. "Hush, baby. It's just a dream. Just a nightmare, honey. Hush, now. I'm here."

He spoke in the low, soothing tones he used with Sonny Buck, and Lanie reached for him, burying her face against his neck. He held her close, his hands soothing over her hair and back. "What did you dream about?"

She tried to find the dream again, but the images were gone, leaving only the terror behind. Breathing in his scent, she shook her head. "I don't remember. Just darkness and being terrified."

Her voice shuddered, and he pulled her closer, rocking her against him. Lanie clung to him, the strength of his arms beneath her fingers. How could he make her feel so safe and so threatened at the same time?

In his arms, she grew still, the intimacy of their position seeping into her brain. He'd pulled her onto his lap, and her nightshirt had ridden up, bare legs resting on his thighs. With their chests pressed together, her face fit into the curve of his neck. She took a deep breath, his scent overwhelming her, heat curling in her abdomen. A slight shift in position, a rearranging of clothes, and she could have him inside her, filling the emptiness as no one else had.

"John." His name left her lips on a shaky whisper, and his muscles tightened under her hands.

For a moment, his mouth brushed against the incision scar on her scalp. He eased her off his lap and stood. "Think you can go back to sleep now?"

She stared at him, and he wouldn't look at her. Didn't he feel it at all? Of course not. Her teeth bit into her lip. He was here for the baby, not her. She pulled the covers to her chest. "I'll be fine. Thank you."

"Good night."

For a long time after he left, she lay staring at the ceiling, missing the warmth of his arms and hating herself for being weak.

John rolled to his side, reciting radio codes. He'd already gone through his repertoire of sports trivia and statistics as well as the sections of Texas criminal code he knew by rote. Nothing worked. He still couldn't get Lanie out of his mind.

The look on her face earlier, when she'd stared at the patched wall, stopped him from going into the other room, taking her into his arms and telling her what he felt. He'd put that look there by placing her in Mitchell's path. If he'd known what would happen, he never would have touched her.

Yeah, right. Tell another one, O'Reilly. Like you could stay away from her.

She'd been a craving, an addiction, from that very first night. The first time, she'd come to him in a sequined black dress, her touch bold and daring on his body. He'd been lost, desperate for more. The passion, always wild between them, flared from a look, a touch, a kiss. And he couldn't get enough—when the lovemaking was over, he still hungered for her. No other woman had made him feel the same way.

He loved her, and it didn't matter. Staring at the silver fish dancing on the wall, he remembered the bargains he'd made with God while she lay comatose. If she got well, he'd walk away. He'd let her go and let her get on with her life.

His actions had done enough damage to her life. It was time he lived up to his end of the bargain.

Sometime during his mental wrestling, exhaustion claimed him. He surfaced from a fitful sleep, senses alert. Something wasn't right. Moonlight filtered into the room, silvery light blending with the amber glow of the nightlight. The angle of light had him lifting his arm to check his watch.

Four A.M.

He bolted upright. Had he slept through Sonny Buck's demand for a three o'clock feeding? Or had the baby even cried?

Horrific possibilities tumbled through his mind. SIDS. Parents who woke to find their babies dead in their cribs. Could Sonny have kicked his covers over his face and suffocated?

In his haste to get to his son, he tripped over his own blanket. The crib was empty. His exhaustion-fuzzed mind refused to take in the information—the duck-embroidered cap at the head of the crib, the soft blue blanket pushed aside. Oh God. Had someone gotten in the house? He'd locked the doors. He was sure of it, but had he set the alarm system?

Mitchell had gotten to Lanie despite the locks and alarm. John's nerves shivered, fear an icy lump in his gut. *Where the hell was his son?* A muffled sound from the other bedroom raised the hair on his neck. Lanie. *Please, don't let anything have happened to her.*

He ran, skidding to a stop at her doorway. The bedside light cast a soft glow in the room. Lanie lay on her side, propped on an elbow, the covers pushed back, and in the shelter of her arm lay a kicking, gurgling Sonny Buck. An empty bottle sat on the nightstand. Relief weakened John's knees, and he groped for the doorframe for support.

Lanie trailed a fingertip along the baby's cheek, and a smile curved her generous mouth. Kicking harder, Sonny Buck chortled, his newest talent. The soft, warm sound of Lanie's laugh filled the room, grabbing John's heart in a vice.

"Look at you," she murmured, a mother's pride filling her voice. She skimmed a finger over the sole of his tiny foot. "You think you're something, don't you?"

Sonny Buck gurgled, his gaze locked on his mother's face.

"You have your dad's eyes, young man, but I do think that's a Falconetti smile." She stroked his head, ruffling his wispy, dark hair. "I'm going to have to keep an eye on you. On a male Falconetti, that smile is lethal to a girl's heart. We can't let you turn into a Lothario, like Vince and Tony. You are going to have to grow up to be a one-woman man. A girl has to know she can trust you."

The words landed like blows to John's solar plexus. He took a silent step back, his gaze locked on the pair in the bed. Sonny Buck cooed, and Lanie pressed a kiss to his forehead. Absolute love suffused her face, and unexpected envy rolled through John's chest. She wouldn't look at him that way again.

He pushed the selfish jealousy aside. This was what he wanted—seeing her connected to their child, knowing Sonny Buck had claimed his place in her heart. The reality jolted through him, a sickening emptiness taking hold of his stomach. She didn't need him around anymore. His time was up.

Chapter Fifteen

The phone tucked between her chin and shoulder, Lanie relaxed into the Adirondack chair and tilted her face to the sun. The sliding glass door behind her stood open so she could hear Sonny Buck if he cried. With John in Houston for the day, they were alone in the house, and she should have felt at peace. Instead, she found herself fidgety and inattentive, drifting from one unfinished activity to another.

Caitlin answered on the third ring, her Bureau voice cool and professional. "Falconetti."

"Hey, it's Lanie." A gull swooped over the water, and Lanie pulled her feet under her.

"Well, hey. How are you?" Affection warmed Caitlin's voice.

"Great, according to my doctors. What are you doing?" Lanie leaned back, letting her cousin's familiar voice settle her jangling nerves.

"Right this second? I'm looking at a set of crime scene photos." A pause hissed over the line. "Lanie? Is something wrong?"

"No, of course not." Lanie winced at her too-cheerful tone. "I'm fine."

Caitlin chuckled. "Oh Lord. Now where have I heard that before?"

"Everything's fine. I'm doing great; the baby's wonderful. I call to chat because I'm at loose ends, and you assume something's wrong. Can't I just call because I miss you?"

Papers rustled. "Sure you can, but if I say you doth protest too much, are you going to bite my head off again?"

Lanie groaned, sinking lower in the chair. "Please don't quote Shakespeare at me. You know I never could stand him."

Caitlin's soft laugh soothed the trembling in Lanie's stomach. "Come on, Lane. It's me. What's going on?"

"Nothing. Everything." Lanie covered her eyes with one hand. "Cait, I'm so confused."

"What's wrong?" Another pause. "Are you still feeling distant from the baby?"

"No. He's perfect." With her eyes closed, Lanie could pull up the feel of him in her arms, his sweet just-bathed scent, the sound of his happy gurgle. A fierce wave of love washed over her. "I can't explain how I feel about him. I've never loved anyone like this."

"Oh, no, it's O'Reilly, isn't it?"

"I don't know. I don't *want* to want him—"

"But you do."

"It's being in this house with him all the time. Watching him with the baby, sharing a bathroom with him so that all I smell is his soap... It's driving me insane." Just thinking about him had heat curling in her. What did that say about her—wanting a man she couldn't trust?

"Isn't his leave almost up? Y'all agreed he would move out then, right? Will that help—having him out of the house?"

He was out of the house today, and every thought she had focused on him. She'd started a load of laundry earlier, and each piece of clothing he owned triggered a memory of the two of them together. Being out of bodywash forced her to use his soap, and now his scent clung to her skin. Even Sonny Buck seemed part of the conspiracy, staring up at her during his feeding with navy eyes so like John's that her heart ached.

"Lanie? Are you still there?" Concern lingered in Caitlin's words.

"I'm here." She sighed. "I don't know if his moving out will help or not. I just... Part of me wants what we had, and part of me knows that wasn't enough."

"I can't tell you what to do, but..." Caitlin's voice trailed away, a deep male drawl an indistinct rumble in the background.

Lanie opened her eyes and glanced skyward. "Cait, am I interrupting?"

"No, that's just Beecham, dropping off reports. Anyway, you have to decide, but I don't want you to settle, Lanie. You deserve it all. Is O'Reilly the guy who can give you that?"

"I don't know." Lord help her, she still wanted him to be.

ଔଌ

The day dragged as Lanie moved through Sonny Buck's routine. With Caitlin's questions running through her head, she was no closer to any answers when John returned home. When his key turned in the lock, she stood in the kitchen with Sonny in her arms, waiting for a bottle to warm, and suppressed a shiver of awareness.

He dropped a bundle of folders on the counter and crossed to pat Sonny's back. The loose papers on top of the folders scattered across the countertop. "Hey. Did you have a good day?"

Lanie watched his fingers cup the baby's head. "We did. He's trying to hold his head up."

"Yeah?" Grinning, John lifted their son from her arms. "You been working out, big guy?"

Holding his head away from John's shoulder for a moment, Sonny Buck graced him with a wide grin. Lanie took the bottle from the warmer, and John reached for it. "He needs a diaper, too. You take a break."

Carrying on an animated conversation with the baby, he went upstairs. Lanie spent a few minutes straightening the kitchen, listening to his voice drift down. Gathering John's papers, she shuffled them into a pile and started to drop them on top of his folders. She paused after seeing her name and read the first few lines. Legal documents. Anger sizzled under her skin. Papers in hand, she stalked upstairs and into the nursery.

John had shed his suit and tie for a pair of sweatpants. A T-shirt hung over the end of Sonny Buck's crib; the empty bottle sat on a small table by the rocker. On the floor, John did sit-ups, Sonny Buck resting against his up-drawn knees. Every time John came up, Sonny smiled and gurgled.

Lanie stopped at John's feet and waved the papers at him. "What is this?"

He glanced at the sheaf of documents, not missing a beat. "Custody and visitation orders."

Cold fear slithered around her spine, chilling the anger for a moment. "You saw a lawyer?"

Curling tighter, he bumped his nose against Sonny Buck's, making the baby laugh harder. "I picked them up from Jeff today. He sent a copy to Troupe Cavanaugh's office for you."

How could he be so calm? Lanie swallowed a frustrated scream. "Damn it, John—"

On this curl, he brushed a kiss on the baby's forehead. "I asked for more visitation time than the law lays out. I was hoping that wouldn't be a problem."

Visitation? She looked at the papers again, reading farther than the primary paragraph. The papers assigned her first custody and an obscene amount of child support. She swallowed, feeling foolish. "John, I can't take this money."

His face hardened for a moment. "It's not for you. It's for him. And I can afford it. I get a raise with the sergeant's rank."

She glanced at the dollar amount again. "And what are you going to live on? Have you looked at rent amounts in Houston lately?"

"Got it covered. I'm moving in with Casey. His roommate is taking a job in Ft. Worth." With a heavy sigh, he collapsed against the rug, one hand holding his ribs. Lanie averted her eyes from the perfect line of his pecs and the dark arrow of hair running between his rippled abs. He sighed. "Hell, I don't think this was a good idea yet. Take him, would you?"

Dropping the papers on the changing table, she leaned down for Sonny Buck. John's woodsy scent enveloped her, and he hissed in a breath when her hair brushed his stomach. She straightened, holding the baby like a shield. "Are you sure you want to move out? We've made it work so far."

Rolling to his feet, he shot her a look. "I'm glad it works for one of us."

"What is that supposed to mean?" Sonny Buck drooped against her shoulder.

"It means I'm not cut out to be your damned roommate," he snapped. "Put him down. He needs to fall asleep in the crib."

"Don't start that perfect dad crap with me." Hissing the words at him, she settled Sonny Buck in his crib. His eyes fluttered closed, and she pulled a white blanket over him. "I don't need you to tell me how to take care of him."

John glared at her. "It kills you, doesn't it? To have to admit I'm a good father."

"Oh, please." She tossed his T-shirt at him. "He's six weeks old. You have plenty of time left to screw up once the new wears off."

The color drained from his face, fury blazing in his eyes. "You little... It doesn't matter, does it? None of what I've done, nothing I will do, is going to convince you, is it? I wasn't sure I wanted him when you were pregnant, and you're going to hold it over my head forever, aren't you?"

If suspecting it was bad, having him say the words was worse. The pain took her breath. She closed her lips against the horrible words bubbling in her throat. Shaking her head, she pushed by him and went into the bathroom, headed for her room.

He followed, his breathing harsh in the small room, and closed a hand on her arm, pulling her against him. "Lanie, I'm sorry. I shouldn't have said that."

Tears burned her eyes, and she squeezed them shut. "But you meant it, didn't you?"

"I want him now." His voice rasped against her ear, the breath hot. "Isn't that what matters most?"

"I don't know." She shook her head, her temple brushing his jaw. Early-evening stubble rasped against the tender skin. "I don't know anything anymore."

Her voice broke, and his groan rumbled through her, too. "Oh hell, Lanie, don't cry. I'm not worth it."

His fingers brushed at the wetness on her cheek, the other hand moving over her arm in a soothing caress. He rubbed his face against her hair, lips a butterfly touch against her incision scar. His chest was hot against her back, her tank top the thinnest of barriers.

He murmured, words she didn't catch, but the rumble of his voice set off tremors low in her stomach. Desire quivered along her nerves, her body coming to life again. She *ached* for him.

Long fingers slid over her arms and shoulders in a gentle touch. She didn't want him gentle. She wanted him rough, hard, wild, like always between them. Her head fell back, and her hands fluttered, seeking a spot to rest. They settled on his thighs, wringing a different groan from him.

"Lanie." His mouth moved along her neck. Shivers tingled through her, and she pushed back, the sudden proof of his arousal pressed against her. "Oh, baby, I've missed you."

This...this she was sure of, his hands slipping from her arms to her hips and up over her stomach. She covered his fingers with hers and eased his hands up to cover her breasts. With the contact, a moan escaped her lips, hanging in the still air. Cupping her, thumbs teasing erect nipples, he rocked against her. Lanie let her eyes drift closed, lost in the sensations of being loved by him again.

Against her ear, his breath rasped hot and moist. One of his hands traveled over her stomach, delving beneath the elastic band of her yoga pants. Anticipating his touch, she trembled, a moist ache between her thighs. His long fingers cupped her through thin silk panties, and the simple pressure wrung another moan from her.

He pulled her closer. "Lanie." His mouth slid up her neck, nipping. "Tell me you want me."

One finger stroked over silk. "Oh, yes."

"Say it," he whispered. "Let me hear it, baby."

Another maddening caress. "I...want you."

He moved, spinning her in his embrace and lifting her to sit on the countertop. Arms braced on either side of her body, he stared at her, his face flushed, eyes dilated. "Touch me. I want your hands on me, Lanie."

Head tilted back, eyes closed, she ran her hands over his shoulders and up his neck. He sighed. "Open your eyes."

She lifted heavy lids. Her gaze locked on his, she let her hands move to his chest, the muscles hard under her fingers. His skin was hot and smooth, the dark hair fine and silky. It grew coarser as her fingers slid down his stomach to the waistband of his sweats. His lashed dipped; he cursed under his breath. She smiled. "Open your eyes, John."

He did, staring at her again. "You make me crazy," he muttered and pressed closer. She smiled, wanting him as out of control as she was. "Feel what you do to me, baby."

She gasped, barely resisting the urge to rub against him like a cat. He eased her back, his hands covering hers where she braced herself on the counter. Trailing a caress up her arms, he traced her collarbone, drifted over her breasts, teasing but not quite touching her aching nipples. He covered her waist with his hands, then slid them to her hips. Lanie swallowed, her tongue darting out to wet dry lips.

His gaze, locked on her face, darkened. Supporting her with his hands, he pulled her closer. "Kiss me."

Her hands tangled in his hair, she lifted her mouth to his. At the first touch of her lips, John's tenuous control slipped. He groaned and took her mouth the way he wanted to take her body. Her hands traced his spine, molding, and he shuddered. He'd waited so long to have her touch him again. Desperate, he pulled her closer still. When her hands slipped beneath the waistband of his sweats, her nails scoring his buttocks, he bucked against her.

John reached for her tank top, breaking the kiss long enough to pull it over her head. The late afternoon sunlight filtered into the room, gleaming on her skin. He cupped her breasts again, lowering his head to worship her. “So beautiful.”

With a moan, she dug her fingers into his hair, holding his head to her body. His own scent lingered on her skin, making him wilder. She was *his*. He couldn’t lose her again.

The need to claim her beat through his veins, but he wanted more than possession. He wanted to be possessed, to have her claim him as well. His tongue circled her nipple, and she sighed, hands moving over his back again. She pushed at his sweats, hands stroking over his buttocks and thighs.

With her touch, joy shot through him. He’d ached for this, to have her with him this way again—the woman he loved, the mother of his child. Child. Oh hell.

He stilled with a groan, burying his face in her throat. Her hands continued to rove, fingers brushing his stomach. John caught her hands in his. “Wait.”

“What is it?” Her voice was a husky rasp, and he lifted his head, staring into golden eyes burning with unfulfilled desire.

“Baby, we can’t,” he whispered, brushing her damp hair away from her face. “You’re not protected, and I—”

Her eyes widened, realization dulling the flame. “Oh my God.” She pushed at him with one trembling hand, grabbing her tank with the other. “What are we doing?”

Fear settling in his stomach, he reached for her. “Lanie, stop. Baby, listen, I need to tell you—”

She jerked the tank over her head. Tears trembled on her lashes. “What was I thinking?”

"Lanie—"

"Don't touch me again." She pushed his hands away. Tossing back her hair, she glared at him. "When did Casey say you could move in? I want you out."

Chapter Sixteen

The phone rang, and John glared at it. If he had to file one more incident report on a stolen lawnmower, keyed automobile, or missing lawn flamingo, he would do someone great bodily harm. The records clerk on duty didn't look up from her computer, and with a sigh, John reached for the offending phone. "Records division. Sergeant O'Reilly."

"You sound really enthused," Casey's drawl greeted him. "Is being a pencil-pushing desk jockey that bad?"

John rubbed his aching temples. Why didn't Casey wait until he got home? "Worse."

"John-boy, how do you feel about fishing?"

The ancient chair gave a plaintive squeak when John leaned back. Suspicion tingled to life in his brain. "I've never done it. Why?"

"You've never... You're kidding."

John grinned at his roommate's shock, the humor a pleasant, if unfamiliar, emotion. He didn't have a lot to smile about lately. "No, I'm not. Are you doing a poll on leisure activities or what?"

"Actually, I'm looking for a partner for the Haven County bass tournament. Tim has come down with the flu, and somehow I don't think having him puke over the side of the boat every five minutes will help me catch anything."

The phone cradled between chin and shoulder, John picked up a pen and tapped it on the desk blotter. He found it hard to believe, but he was actually tempted. "I don't know."

"Look, John, you don't have to even do anything but sit on the boat. I've already paid the entrance fee, and I don't want to forfeit that."

Head tilted back, John stared at the ceiling. The tournament was the largest fundraiser for the Haven County Sheriff's Department. This year, it also served as a memorial for Steve Martinez. Somehow, he felt he owed Martinez this much. "All right. I'll do it."

"Great. I appreciate it, man. See you tonight."

"Yeah." John replaced the receiver and jammed the pen back in the cup on his desk. At least he'd have something to fill the empty hours Saturday since it wasn't his visitation weekend with Sonny Buck. Normally, he'd see his son this evening, but Lanie had emailed him earlier, begging off since friends planned to throw her a belated baby shower. The days until Tuesday, his next scheduled visitation, stretched before him.

For six weeks, his life had revolved around Lanie and his son. In the last two, he'd learned what shaking an addiction felt like—being deprived of Sonny Buck's presence had to be as bad as any crackhead's withdrawal. Even worse was being without Lanie. Dreams of her invaded his sleep. He woke at night, his body hard and aching, and reached for her before he remembered. Twenty times a day, he found himself checking his voice mail, just to see if he'd hear her voice. He never did.

Rebecca, the younger of the two clerks, drank coffee spiked with vanilla and cinnamon; the scent drove him crazy. A single whiff dredged up memories of Lanie—her arms wrapped around him, her mouth on his skin. Over and over, he relived climbing in the tub with her the night Mitchell blew all their lives apart. His body reacted to the memory of her wicked smile, her warm, wet fingers sliding around his erection, the feel of her body around him. He smothered a groan and pressed the heels of his hands into his eyes, willing the errant desire away.

Looking back, knowing what he'd lost, he wished he'd savored that night—every touch, every kiss, every sigh.

Hell, he wished he'd called a tow truck for Beth.

While he was at it, he wished he'd had enough damn sense to know that Lanie was the woman he loved—and that he'd told her when she might have believed him.

ଓଃ୭ଃ

Lanie eyed Caitlin seated on the floor by the coffee table and sighed. She could see her own tension echoed in the tight line of Caitlin's shoulders. Outside lightning crashed again, rain sheeting against the windows. With resignation, she waited for the lights to go out.

Cradled against her shoulder, Sonny Buck scrunched up his entire body and wailed. This new evening ritual had started a week ago—three to four hours of inconsolable screaming. When he stopped to catch his breath, his little body shook with raspy sobs. Tuesday night, even John's soothing touch had failed to work. Tonight, Sonny had screeched through her entire abbreviated baby shower.

A glance at the clock over the mantel told her they had another hour or so until he quieted. Her stomach clenched, and she held him closer, brushing her lips against his head. If possible, his body tightened further, and Lanie tried to squash the feelings of rejection and inadequacy. Why couldn't she figure out what was wrong?

Closing her eyes, she listened to the wails building in the room. She knew it was silly, but they almost sounded like accusations. The crying hadn't started until John moved out, and she couldn't help wondering if there was a connection. Sonny Buck had bonded with his father; he had to miss him, miss the stability of John's presence.

"Lanie?" At Caitlin's quiet voice, Lanie opened her eyes. Caitlin stacked opened gifts on the coffee table. "How are you handling the formula measurements?"

Trust Caitlin to bring up her shortcomings. She shrugged off the bitchy thought. "My therapist suggested I take pictures of the measuring cups and the containers. I put them on the wall and just follow the steps. Believe it or not, it works. I haven't screwed it up yet."

"Sounds like you're getting along okay without John."

"Yeah." Lanie feathered her fingers over the baby's head. She moved through Sonny Buck's daily routine, but the house seemed incredibly empty with just the two of them. She missed her job, and as badly as she hated to admit it, she missed John. The old cliché made her want to laugh—she couldn't live with him; she couldn't live without him.

Glancing up, she flinched under Caitlin's knowing gaze. She'd never been able to deceive Caitlin. Needing to get away, she turned toward the stairs. "I'm going to see if a warm bath will help him relax."

An hour later, a quiet, drowsy Sonny Buck in his crib, Lanie wandered back downstairs. She didn't glance at the foyer and its memories, steeling herself to join Caitlin in the living room.

Still seated on the floor by the coffee table, Caitlin didn't look up. "I'm making you a list of gifts and who sent them. I'll help you with thank-you notes while I'm here, if you like."

"That would be great." Lanie gathered empty paper cups and plates from the room and added them to the trash bag.

Caitlin capped her pen and laid it on the pad. She looked up, catching Lanie's gaze. "You love him, don't you?"

"Sonny Buck? More than I can say."

"I don't mean the baby. It's obvious you love him. You're a great mother."

"Thank you, but I think he's just an easy baby." Lanie forced a laugh to cover her discomfort.

"You didn't answer the question." Caitlin pinned her with the look Lanie suspected her cousin used with recalcitrant suspects. Pure steel under satin refinement.

Feeling trapped, Lanie walked to the glass doors and stared out at the drizzling rain. "I don't know how. He's not the man I thought he was." She remembered his anguish and the cryptic comment about his mother. "There's so much I don't know about him. How can I love him?"

"I don't know. But you're miserable with him gone, aren't you?"

"And I'd be miserable with him here. I'd always wonder if he was thinking of Beth, if he wanted her instead." She glanced at Caitlin over her shoulder. "Could you live with that?"

"Probably not." Caitlin wrapped her arms around her knees. "I hate seeing you unhappy."

Lanie turned away from those all-seeing eyes. With a fingertip, she traced a raindrop's path down the window. In the weeks since the night she'd given in to the temptation of John's touch, she'd wrestled with her feelings and what they meant.

With the memory of his mouth on hers, desire tingled in her abdomen, and she squashed it. She had only one option. “It’s the lesser of two evils, Cait. I’d rather be alone than end up like my mother, living with a man she could never really have. And I won’t do that to my baby, either.”

Silence lay between them for long moments, and when Caitlin spoke again, her voice was too cheerful. “Did you decide if you’re going with us tomorrow night?”

Lanie sighed, her gaze on the tear-like droplets glistening on the glass. “I don’t know. I’d love to get out for a while. I could find a sitter, but I bet nothing in my closet fits.”

“Sounds like a great reason for a shopping bonanza. Come on. It’ll be fun.”

Anticipation shivered over Lanie’s skin. A new dress. Dinner. Music. A little dancing, and a night when she could feel like the old Lanie. A night to help her forget John O’Reilly ever existed. She turned, grinning. “You’re right. It does sound like fun. In fact, it sounds like just what I need.”

“Well, I’m going to get out of here.” Caitlin rose, brushing at the seat of her jeans. “I’ll come by around nine.”

As Lanie closed the door behind her cousin, the phone rang. She hurried to pick it up, not wanting the upstairs extension to wake the baby. “Hello?”

For a second, silence shimmered on the line, and her nerves tingled. John cleared his throat. “Hi. I was calling to see if Sonny had a better evening.”

Eyes closed, she leaned against the hallway wall. The deep roughness of his voice conjured recollections of them together, dark whispers of what he wanted from her, what he wanted to do to her. “About the same. He’s asleep now.”

“Did you call Dr. Ridley? What did he say?”

"It's probably colic. It lasts about a month."

"A month?" The distinct squeak of shifting bedsprings carried over the line, and Lanie pictured him lying in bed, wearing just his boxer briefs. Her mouth went dry.

"That's what he said." God help her, she was grateful for the inane conversation, the opportunity to bask in his voice.

"I get off at five every afternoon. If you need help, I can come over and—"

"We're fine." The words emerged sharp and brittle, but she couldn't handle seeing him every evening, knowing he'd leave.

Silence stretched over the line. "Fine." His voice was clipped, harsh. "I'll see him Tuesday, then. Good night."

The line went dead, and Lanie stood for a long time, leaning against the wall, the phone pressed against her lips.

cs80cs80

John jogged up the stairs to the small apartment he now shared with Casey McInvale. He could feel the weight of the fundraiser dinner-dance ticket he carried in his pocket, the outline burning into his skin. Casey had laid it on him after the fishing tournament that morning, and the ticket was pure temptation—an excuse, an opportunity to see Lanie. Not even a game of tennis at the Y had pushed it from his mind. Already, his resolve weakened.

He tried to shrug off the despondency settling on him—he'd given Lanie time and space, and he was no closer to getting through to her than he'd been when she'd awakened in the hospital, looking at him with hatred in the golden depths of her eyes.

On the landing, he sorted through his keys, still not used to looking for the brass key instead of the silver one to Lanie's door. The key stuck in the lock, and he cursed under his breath, jiggling the handle. Finally, the door swung inward, and he stepped into a raucous blend of familiar voices.

"O'Reilly! About time you got here." Casey stood in front of the mirror by the front door, straightening his tie. "Look who's here."

Hank Starling and Alison Rivers, the detectives who had shared the desks adjacent to his and Beth's, greeted him with derogatory teasing about desk jockey spread and pencil pushing assignments. He laughed, but his attention was on the other occupant of the room. Beth stood by the kitchen door, a bottle of sparkling water in hand, a dark blue dress setting off her copper hair and fair skin.

She smiled and crossed the room to envelop him in a warm hug. "Smile, O'Reilly. I'm not going to bite you."

He returned the hug, glad to see her eyes were bright and clear. "I wasn't worried about that, Cameron."

No shivers of sensation moved over his skin. His nerves didn't jerk. The only emotion tugging at his heart was simple pleasure that she lived. His eyes closed, with Beth's arms around him, the only face he saw in his mind was Lanie's.

"God, you smell." She stepped back, her nose wrinkled. "What have you been doing?"

With a sheepish grin, he tugged a hand through his hair. "Playing tennis. What are you doing here?"

"I got a personal invite from Sheriff Burnett to Haven County's fundraiser dinner." She shrugged, still smiling, although shadows slipped into her blue eyes. "I figured since his guys saved my life, showing up was the least I could do."

The ticket in his pocket took on extra weight. “Where’s Nicole? How’s she doing?”

“Better. She’s making friends and settling down at school. The little girl across the hall from our place is in her class; she’s spending the night over there.”

John waved a hand at the others. “I guess you guys are making a night of it, huh?”

Casey leaned against the foyer wall and grinned. “I graciously offered to escort Ms. Cameron since my lovely and understanding significant other had to work an extra shift.”

“And *we’re* making a night of it, O’Reilly,” Alison put in. Seated on the sofa arm, she tugged the skirt of her little black dress closer to her knee. “You still owe me a dance from New Year’s.”

“You’ll have to take another raincheck, Rivers. I’m not going. I need an early night.” Beth’s presence made his decision for him. He could imagine Lanie’s reaction if he showed up with Beth, even in a group.

“That desk job is already getting to him,” Hank said.

“Shut up, Starling.” Beth stared John down, her eyes narrowed. “We’re not taking no for an answer, O’Reilly.”

With a harsh laugh, he slumped into the recliner. “How about ‘hell, no’ then?”

Casey jingled his keys. “Starling, Rivers. Let’s go pull the car around. We’ll let Cameron work her persuasive wonders on him.”

The others filed out, leaving John and Beth staring at each other. She crossed her arms over her chest, tapping one foot. “Now what’s going on?”

Pushing the chair back, John folded his hands behind his head. “Nothing. I just don’t feel like socializing.”

"No." Beth waved a hand around the room. "I mean, this. You moving out. The desk job. The fact you look like walking crap."

He resisted the urge to jump to his feet and pace. "I took the desk job so I could spend time with my kid. I moved out because Lanie wanted me out. And maybe I look like crap because that's what my life has turned into."

Beth's eyes narrowed further, gleaming blue slits. "Poor baby. Having a little pity party, are we?"

Fury sizzled on his nerves. Slamming the chair to an upright position, he shot to his feet. "Don't give me that, Cameron. I don't need it from you. Remember, I've seen you in worse condition than I'm in."

She smiled, surprising him. "Good. You haven't forgotten how to fight. What are you doing, just giving in? Is that your plan, O'Reilly? Give her everything, including your back to use as a door mat?"

He jerked his fingers through his hair. "She doesn't *want* me anymore. What am I supposed to do? Hang around outside her door until she takes pity on me and takes me back?"

"If that's what it takes, yes. Have you tried telling her you love her?" She pointed from his head to his feet. "It's obvious you're pining away for her. God knows, you didn't go to hell like this when I dumped you."

"I can't tell her." The words hurt his throat. "She wouldn't believe me."

With a disgusted sigh, Beth grabbed her small beaded bag from the sofa table. "You know what, O'Reilly? You're hopeless. Stay here; wallow in self-pity. And in six months, when you eat your gun, maybe Lanie will show up for your funeral."

Chapter Seventeen

Lanie adjusted Sonny Buck's blankets. After his evening screaming bout, he'd taken a bottle and fallen into an exhausted slumber. She smiled, stroking his cheek while he sucked his fingers, his newest discovery. A warm rush of love suffused her body. He changed so much every day.

Guilt chilled the warmth. She couldn't imagine losing these moments, and part of her regretted telling John he couldn't come by every evening. She hated it, but even so, her sense of self-preservation was stronger than the regret.

A soft rustle of beads signaled Caitlin's presence. Lanie glanced up to find her cousin watching her from the doorway. A tense smile curved Caitlin's mouth. "Tristan's here. Ready to go?"

Lanie brushed a fingertip over her son's wispy hair. "Leaving him is harder than I thought it would be."

Caitlin crossed her arms over her midriff, her dress's silver beading clicking with the movement. "It will do you good to get out. Tristan has your cell phone number, and mine, if anything happens. We'll even call it an early night."

Lanie smiled. "You convinced me."

They went downstairs, Lanie wondering if the scandalous heels she'd chosen were really a good idea. When was the last time she'd worn high heels anyway? Probably that first, and only, Valentine's Day with John, just weeks before she discovered she was pregnant. His eyes had flared when he'd glimpsed the strappy, stiletto sandals, and she'd ended up leaving them on while he made love to her.

Putting his reaction to those dangerously high heels out of her mind, she enjoyed the feel of her new red dress. The silk shifted like caressing fingers over her skin, the asymmetrical hem fluttering about her legs. Knowing the scarlet hue set off her hair and skin, she felt attractive for the first time in what seemed like forever. With an artfully messy updo covering the incision site on her scalp, she could even let herself forget the scar and still-bare spot.

Dennis lounged against the banister, and his playful, appreciative whistle boosted her spirits further. He wrapped an arm around Caitlin's shoulder and grinned. "Ladies, I am going to be the envy of every guy at this shindig."

Excitement tingled under her skin. Music and dancing were old loves, and she felt their call tonight. With Tristan's reassurances relieving her last remnants of maternal guilt, she followed Dennis and Caitlin to the car.

The historic Seaview Hotel rose above the beach with restored twenties splendor. Images of crystal chandeliers and a polished ballroom floor danced in Lanie's head as Dennis handed his car off to a valet. In the spacious lobby, small groups congregated, talking, laughing, and sipping drinks. Surrounded by friends and acquaintances, Lanie relaxed further.

Moving through the lobby, they stopped several times as Lanie fielded hugs, handshakes, questions about her health and congratulations on her baby's birth.

When they walked away from the last group, Dennis glanced at his watch. "We've got a while before dinner. How about if I go to the bar and get us something to drink?"

Grateful, Lanie smiled. "A white wine would be wonderful."

Dennis nodded. "What about you, Cait?"

"Make it two."

"Be right back." Dennis disappeared into the chattering, laughing crowd.

"Are you tired?" Caitlin fingered the fringe of beads at the hem of her dress. "Do you need to sit down?"

Lanie shook her head, the noise of countless conversations pressing in on her. A slight ache began at her temples. "But when Dennis gets back, I wouldn't mind stepping out for some air."

"Hey, gorgeous, fancy meeting you here." Casey's enthusiastic voice brought a smile to her face, and she turned to greet him. The smile froze on her face, her breath strangling in her throat. Standing with Casey, hand tucked through his elbow, was Beth.

Lanie stopped herself from taking a step back. Beth's split lip had healed, and wearing a dark blue dress that hugged her curvy, petite figure, she radiated beauty and confidence. She stared at Lanie, a smile on her lips and something like anger crackling in her bright blue eyes. Lanie's gaze darted away, seeking John. Acid bitterness curled in her. He wouldn't be far away.

The impressions jumbled through Lanie's mind in seconds. If Casey noticed anything amiss in her reaction, he didn't show it. He wrapped her in a quick, hard hug and stepped back, whistling. "That is some dress, Lanie. You look awesome."

Pride forced her to widen her smile. She curved her fingers around his forearm, a teasing, flirtatious gesture. "You don't look so bad yourself, McInvale. Where's Lisa?"

Casey grinned. "She had to work, so I'm making the extreme sacrifice of escorting Beth tonight. It's a hard job, but—"

"Oh, stop," Beth commanded. She smiled at Lanie again. "You're looking very well, Lanie."

"Thank you." Lanie struggled to keep her voice even. Beth wasn't to blame for the mess Lanie's life was in. She couldn't help the way John felt about her. "You look great."

"We sound like a mutual admiration society." Casey's lighthearted enthusiasm did little to alleviate the tension. He glanced at Caitlin. "Gorgeous, you want to introduce me?"

Her mind whirling, Lanie made the introductions automatically, including Dennis as he returned. Sipping her white wine, she scanned the crowd again. No John.

"John should be along in a little while," Casey said, as though reading her mind. "He didn't want to come, but Beth worked her magic on him. He was in the shower when we left."

Anger washed Lanie's vision with a haze, and she swallowed past the lump of jealousy in her throat. Of course, he'd show up. Beth was here. She turned to Caitlin. "You know, I am a little tired." She winced at the brittle tone of her own voice. "Let's see if a table is available yet."

Casey glanced around at the crowd. "That's the best idea I've heard yet. Tell you what—we'll find Hank and Alison and join you."

Her only reply a tight smile, Lanie spun and walked away.

☙❧

Dinner turned out to be a miserable affair. The Seaview cuisine, famous throughout Texas, tasted like dust and ashes in Lanie's mouth. She pushed baby salad greens around her plate, unable to eat more than a bite of the spiced cornbread croutons. Conversation bounced around the large table, Casey kept the air lighthearted, but Lanie couldn't forget the empty chair between Hank and Casey.

Finding Beth's narrowed gaze on her every time she looked up didn't help either. Beth reminded her of a cat, waiting to pounce on it prey. Spearing a cob of baby corn and dipping it in the light house dressing, Lanie swore not to give her the opportunity. As soon as dinner was over, she was out of there. She would use Sonny Buck as an excuse and catch a cab.

The escape route made her feel marginally better. Commanding her stomach to settle down, she took a long sip of ice water.

A server approached to remove their salad course. He eyed the untouched plate in front of the empty chair. "Is your other party not joining you?"

"The other party is here." John's deep voice turned every bite Lanie had eaten into a lump of ice in the pit of her stomach. She glanced up to find him standing behind Hank's chair, his unreadable gaze steady on her. He clapped Hank on the shoulder. "Shove over, would you, Starling?"

With good-natured grumbling, Hank shifted to the empty chair, which left John seated at Lanie's right. Along with his woodsy scent, his warmth enveloped her, and the muscles low in her stomach trembled. Aware of his gaze on her face, she lowered her eyes and fiddled with her napkin, wondering why he hadn't asked Casey to move so he could sit next to Beth.

The interrupted conversation picked up again. The waiter began to place the main course, and John shook out his napkin, his elbow brushing Lanie's bare arm as he spread the linen square in his lap. He tilted his head toward her. "Who's with Sonny Buck?"

She didn't look at him, his voice doing crazy things to her nerve endings. "Tristan. He was asleep when I left." She lifted her goblet again, wetting her dry throat. "You didn't tell me you were coming."

He leaned back to give the server more room, his arm around the back of her chair. When he spoke, his breath stirred the hair at her temple. "I didn't know until this afternoon."

"Beth convinced you, huh?" She picked up her fork, using the action as an excuse to scoot away from his enticing heat.

"In a way." He straightened and reached for his own fork, but didn't drop his arm from her chair. "But I'm not here because of Beth."

With his torturous presence, there was no way she could eat. Lanie choked down a few bites of grilled seafood and vegetables, his every movement filling her with tingling awareness. Hoping to be distracted from his appeal, she tried to focus on the current topic of discussion at the table.

Casey laughed and waved his fork in John's direction. "This is how spoiled the kid is going to be—it's March, and O'Reilly is already hiding Christmas presents in the closet."

John grinned. "One. I have one gift for him stashed up there, McInvale. Stop exaggerating."

Through lowered lashes, Lanie shot a glance at John. He was already Christmas shopping for Sonny Buck. Thinking ahead. Planning to be a father for the long haul.

Turning his head, he caught her looking at him and grinned. He leaned closer. "Wondering what's in that closet for you?"

Ignoring the warmth pooling in her stomach, she pushed pure ice into her voice. "Save your money, O'Reilly. I don't want anything from you."

He straightened, the skin around his mouth taut and pale. "You're not going to give an inch, are you, Falconetti?"

She shot him a look. "Do you expect me to?" Folding her napkin and laying it by her plate, she rose. "Excuse me a minute. I'm going to call and check on the baby."

The hotel had a large stone patio off the lobby, and she drank in grateful breaths of the cool sea breeze. A quick call to Tristan confirmed that Sonny Buck still slept peacefully. Tucking the cell phone back in her small bag, she walked to the balustrade and stared out over the waves.

"You know, Lanie, he's not going to hang around and let you kick him in the gut forever." Beth joined her at the railing. "Don't you think he's been punished enough?"

Startled, Lanie shot her a wary glance. "What are you talking about?"

Beth matched her glare for glare. "He was a shallow jerk, and he followed his libido into your bed. I don't remember you asking for hearts and flowers at the time. When the condom broke and you got pregnant, he took responsibility. He avoided the emotional involvement, but a lot of guys would have just walked away and left you to handle it on your own. He didn't."

Nerves trembling under her skin, Lanie feigned a bored air. "And how is this any of your business?"

Looking unimpressed, Beth folded her arms over her chest. "Because he's probably the best friend I've ever had and you're ripping him apart. He loves that baby, and for some unknown reason, he loves you. And instead of thanking your lucky stars that he does, you're still punishing him for what Doug did."

Anger sparked to life, burning away the nerves. "You think this is about Mitchell? This is about—"

"Me," Beth finished for her. "Or what you think John feels for me. About him not telling you about our past. Then why aren't you blaming me? I'm the one who wouldn't let him, who made him keep my secrets, even when he didn't want to."

"I can't—"

"Blame me because I'm a victim, too?" Beth's laugh was harsh, ugly. "Yeah, it's not real PC to blame a victim. But don't you see, Lanie? John was Doug's victim, too. He robbed me of my life, Nicole of hers. He stole your baby's birth from you. And he stole John's chance to sort his feelings out in his own time. You know, he would have figured out that I wasn't the woman he really loved, probably about the time he helped you bring his son into the world. Doug robbed you both of that experience."

Lanie didn't want to listen, didn't want to think about the weird kind of sense Beth's words made. She locked trembling hands onto the carved stone railing. "I can't believe you're making excuses for him. He should have told me."

Beth pinned her with another look. "And what secrets do you keep from him? Does he know everything about you? He has his share of ghosts, Lanie, and they kept him from confiding in you. You just never bothered to find out what they were."

Speechless, Lanie stared at the other woman, confused thoughts tumbling in her head. What kind of ghosts? Like his mother? Had she been that wrong about him?

"One more thing," Beth said, rubbing at her arms. "You're going to drive him away, and some other woman will welcome him with open arms. Can you live with that? Think about it,

Falconetti. That stubbornness of yours isn't going to keep you warm at night when he's in someone else's bed."

Hands tucked in his pockets, John leaned against the wall and watched the couples on the dance floor. His own future stretched before him, grim and empty. He could give Lanie all the time from here to infinity or tell her how he felt every second of that period, but none of it would matter a damn. She wasn't coming back to him.

Head tilted back, he closed his eyes, not able to handle watching the happiness of others any longer. Beth had thrown that crack about eating his gun at him, but he didn't even have that option. He couldn't, wouldn't, do that to Sonny Buck.

A light, familiar touch on his arm snapped his eyes open. Lanie stood beside him, her golden eyes shadowed. He straightened, nerves thundering in his stomach. "What's wrong? Is it Sonny—"

"He's fine." She swallowed, and he watched the fine muscles in her neck work. Her collarbones stood out above the deep neckline of the red dress, the line of her cleavage inviting his touch. In his pockets, his hands clenched tighter. "I'm ready to leave, and I thought... I thought you might like to come with me."

He wanted to read something into her invitation, to believe some miracle he didn't deserve had occurred to change her mind. Instead, he glanced at his watch. Ten o'clock. The baby would wake for a feeding around eleven. He hadn't seen his son in four days, and he couldn't miss this opportunity.

"Yeah, I would." He gestured toward the dance floor. "I'll drive you. Do you need to let them know you're leaving?"

She nodded, still gazing at him with that unreadable expression in her eyes. "I'll meet you out front."

The valet pulled his car around, and John leaned against the passenger door. A couple of minutes later, Lanie walked out, and the breeze molded the silk of her dress to her body. John stared, his hungry gaze following the curves and planes of her form. Eyeing the line of her thighs, he felt the familiar heaviness settle in his groin.

Forget it, O'Reilly. She invited you home to see the baby. She's not interested in anything else.

He straightened and opened the door as she approached. She smiled, her hand grazing his upper arm. "Thank you."

His body jumped under the brief touch, heat zinging from the point of contact to his groin. Dragging in a deep breath, he crossed to the driver's side and slid behind the wheel. Lanie twisted to fasten her seatbelt, the skirt of her dress riding high on her thighs, knees angled toward the gear shift.

When he shifted gears, his wrist brushed the bare skin of her legs. The brief drive to what had been their home was torturous. Surrounded by the evocative scents of cinnamon and vanilla, John was bombarded by memories of other journeys, when he'd been free to stroke a hand up her thigh, or her hands had roved over him, making him crazy.

The Clapton CD changed tracks, the distinctive strains of "Wonderful Tonight" filling the car, and Lanie sighed.

"I love this song." She leaned forward to turn up the volume. Her breast brushed against his hand on the gearshift, and he sucked in a harsh breath, the tightening in his groin growing. If he didn't know better, he'd think she was deliberately trying to drive him crazy.

He turned into her driveway and jumped from the car, coming around to open the door for her. She walked ahead of him up the walk and stairs, and he found it impossible to keep his gaze from the sway of her hips under red silk. Sonny Buck better wake early, or he risked having an insane father.

Once inside, Lanie greeted Tristan, and John listened in disbelief as the young woman told them Sonny Buck had indeed woken early, taken his bottle and gone back to sleep. Irritation jerked under John's skin. He'd endured the torture of her seductive presence for nothing.

He stood in the living room, glaring out at the waves, while Lanie walked Tristan to the door. When she returned, he watched her reflection in the glass, his chest aching. God, he wished she still wanted him.

He wanted her to love him.

Jerking a hand through his hair, he turned. "I should go."

A nervous expression flitted across her face. She walked toward him. "We need to talk."

That was never a good phrase to hear from a woman. He had a sickening premonition that she was going to ask that his visitation hours be changed, shortened, and he prepared himself for a fight. He'd lost her. Damned if he was giving up any more time with his son.

She didn't stop until she stood directly in front of him, so close he could see the tiny pulse in her throat. He stared down at her, his heart pounding, knowing that if she got any closer, she'd be able to feel exactly what she did to him. "Lanie, can't this wait? We're both tired—"

Leaning up, she covered his mouth with hers.

Chapter Eighteen

Heat exploded with the fusion of their mouths. Lanie wrapped her arms around John's neck and pressed closer. Through the thin silk of her dress, the line of his body burned into her skin. She felt everything—the ripple of muscles, his heartbeat, outline of shirt buttons, his belt buckle, the thickening ridge of his erection against her abdomen.

His hands spread over her back. She opened to him, drawing his tongue into her mouth with a soft, sucking motion. The groan that rumbled in his chest vibrated through her, sending a thrill along her nerves. She'd missed this, missed *him.* An ache of desire swirled in her and pooled between her thighs. She moaned and pressed closer still, wanting him all over her.

One second he was kissing her, and the next his hands were at her hips, putting her away from him. He glared, chest heaving. "What kind of game are you playing now?"

She flattened her hands against his chest, his heartbeat thudding under her palms. "I'm not playing anything."

He backed up a step and pushed a hand through his hair. "Thought you said you didn't want anything from me."

Confused, she shook her head. Why was he doing this? Wasn't she offering him the one thing he'd always wanted from her? "I want you."

His strained laugh assaulted her ears. "You could've fooled me. You know, Lanie, I don't think *you* know what you want."

Stepping around her, he headed for the foyer. Stunned, Lanie stared after him for a moment. Anger and rejection washed through her. He couldn't just walk away, could he? She followed him, her fingers closing around his on the door knob. "That's it? You're just leaving?"

She felt his shudder before he jerked his hand out from under hers. He straightened, his bad temper crackling, seeming to fill the small area. "Yeah, I'm leaving."

"John, don't go." Angry desperation trembled in the words. If she let him walk out, she was afraid it was all over—he wouldn't be back.

"Give me a reason," he snapped. He waved a hand toward the living area. "And not what you were offering me in there."

The words hurt. She narrowed her eyes at him, fighting off the urge to screech in frustration. "It never bothered you when I offered you that before."

He jammed his hands in his pockets. "Yeah, well, I didn't know then what I know now. Are you going to get the hell out of my way or not?"

She leaned forward, in his face. "What do you think?"

"Don't start with me, Lanie. It's not a good idea right now." A tense warning lurked in his voice.

"I tried starting with you. You weren't interested."

His hands shot out and closed on her shoulders. He pushed her against the wall, his lower body in intimate contact with hers. He was erect, and Lanie gasped, staring into navy eyes so dark with frustrated arousal they seemed black. "That's how interested I am, Falconetti. I could take you right here, right now, but I want more than just sex between us."

"What do you want?" Her voice emerged a raw whisper, her gaze still locked on his. A different ache spread through her body, a need for something more than his possession.

He shifted closer, until she didn't know where he ended and she began. "I want all of you. I want everything. I want you wrapped around me, but I want it to be because we love each other, not because we've got an itch. I want you to trust me."

Her harsh laugh bounced off the walls in the small area. "You want me to love you? To trust you? I don't even know you."

"But you were willing to screw me anyway, weren't you?" He released her shoulders, hands resting against the wall on either side of her neck. "Or were you going to get me all tied in knots again before you pushed me away and blamed me for it? I make a hell of a whipping boy, don't I? Am I standing in for your father? Paying because he didn't love your mom?"

She stiffened, everything turning to ice. "You bastard. Why don't we talk about your mother?"

He paled and dropped his hands, stumbling away from her. "I'm out of here. I don't need this."

The piercing cry from upstairs raised the hair on Lanie's neck and sent dread racing through her. John's face reflected her own fear. He sprinted for the stairs, a mere step ahead of her. Lanie stumbled in the heels and cursed, stopping to rip off the offending shoes.

When she reached the nursery, John already had Sonny Buck in his arms. The baby screamed, arms and legs jerking. John looked at her, his face white with fear. "He's burning up."

"I'll call Dr. Ridley." She dashed for the cordless phone in the bedroom, hearing him moving about in the nursery. One hand holding her address book open, she punched in the number and almost screamed when the all-night pizza joint downtown answered. She hung up without an apology. Fighting down frustrated tears, she rushed back to the nursery.

John had the baby care book open on the dresser, Sonny tucked against his shoulder. The screams had stilled to shuddery sobs and sniffles. He looked up as she entered the room. "What did he say?"

The tears overflowed. Filled with an urge to throw herself into his arms and sob out her fear and inadequacy, she held out the phone. "I can't even dial the number."

Comprehension dawned on his face, and he groaned. "Oh, baby, I'm sorry. I didn't think. Here, take him, I'll call."

He shifted their son into her arms and took the phone. Lanie cradled the baby close, and he snuffled into her shoulder, his tiny head hot against her cheek. Fear curled through her. He had to be all right. She couldn't bear it if anything happened to him. Her arms tightened.

"All right. Thank you." John dropped the phone on the dresser and looked at her. "Answering service. They'll have the doctor call us. We're supposed to take his temperature."

Lanie nodded, panic gripping her throat. "There's a digital thermometer in the changing table basket."

John went for it. Straightening, he motioned at his ear. "We don't have one of those ear ones?"

"No. I was going to—"

He waved the words away, looking at the baby book again. A grimace crossed his face. "Rectal temperature? You've got to be kidding me. I can't do that to him."

"You can take it under his arm. I remember that from another book." Her hair was falling, and she tossed back loose strands the best she could.

John reached for the baby. "Give him to me."

When John laid him on the changing table, Sonny Buck burst into fresh screams. John winced and lifted the baby's sack gown. With the thermometer under his arm, they waited. John cupped the baby's head in his hand and whispered soothing nonsense.

Lanie hovered, glad for his presence. The incident with the phone number unnerved her. What if John hadn't been here? Insecurity crowded in on her.

After a shrill beep sounded, John pulled the thermometer from under Sonny Buck's arm. Lanie reached for the baby and lifted him back to her shoulder, rubbing his back in a soothing motion. "A hundred and one point two," John said, looking ill. "God, that sounds high."

The phone rang, and John snatched it up. "Hello?"

Lanie listened as he explained the baby's condition and told the doctor how high the temperature was. He rubbed a hand over her back, a distracted, soothing caress, and Lanie leaned into his touch, grateful for his strength.

"All right. We're on our way." Clicking off the phone, John dropped it on the dresser again. His thumb rubbed over her spine, and the corners of his mouth quirked in a tight smile. "Dr. Ridley is going to meet us at the emergency room."

The short drive and brief time spent in the waiting room stretched until Lanie's nerves threatened to snap. Sonny Buck kept drifting into an uneasy sleep, only to jerk awake and squall again. She refused to leave him in the carrier and lifted him into her arms. John rubbed his palm over her knee, a quick supportive gesture, and again gratitude for his solid presence suffused her.

A nurse appeared and called them back to a small, curtained area. With smooth, efficient movements, she checked Sonny Buck's temperature and other vital signs. Lanie watched, keeping a hand on the baby's head. She glanced up to find John staring at the plaid curtain, jaw clenched, a haunted expression on his face.

"Dr. Ridley will be with you in just a moment," the nurse said and pulled the curtain behind her.

"John?" Lanie laid her other hand on his arm. "Are you okay?"

He turned anguished eyes in her direction. "I hate this place. I keep remembering you lying in one of these damned cubicles and all that blood...knowing it was my fault you were here, that it would be my fault if you died."

Beth's insistence that he was as much a victim as anyone else echoed in Lanie's head. She tightened her fingers on his wrist. "You didn't—"

"All right, let's see what's wrong with our Sonny Buck tonight." Dr. Ridley pulled the curtain closed behind him. Lanie dropped her hand from John's arm, glad the doctor was here for her baby yet aware that some intangible opportunity had just passed her by.

Arms wrapped around her midriff, she watched Dr. Ridley's quick examination and answered the questions he threw out while listening to Sonny Buck's heart and lungs, palpated his stomach, and looked in his nose and mouth. The noncommittal noises he made while doing so intensified her worry and impatience. She glanced at John. The tightness of his features reflected her own edginess. He caught her looking at him and sent her a tight, reassuring smile.

"Oh, here's the problem," Dr. Ridley said, looking into Sonny Buck's minuscule ear with an otoscope. "Does he seem more comfortable tonight in an upright position?"

John dragged a hand through already disheveled hair. "Yeah. Every time we had to lay him down, he screamed."

Nodding, Dr. Ridley clicked off the instrument's light and replaced it in the rack on the wall. "He has a middle ear infection, and a prone position increases the pressure."

"An ear infection?" Lanie remembered the heart-rending screams and shuddered. "Are you sure that's all?"

A smile quirking at his mouth, Dr. Ridley nodded again and pulled his prescription pad from his pocket. "They're a little more common in bottle-fed babies, and they have an exasperating tendency to come on at night. Acetaminophen every four hours for the fever and pain will make him more comfortable, and we'll start him on a course of antibiotics to clear up the infection. Make sure he takes the antibiotics for the entire ten days, and I'll want to see him in the office next week."

John took the prescription slip, and Lanie smiled at the pediatrician. "Thank you."

He grinned and pulled the curtain aside. "Anytime. Call if you have any questions or if he gets worse. The nurse will be in with your discharge papers in just a bit, and I'll have her give him his first dose of acetaminophen."

Again, the curtain isolated them together. Sonny Buck squirmed, fussing, and John picked him up, whispering against his forehead. Lanie watched them, that funny little ache in her chest again. "I'm glad you were here."

Over the baby's head, he shot her an unreadable look. "Yeah, me, too."

Bats fluttered in her stomach. She swallowed. Was this how boys felt asking a girl out for the first time? "Would you like to stay with us tonight? You can use the daybed—"

He half-turned away from her, shifting the baby's weight from one arm to the other. "That would be great. I really don't want to leave him."

Lanie closed her eyes against the picture he made with their son. She didn't want him to leave her, either.

ꕥ

Wearing a soft cotton nightshirt, Lanie padded through the bathroom to the nursery. John lay on the daybed, eyes closed, Sonny Buck asleep on his chest. One long-fingered hand rested on the baby's back, keeping him secure. Lanie's throat tightened. Everything she wanted was before her, and she'd never felt farther away from it.

Intending to move the baby to his crib, she crossed the room and circled John's wrist with her fingers. His eyes snapped open, and she stared down at him in the dim light. Lanie swallowed. "I'm going to put him in the crib."

He moved his hand, surrendering the baby to her. As she slid her hands under their son, her fingers brushed John's bare chest. Recalling his heartbeat under her hands earlier and the rejection in his eyes, she stepped away.

Cloth rustled on the daybed behind her. She settled Sonny Buck in his crib and pulled his blanket about him. The daybed springs creaked, and John's bare feet whispered against the floor. She stroked the baby's forehead, skin now cool to the touch. "Are you really stashing Christmas presents for him?"

"Yeah." John's soft laugh filled the room. "I'm looking forward to him believing in Santa. I never did."

A picture of John as a little boy with dark lashes and navy eyes like their baby flashed in her mind, and her heart ached. "My mother loved Christmas. She played Santa Claus every year, even after I'd figured out he wasn't real. I'd have gifts from her under the tree days before Christmas, but my Santa gifts never showed up until Christmas morning. She hid them, but as hard as I tried, I never could find them."

"Lanie, about what I said earlier, about punishing me because your father didn't love your mother—"

"He didn't." She turned to face him, her hands clenched on the top rail of the crib. Clad only in his boxer briefs, he sat at the edge of the daybed, watching her. She glanced away before meeting his gaze again. "He married her because she was pregnant with me and my grandfather forced him. He'd become engaged to another girl after that summer fling with my mother. He hated being married to her, and he resented me."

John shook his head. "Why not just divorce her?"

She laughed. "Sounds reasonable, doesn't it? But there hasn't been a Falconetti divorce in... Well, who knows if there's ever been one. Grandfather expected him to live up to his responsibility by marrying her, and he expected him to stay in the marriage, whether they were happy or not. The weird thing was, my mother seemed happy. She'd wanted him, and she got him. And me."

"She loved you." The statement held quiet certainty.

A smile tugged at her mouth. "She did. I remember being small, and she would come into my room and just hold me close. She always smelled of this rose perfume...and she was always there to do the silly things that little girls want to do. I used to play in her makeup and her jewelry box, and she would let me fix her hair... She had this long blonde hair, almost to her waist."

He continued to watch her, and she turned away, resting her hand on the baby's back, his breathing steady under her fingertips. Remembering, she shuddered. "As I got older, I could see she hid a lot of things behind that bright smile. The nights my father didn't come home, she would sit in the living room and wait. Or he would come home, and I'd lie in my bed and listen to the yelling downstairs. My mother crying. I hated him for making her cry."

The bedsprings creaked. His hands cupped her shoulders, and he pulled her back against him. The warmth of his skin burned through the thin cotton of her nightshirt. Lanie closed her eyes, soaking in the feel of him. "The summer I was fifteen, he stayed gone more and more. And she just kind of faded. He came home one day... I remember it was in the middle of the afternoon. Cait and I had been playing tennis, on one of those days when it's so hot you can hardly breathe. We were in my room; the door was open. We could hear them down the hall."

"Lanie." His breath whispered over her ear. "You don't—"

"He told her he was leaving, that he loved Carol, and Mom screamed at him that he couldn't leave. She was pregnant. And he told her that she'd trapped him that way once, but it wasn't going to work again. He packed a bag and walked out. The house was huge—the bedrooms were on the third floor, and the master suite had a balcony that overlooked the stone patio by the pool. She jumped. I heard her scream his name and—"

"Oh God, baby, don't." His arms came around her, rocking her against him.

Unshed tears dammed in her throat. Lanie covered his wrist with her hand. "It was only July, and she already had Santa presents in the closet. We found them when we were packing her things afterwards. My father married Carol the following spring, and I had to live with them in that house."

His arms tightened.

She swallowed against the tears. "When I got pregnant... My mother drilled into me that loving a man wasn't worth what it took from you. She didn't want me to ever feel the way she did about my father. When I got pregnant, it was like I was living her life all over again."

"That's why you wouldn't marry me." His voice rasped against her ear.

She nodded, his nose brushing her temple. "I couldn't do it, trap us into something like that. We'd only been together a few months, and all we had between us was the sex even if we were living together. I couldn't do that to him. Or us."

"I'm sorry," he whispered. His lips brushed her jaw. "So, so sorry."

"John." She moved, turned in his arms. Their gazes locked, and she stared up at him. "I know you want more than what we had, but I can't do that right now. Too much has happened; too much has changed. We don't even *know* each other."

He traced the line of her lips with his index finger. "We can change that. Give me a chance, honey. A real chance."

Possibilities danced before her. A man who loved her. A family. Forever. Squashing the spurt of cynicism that said she was courting trouble, Lanie nodded. "I can do that."

Chapter Nineteen

After zipping her jeans, Lanie turned sideways and looked at her reflection. She sighed, remembering the sets of crunches she labored through before bed every night. Obviously, Sonny Buck had ruined her flat stomach for life. Turning away, she grabbed her white long-sleeved T-shirt and tugged it on.

Nerves fluttered in her stomach. The days of John's scheduled visitation crawled now, since they'd turned those evenings into date nights. They spent the evening with the baby, and when Sonny Buck was tucked in for the night, they spent time with each other, doing something they'd never really done before—talking. Lanie checked the clock a hundred times a day, counting off the minutes until John arrived.

She brushed her hair, arranging the heavy mass so it covered her incision scar. The hair was slowly returning, but she still looked like the victim of a really bad barber. She replaced the brush on the dresser and opened her jewelry box. The silver infinity pendant lay on top, glittering and mocking. Her fingers hovered over it for a moment before she pulled out a silver choker with a turquoise slide instead.

The doorbell rang, and she closed the lid. While jogging down the stairs, she closed the choker about her neck. Anticipation making her giddy, she opened the door. "Hey."

"Hey, yourself." On the porch, John grinned at her. His hair still shower-damp, he wore jeans and a black golf shirt. He hefted a plastic shopping bag. "I hope Chinese is okay."

Her mouth watered, more from his clean scent than the food. "Sounds great."

His grin widened. "Do I get to come in?"

"Oh!" Laughing, Lanie stepped back and wiped damp palms down her jeans. "I'm sorry."

He moved by her into the house, brushing his mouth across her cheek. Her skin tingled under the brief caress. She followed him to the kitchen, appreciating the way the faded denim hugged his thighs.

"Where's Sonny Buck?" he asked, pulling paper cartons from the bag.

She dragged her gaze from the muscles moving beneath his shirt. "He's asleep."

He stopped, staring at her. "You're kidding."

"His schedule's been off all day." She resisted a smile at his disappointed expression—he looked like a little boy who'd just been told his best friend couldn't come out and play. "Give him an hour or so."

"I guess," he grumbled and pulled a crab rangoon from a carton.

Laughing, she opened a container of shrimp with broccoli. "Careful. I'll think you want to see him more than me."

"Hardly." He shot her a look, the hot "eat you alive" expression she hadn't seen since the night Sonny Buck was ill. Sudden arousal tingled in her stomach before he dropped his gaze. He tugged chopsticks from the shopping bag and clicked them at her. "Want to eat in the living room?"

What she really wanted was to forget the agreement they'd made to get to know each other before they made love. She wanted to drag him upstairs, pull his shirt free from his jeans, press her lips to his stomach. Heat flashed through her with the images. Looking at her own bare feet, she swallowed and forced a cheerful tone. "Sounds great."

Stomach full, John stretched out on the carpet, hands behind his head. Just being here, in Lanie's presence, knowing Sonny Buck was safe and secure upstairs, filled him with a lazy satisfaction. The day's stress began to ease out of his body. He could stay right here and never move again.

Lanie's toe nudged his ribs. "All right, O'Reilly, you still have to help clean up, even if you did buy dinner."

He didn't open his eyes, but a grin tugged at his mouth. "Tell you what, Falconetti—I'll stay here, you clean up, and I'll let you take advantage of me later."

The toe nudged a bit harder. "Nice try, but that's not part of the deal."

With an exaggerated groan, he rolled to his feet. While Lanie collected their used glasses, he gathered cartons and took them to the kitchen. Resigned, he eyed the almost-full trashcan. He didn't live here anymore, and still she left this chore for him. "Lanie, I'm taking out the trash."

Outside, he tossed the bag into the curbside container. Sea air rolled in, hazy under the streetlights. The clean, damp smell filled his nose. Taking a deep breath, he turned towards the house. Light spilled from the windows, falling in squares on the postage stamp yard. He blinked, nerves shivering under his skin. His dinner solidified into a cold lump in his gut.

Shaking off the feeling, he jogged up the front steps. He'd left the front door open, and the foyer light cast a square of light on the small porch. His stomach tightened further, images of running through this door with Dennis Burnett on his heels flashing in his head.

The bathroom door stood open, the light on and shining off the white tile floor. He froze, Lanie's exasperated voice washing over him. "John? You're not going to believe what I did. I cut myself on that chipped sink edge, and I can't get the first aid kit open. Damned child resistant latch. Help me, would you?"

Help me. His mother's voice pounded in his head.

His back against the wall, he stared at tiny drops of blood against that white tile, the red running together into a haze over everything. Nausea churned in his gut, and he closed his eyes, struggling for breath. In the dark, images swirled—Lanie's still body, blood, his mother's open, staring eyes.

"John?" Concern hovered in Lanie's voice. She touched him, a firm hold on his arm. The metallic scent of blood rushed up his nose. His stomach heaved, and he bolted for the door.

He made it as far as the porch and leaned over the railing, a helpless retching shaking his body. A dim awareness of Lanie's gentle touch on his back invaded his consciousness, and he focused on that warmth, trying to break free of the dark mire holding his mind prisoner. Stroking his hair, she whispered to him, soothing words she used with Sonny Buck.

Finally, the heaving stopped, and he rested his damp face on the railing. Tremors racked his body, his knees threatening to give out. Lanie's lips brushed his nape. "John, come on. Let's get you inside."

He rotated his forehead on the cool painted rail. Throwing up like a wet-behind-the-ears rookie, over a little blood. Losing it in front of the one woman who needed him to be strong. He sagged and felt her hands buoy him up.

She pulled him toward the door. "Come on."

When he wanted to move under his own power, his body refused to cooperate. He leaned on her heavily, her shoulder under his arm, her arms about his waist. Moving like clumsy participants in a three-legged race, they made it to the couch. She pushed him down and pulled away. "I'll be right back."

Sprawled where she left him, John closed his eyes. Humiliation crawled under his skin. Weakness wasn't an option, and showing vulnerability in any form was a good way to get kicked in the gut. He'd learned that lesson at a young age, and life had underscored it for him over and over.

"Here." Lanie pressed a glass into his hands, and he opened his eyes, staring into a golden liquid the color of her eyes. She smoothed a cool, damp cloth over his face.

He jerked his head away and tried to push the glass back at her. "I don't want it."

"Tough cookies." She slid a hand into his hair, holding his head still and bathing his face. "You're shaking, your face is white as a sheet, and your mouth probably tastes like crap. Drink it."

His gaze locked with hers for a moment. She watched him with a look that said she wouldn't give an inch, and he was too exhausted to fight her. With a muttered curse, he tossed off the liquor. The Scotch burned all the way down, and for a moment, he feared he would throw up all over again.

She nodded, grim satisfaction firming her generous mouth. "I'm going to take care of my hand." His gaze dropped to the white rag wrapped around her palm, and his stomach lurched again. He closed his eyes, willing the bile down. "Stay here."

Stay here? Didn't she realize he didn't have enough strength left to move? He listened to her move about and tried to still the tremors in his arms and legs. Every sound jerked along his already jangling nerves.

"John?" Her hand curved along his jaw; the couch dipped beside him with her weight. He opened his eyes to find her kneeling next to him, her golden eyes dark with concern.

The sympathy chafed. "I'm fine."

"Liar." Her fingers slid behind his nape, working at the knotted muscles there. He stifled a groan. "Face it, O'Reilly, your inviolate male ego is shot to hell. Neither one of us is fine right now. Shut up and let me help you."

Her fingers worked magic on him, easing the painful tension. His eyes closed. Drawn to her, he slumped sideways. His face brushed her shoulder. The warm scents of vanilla and cinnamon enveloped him, soothing the remembered fear away. "You get off on giving orders, don't you?" he mumbled, his lips numb.

Her fingers moved into his hair. "Just with you."

With a sigh, he pressed his face against her collarbone and let his arms wrap around her waist. He wanted to get lost in her, allow her to absorb him. The fear and trembling faded, leaving warmth and something he couldn't define in their wake. Something he hadn't experienced in years. He tried to pin it down, but it fluttered and moved, dancing just out of reach.

She massaged the length of his spine, and he groaned, pulling her closer. "You can order me around all you want, if you just keep...doing...that."

"We're going to talk about what happened later. You know that, O'Reilly." Her words ruffled his hair, fingers moving up his back.

Boneless, he moaned and nodded, her skin like silk under his cheek. "Yeah, I know." Right that moment, he didn't care. The stress—days and weeks and years of it—evaporated under her touch. He just wanted her to go on touching him, wanted to let himself be touched.

Peace. That's what it was. He'd forgotten what it felt like. The idea flitted through his mind before vanilla and cinnamon and darkness took him under.

ଔଡ଼ଔ

"Shhh." Lanie held a finger to her lips and smiled at Sonny Buck. He chortled harder and kicked, splashing his bath water everywhere. "Your daddy is asleep downstairs."

She tiptoed her fingers up his pudgy tummy, and his navy eyes widened. He threw out his arms and looked surprised when water spattered his face. Laughing, Lanie slid her hands under him and lifted. With a bright yellow towel wrapped around his wiggling form, she carried him through to the nursery.

"I know this is a scary thought, kid, but I think I'm beginning to get a handle on your dad." She rubbed lotion over tiny arms and legs, lingering over elbows and knees. Sonny Buck cooed. She smiled and touched the curve of his mouth. "Well, kind of. He's a tough guy to figure out."

The episode in the foyer, his reaction, disturbed her. She had no doubt it was tied to the night Mitchell held her hostage, but she'd seen something deeper, something darker in his anguished gaze.

I saw it happen with my mother.

His words returned to her, and she closed her eyes, seeing again a small dark-haired boy with big navy eyes and long, dark lashes. What had he seen?

Under her hands, Sonny Buck kicked, bringing her back to reality. Her baby's father lay asleep downstairs, and even though she'd learned many facts about him during their recent conversations—he'd graduated third in his high school class, gotten through his first year of college on a tennis scholarship, lost his virginity at fifteen to the girl next door—she still didn't know him. And despite her claim that she was getting a handle on him, she still had no idea what made him the man he was. The man who, more and more, was making his way into her heart.

Could she fall in love with a man she already loved? Or had what she thought was love really been infatuation and a strong attraction? The closer he got, the more confused she became.

She dressed Sonny Buck for bed and rocked him, her thoughts on his father. When his eyes began to droop, she tucked him into the crib. Silence descended on the house. She put away Sonny's bath items and went to change her damp clothes.

The jeans and T-shirt went into the hamper. She pulled on loose lounge pants and a trim T-shirt. Unclipping the choker, she moved to the jewelry box to put it away. The infinity pendant glinted at her again, and she lifted it, letting the chain drift over her fingers.

She slid the necklace over her head, and the pendant fell beneath her shirt. The cool metal lay between her breasts, soon warming with her skin.

Turning out the light, she left the room and went downstairs to wait for John to wake up.

He was being watched. The awareness prickled along his skin, drawing him from the best sleep he remembered. John opened his eyes to flickering light—the fireplace and the large candles on the coffee table. Memory rushed in, and he groaned, rolling to sit on the edge of the couch.

"Feel better?" Lanie sat on the floor by the fireplace, her arms linked around her up-drawn knees.

Rubbing a hand over his eyes, he dodged the question. His body felt rested, but his mind felt like an exposed nerve, a wound with the scab ripped away. "What time is it?"

"A little after midnight."

His head jerked up. He'd slept for hours. Remembered humiliation burned along his skin. Not looking at her, he ran a hand through his hair. "God, I've got to go. I'm sorry—"

"Oh, no, you don't." Moving with a lithe grace he hadn't seen in months, she came to her feet. "You're not going anywhere, O'Reilly. We said we were going to talk."

The idea of exposing those images to the light scared the hell out of him. He stood up, his body drained and lethargic. "There's nothing to talk about."

With a disgusted sigh, she turned away, staring into the flames. "Yeah. That was nothing making you physically sick."

Irritation jerked along his nerves. He should have known she was going to push this, that she wouldn't let the dark memories settle back to the bottom of his soul. He should have known his plea for a chance, his plan for them getting to *know* one another was going to come back and bite him on the ass. He gritted his teeth. "It was the blood, okay?"

"Oh, the blood." She nodded, a knowing expression on her face. "You're a freaking homicide detective—"

"*Your* blood, Lanie. Your blood and that white floor and what could have happened. Yeah, I freaked out and lost it." He pushed a hand through his hair again, wanting out of this conversation. "Is that enough for you? Are we done now?"

“Yeah, I think we are.” Her soft voice lifted the hair on his nape, and he shot a look at her. She watched him with narrowed eyes, her jaw set in a familiar, stubborn line.

He threw out his hands. “What?”

“So this is the way it’s going to be? I pour out my heart to you, but all you give me are meaningless facts and nothing of substance? I’m the only one at risk?”

“Damn it, Lanie—”

“Well?” She crossed her arms over her chest.

Anger exploded in his chest, and he struggled to kill it. He wanted to shake the stubbornness out of her; his memories wouldn’t let him touch her in anger. “What do you want to know?” He snarled the words between clenched teeth, and her eyes widened. He reined the anger in. “What do you want me to tell you?”

A visible breath shook her body. She moved toward him, the stubbornness gone from her face, replaced by something softer. She didn’t touch him, but stopped inside his comfort zone, her head tilted back so their gazes met. Again, the urge to lose himself in her, in those eyes, surged through him. Her lips parted on a whisper. “I want to know who you are. I want to know what’s still eating you alive.”

A shudder ran through him. He let his lashes fall, closing out those golden eyes. She would ask the one thing he didn’t want to give, and he had no doubt that if he couldn’t give it, this was it. End of the road.

Damn it, she had to do everything the hard way.

“My father was a beat cop. Lower East Side.” He plunged into the story, knowing that was the only way he could get it out. His stomach clenched. “He died when I was three. The old cop cliché—walked in on a robbery in progress at a corner grocery and the perp blew him away before he ever got his gun out of his holster. His partner killed the perp."

"I'm sorry." She touched him then, her hand warm on his arm. He wished she hadn't, but he couldn't pull away.

He shrugged and opened his eyes. "Don't be. I don't remember him anyway. He's just this young guy in a picture my mom had. I have his eyes."

A sad smile curved her mouth. She reached up, caressing his jaw. "Then so does Sonny Buck. What happened?"

"What do you mean?"

"That's not all, is it?"

"No." He did pull away then, rubbing a hand over his mouth. "A few months later, my mom married again. To my dad's partner. I guess having him around helped her feel like my dad was still there. She'd have been better off alone."

"What happened?" Behind him, her voice was soft.

"He killed her." Her gasp filled his ears, and he laughed, a raw, harsh sound. "Oh, it took him a couple of years. Guess he needed to break her down first."

"Oh God, John. I'm so sorry." From behind, her arms came around him, hands flat on his chest. The comfort in her touch chafed at him, yet he never wanted her to let him go. Her cheek rested against his back, the only warmth he could find on his entire being. He was so damned *cold.*

"It was my fault."

The arms encircling him tightened. "No," she whispered. With weird detachment, he realized he could feel her lips moving, even through his shirt. "Oh, no. It wasn't—"

"He was going for me, and she got between us. I'd done something... Hell, I don't even remember what. Shouldn't I remember that? And he went for his nightstick." He pulled away from her and rubbed a hand over his nape, the muscles like a knotted rope. "We had this cheap white linoleum floor."

Lanie made a noise behind him, a small, fearful sound.

Hands spread in front of him, he made a circle with his fingers. The memories beat in his brain, the nausea pushing at his throat again. The urge to run pounded under his skin. "I remember watching the blood spread out under her ear. Brain hemorrhage. She died a couple of days later."

The words fell between them. He listened to the silence thump against his ears for a moment before turning to face her. She stared at him, her face white, and he shrugged. "Usually, I manage to forget about it. Every once in a while, there'll be a crime scene that... Beth scraped me up off a barroom floor after a bad one, but I didn't want to turn into one of those washed-up, has-been cops who drink away the job stress. I'd go to the courts, hit a few tennis balls, wear myself out so I could sleep."

She continued to stare at him. He'd seen that look before, too often on too many faces—new teachers, new foster parents, the little blonde he'd had a crush on all through eighth grade. Somehow, finding out about his past always seemed to change people's perceptions of him. Like they expected him to snap, go off the deep end and off someone, too. He'd thought maybe with her, it would be different.

Looked like he'd been wrong.

Tucking away the pain of that realization, he bounced on his heels, once, twice. The need for physical activity burned in him. He forced a grin, had to clear his throat before he could get any words out. "I know you're tired. I'm sorry about earlier and for crashing on you, leaving you with the baby. I'm going to head home."

He walked by her and to the door, the flight syndrome pounding in him. Halfway down the steps, he heard her voice, a note of panic in it. "John, wait. Please don't—"

"I'll call you." He called the words over his shoulder before sliding into the driver's seat. Aware she stood at the door, he backed out without looking at the house. Once on the street, he didn't use the rearview mirror until he was sure the house was out of sight.

Chapter Twenty

"Casey, I know it's the middle of the night!" The three wrong numbers she'd gotten while trying to dial Casey's number had made the late hour more than clear. She'd been cussed out in two different languages. The need to scream at John's roommate shivered under Lanie's skin. Fear trembled in her stomach. "I just... I need you to call me as soon as John gets there."

"I'll tell him to call you," Casey mumbled, half-asleep.

"No. He won't do it." Frustrated, she squeezed her eyes shut, remembering the awful blank look on his face. "This is important, Casey. Wake up and listen to me."

"You two have another fight?"

"No. But you've got to call me, as soon as he walks in the door." Opening her eyes, she glanced at the mantel clock and calculated the driving time to Houston. Frustration curled through her. Probably had that wrong, too. "Hell, call me if he's not there in an hour. If I don't hear from you, I'm calling back."

"Hour. Got ya. Call you back." The line went dead.

Lanie resumed pacing the living room, anger and foreboding fighting for dominance in her gut. Fear that he would do something stupid and get himself killed. Fury that he could just dump his past on her and walk out. That wasn't the way it was supposed to work. He'd cheated her of giving him the support and comfort he'd shown her the night she'd told him of her mother's suicide. The sensation was like having a lover get her almost there and roll away to fall asleep.

Damn it, if he didn't get himself killed, she might wring his neck herself.

But first, she'd wrap herself around him and take away as much of the pain as she could.

She stopped at the glass doors, staring out at the dark ocean. His revelations explained so much—why he'd stayed when he learned she was pregnant, his involvement with Beth, his guilt over Mitchell's actions, his strong bond with Sonny Buck. He stepped up to his responsibilities, but not his emotions. From those, it was easier to run—to use tennis or sex as an outlet.

Oh, you're one to talk, Falconetti. If O'Reilly uses sex for release, you use it for control. Have you ever really given yourself over to him?

Cheek pressed to the cool glass, she eyed white caps rolling ashore. A shudder played over her skin. If telling him about her mother had been hard, the idea of turning sex into an emotional connection was even worse. Sex had always been about her rules, no one else's.

They'd taken turns sharing trivia about their lives and their worse memories. They shared a child. Could she throw out the rules, share herself with him?

An hour later, after Casey called and confirmed that John hadn't made it to Houston, she was beyond caring about her rules, her wants, her need for control. She wanted John, safe, sound, and with her. Tears trembled on her lashes, dread setting up an icy residence in her veins.

The grind of a key in the lock had her running for the foyer. She pulled the door open before he could. “Where have you been?”

Sweaty and disheveled, his hair stood out from his head. His shirt had come untucked, and the hems of his jeans were wet, covered in the same damp sand that coated his shoes. Face still pale, he tucked the key she’d let him keep for emergencies into his pocket. He stared at her, his navy eyes intense. “Figuring out there’s nowhere left to run.”

“Oh, John.” Her eyes closed, and relief left her giddy. She lifted her lashes to find him still watching her, the same hungry look on his face. Without speaking, she held out her arms, and he fell into them.

His body trembled against her, and she managed to push the door closed before his knees gave out. They slid down the wall, arms around each other, his face pressed to her throat. Against hers, his skin was cool and damp, and Lanie pressed closer, trying to transfuse her own warmth into him.

A sigh shuddered through him, and he tightened his arms. Her hands roamed over his back, hungry to make sure he was real. They sat that way for long moments, not speaking, before Lanie tilted her head back to look into his face. She moved her hands up his neck, running her fingers over the planes and angles of his features. His eyes closed, a soft sound escaping his lips. His woodsy scent, mingled with fresh, male sweat and salty ocean air, surrounded her.

The beginnings of a cry wafted down the stairs to them, and for once, Lanie didn’t jump to see what the baby needed. John nuzzled his nose against her temple. “He’s hungry.”

She pressed his cheek against hers. “I know. Why don’t you take a shower while I feed him?”

The cries grew louder. His mouth brushed her ear. "You'd better hurry. He's demanding, now, instead of asking."

They disentangled, and Lanie watched him walk up the stairs, a thrill of anticipation settling in her abdomen. She turned away, and his voice carried to her while she warmed a bottle.

She paused in the nursery doorway. Sonny Buck cradled in his arms, John shot her a lopsided grin. "He's grown."

She crossed the room to take the baby. "Like a weed." He clamped down on the bottle with hungry glee. Settling into the rocker, she glanced up at John. "Take a shower."

"Yes, ma'am." Pulling his shirt over his head, he gave her a glimpse of the long, sloping muscles in his back before disappearing into the bathroom.

Eyes closed, Lanie rocked the baby while he ate. The sound of running water filled the room, and she pictured water sluicing over the muscles she'd seen, down over thighs and calves. Heat poured through her body, pooling, flowing out, tingling.

She wanted him. Not the old seeking-physical-gratification wanting, but wanted *him.* Wanted to give herself to him, lose herself in him.

As she tucked the baby back into bed, the shower stopped. Nails cutting into her palms, she walked to the bathroom. John pushed the shower curtain back, reached for a towel and froze, his gaze locked with hers.

Droplets trailed down his neck, over his chest, and into the arrow of hair on his abdomen. Her gaze dropped lower, warmth tingling along her skin. The muscles shifted in his legs as he stepped from the shower. Her breath coming in shallow bursts, she lifted her gaze back to his.

One second, she stared into navy eyes; the next his mouth covered hers. He tangled a gentle hand in her hair, his lips teasing hers apart. Her hands roamed his arms and shoulders, the skin slick and wet. The thin T-shirt she wore soaked up water from his skin and clung to her; she felt every line of his body along hers.

The kiss went on and on, and the heat pooling in her core spread out along veins and nerves, suffusing her being. He was hot, too, his skin fiery where she touched, warming the wet fabric that should have been clammy against her skin. Heat built around them, between them. Just a kiss. If just kissing him was hotter than anything they'd done before, what would making love with him be like? All of this felt so new.

His hands cupped her face, and he pulled his mouth from hers. "Lanie," he whispered against her temple. He rubbed his cheek against her hair, and his sigh trembled through her.

He lifted his head and stared down at her, unsmiling. His fingers moved over her face and neck, smoothing damp hair from her skin. Desire and something deeper burned in his eyes.

Strengthened by that flaring emotion, Lanie stepped away from him but not before sensing the sudden tension in his body, preparation for a blow of some kind. Holding his gaze, she smiled and reached for the hem of her T-shirt. She lost contact only long enough to pull the wet garment over her head.

The infinity pendant swung free, tapping the skin between her breasts, and his swift indrawn breath filled the room. His eyes flared hotter, and as she skimmed the lounge pants down over her hips and thighs and stepped out of them, she stared into those eyes, thinking he was going to burn her alive.

And Lord help her, she wanted him to.

His gaze dropped, traveling down her form, and for the first time, she faltered. She didn't look the same as he remembered.

Fine white stretch marks marred what had been her flat, smooth stomach. And farther down, the Cesarean scar, faded to a thin, pink line. She closed her eyes.

A finger touched her collar bone, and she startled. A trail of fire followed the line of the silver chain, traced the pendant's outline between her breasts. Her nipples tingled, hardened.

"Open your eyes." Even his whisper burned.

She lifted her lashes and looked into his face. He stared at her, his gaze on the necklace. Bending his head, he followed with his mouth the path his finger had taken. Her hands clutched at his shoulders for support.

He moved lower, his lips worshipping her, caressing the stretch marks, stroking over the scar. His finger danced over the tiny square patch above her hipbone, and he grinned against her thigh. "Different precautions, baby?"

His finger moved over the skin of her inner thigh, and a gasp trembled on her lips. She burned already, and he hadn't even touched her, not really. "Look what happened the last time we used a condom."

"Yeah." His teeth grazed her skin, a light, nipping caress. "Isn't he great?"

She never got a chance to reply because his tongue touched her, stroking, devouring, and her knees buckled. He laughed, a low sound of pure male satisfaction, and held her to him. His mouth moved against her stomach. "Let me take you to bed. I want to make love to you."

Her hands tangled in the dark thickness of his hair. "Yes."

With a swift motion, he stood and lifted her against him. Lanie wrapped herself around him, holding on, ignoring the nerves fluttering in her stomach. This was more than just sex, and the sense of exposure was worse than offering her virginity to the boy she'd never given a chance to break her heart.

He laid her on the bed, hands in her hair, his leg between her thighs. In the dim light, he stared down at her with a crooked grin. "I'm scared to death. I've never done this."

She knew what he meant, but she wanted the words. "Done what?"

"Made love like it matters." He lowered his head and feathered his mouth over her. The simple caress tingled all through her body, intensifying the ache between her legs. "Made love to the mother of my child."

The words alone did more than any touch to her body, although he took his time about that, too. He worshipped her with his hands and mouth, stroking, caressing, turning her to molten heat. His hands slid down, skimming her curves, stroking her thighs apart. He moved, erection hot and intimate against her.

Cupping her hips, he slid inside, a slow, deep movement that took her breath. His eyes closed, opened, stared into hers. Pleasure tightened his face, and he moved within her. Fire and tension built, grew, flared in her. "Made love to the woman I love."

"Oh, John." The words curled in her, joining the fiery pressure that coiled and tightened until she came apart and burned in his arms. Above her, he gasped and pushed deeper, a groan rumbling next to her ear.

He collapsed, his elbows keeping most of his weight from her. Breathing hard, Lanie closed her eyes. Enveloped by him. Shattered, sheltered, and secure.

ଔଷଔ

John opened his eyes, blinking at a familiar ceiling. Tentative rays of dawning sunlight poked into the room. His body ached deep in the muscles, but a hazy satisfaction curled through him. Still asleep, Lanie sprawled on his chest, a leg thrown over his thighs. She held on to him, possessing him.

He loved it.

Threading his fingers through the dark silk of her hair, he kept his touch gentle near the ridge of her incision. She shifted in her sleep, moaning into his chest, thigh brushing his early morning erection. The sensation shot through his body, and he smothered a groan. He wanted nothing more than to stay in this bed with her.

However, the hell on earth known as the Houston P.D.'s records division awaited him, as well as the commute into the city. Another groan, one of disgust rather than pleasure, rumbled in his chest.

Lanie moved, her fingernails digging lightly into his ribs. Her lashes lifted, and she smiled at him. A catlike stretch pressed her body closer. "Good morning, O'Reilly."

He made a noncommittal sound. With her looking at him like this again, even desk duty didn't seem so bad.

Her hand eased down his side to his hip. Her eyes drifted closed again, and she sighed. "What time is it?"

Everything she did drove him crazy. That little sound she purred in the back of her throat made his erection jerk like it had a mind of its own. He gritted his teeth. "Time for me to get up if I'm going to be on time for work."

Her sultry laugh was that of the naughty lover he remembered. She brushed him with her knee, and arousal shot through his gut. "Feels like you're already up."

He wanted to give in. "I've still got to drive into the city, take a shower, get dressed—"

"You can shower here." Her mouth moved along his stomach. "One of your suits is in Sonny Buck's closet."

"I'm supposed to be in uniform." He gasped out the words as her mouth had moved lower, eradicating his ability to breathe.

Her fingers stoked his inner thigh. "Any other excuses?"

His fingers dug into the sheets. "You're going to make me late."

"Do you care?"

"God, no."

ଔଓ

In the end, he was only five minutes late. He busted every speed zone between Cutter and Houston and arrived in the precinct wearing his charcoal suit instead of his uniform. Almost feeling like his old self, he grinned at Joyce Haynes, the bitter-because-she'd-flunked-out-of-the-academy records clerk. "Morning, Haynes."

The woman hated his guts. She glared at him. "You're late. And where's your uniform?"

He decided not to point out that technically he was in charge and he didn't give a damn about her opinion. He gestured at her overflowing in-box. "Want some help?"

She cast him a suspicious look before handing over a third of the stack. John flipped through them—wants and warrants to be entered into the system. He ached for a good, cold case to sink his detective's fangs into. Joyce crossed her arms over her skinny chest. "You're in an awful good mood."

A grin quirked at his mouth. "Yeah. I am."

As the morning progressed, some of his good humor faded. The repetitive, mindless task of entering data allowed him too much time to think, too much time to remember. By twelve o'clock, a nameless dread had taken up residence in his gut.

The night before, he'd been too focused on Lanie, on showing her how he felt. The second time they made love, he'd whispered "I love you" over and over, wanting to imprint the words on her skin, her mind, her heart. She'd responded with passion and eagerness. The intimacy of the experience had blown his mind. Only now was he coming back to reality.

You idiot, O'Reilly. Don't you see what's wrong?

Muttering a curse that made Joyce turn around and glare at him, John rubbed a hand over his face. He'd given Lanie everything last night—his vulnerability, his body, his love. He'd already had her vulnerability. She returned the gift of her body. He told himself that she loved him, that she wouldn't have let him back into her bed without it. He told himself he was being an idiot, that he was looking for trouble where it didn't exist. She loved him. She had to.

She just hadn't given him the words.

Chapter Twenty-One

Naked, Lanie lay sprawled in sheets that still bore John's scent. Beyond the window, sunlight sparkled off the water, and although Sonny Buck would be up soon and she should shower while she had a chance, she didn't move. John's scent was still on her skin, too, and she didn't want to wash it or the memory of his touch away yet.

Arms wrapped around his pillow, she hugged it close, warmth and satisfaction surging through her. *I love you.* He'd whispered the words over and over, a mantra against her skin while he made love to her once more. Even more than the words, his actions—sharing his old hurts, returning to her, making love to her the way he had—proved it. She closed her eyes, dreaming of a future with him.

Her fingers drifted down, playing with the edge of the birth control patch. Another baby. She smiled at the thought, envisioning a little girl with those navy blue eyes and long dark lashes. The image jerked her musings to a stop. Another baby? No. What they had between them now was more than she'd hoped for. This was their future—being together, raising their son, nothing but love to bind them, nothing to make John feel trapped.

"What are you doing, Falconetti?" she whispered into the pillow. "There you go again, rushing, without looking where you're going."

With reluctance, she rolled from the bed. The baby she had now would be awake any time. She needed to shower and get ready for the day, which stretched ahead of her, the empty hours offering plenty of time for daydreaming.

After breakfast, she put Sonny Buck on a pallet in the living room floor to play. On his stomach, he lifted his head and grinned when he saw her. His comical pushups made her smile. She brushed her fingers over his head. "You are scintillating company, my boy."

She sighed and stretched out on the floor facing him, her chin resting on her hands. He was just over two months old. If her pregnancy and delivery had gone as planned, she'd have already returned to work. Light duty, surely, but work just the same. And as much as he fulfilled her, she still missed the excitement of being a road cop.

That wasn't in her prospects anymore, and she didn't want to face indefinite desk duty. What would she do when she was completely well? That part of her future stretched before her, dark and hazy. She shrugged off the cold knot of worry. She was alive. She had a healthy child and a man who loved her.

The rest would fall into place.

The afternoon mail killed her optimism. Tucked in with her electric bill and a credit card offer was a statement of her hospital charges. The total amount kicked off a sick wave of nausea in her stomach.

Oh, good Lord. Her entire college education cost less. Facing unemployment, and her level of unsecured debt had just grown by an obscene amount. She leaned against the wall and stared at the numbers again.

Suddenly, sinking her inheritance from her mother into this house so she could afford the luxury of living on the ocean didn't seem like such a good idea. She looked at the statement again and tried to figure out what would be left to pay after her insurance plan paid its percentage. *Damn it. Basic math. Why can't I do freakin' basic math anymore?* Her mind refused to wrap around the numbers, and she leaned her head against the wall, frustration and insecurity washing through her.

She couldn't do this to John. She wouldn't burden him with her debts, her deficiencies. She'd be his equal or nothing. Images of being in his arms flashed through her mind. His deep voice whispered over her again. The idea of giving that up, of never having that intimacy with him again, sent a stab of actual pain through her stomach.

The hazy daydreams of a future with him evaporated—an oasis that didn't exist and never really had.

ଓଃଃ

John slammed the racket into the ball and watched it ricochet off the practice wall. He smashed into the return, and the impact jarred all the way up his arm. Thoughts jumped around his mind, echoing the movement of the bright yellow ball on the court.

She wore the damned necklace again. Wasn't that enough?

Another crashing forehand. Sweat trickled down his brow.

No. He wanted the words. He wanted to hear her say she loved him.

The ball bounced back at him. *Don't push so hard. Give her time.*

Impatience added force to his return. How much time? He had a vision of Sonny Buck in a graduation gown and himself with gray in his hair, still waiting for Lanie to confess her feelings. What should have been funny, wasn't.

The yellow missile veered to the left, and he had to run for it. *As much as she needs. Remember what she's been through. And not just with Mitchell. All of it. Her parents, everything. She needs you. Aren't you the guy who prides himself on meeting his responsibilities?*

He missed the ball, and it bounced away, dribbling to a stop by the net. Dropping his racket, he leaned forward, hands on his knees. His lungs heaved, a slight ache in his barely healed ribs. He squeezed his eyes shut. What if he failed her? What if he wasn't enough? What if she couldn't ever give him the words?

Straightening, he shook off the doubts and focused on what he had, what he could hold on to. He went to pick up the ball. She was wearing his necklace again. For now, that was all he had. That would have to be enough.

ଓଃଛଠ

As much as possible, Lanie let the myriad tasks of motherhood soothe her jangling nerves, but always in the back of her mind was the hospital statement lying on the kitchen counter and her lack of employment prospects. But once early evening came with Sonny Buck bathed and in bed for the night, all the worries rushed back in like waves on the beach—one right after the other.

She had a huge debt hanging over her head.

She didn't have a career anymore. Disability insurance didn't last forever either.

She had a son who was going to learn more about math in the third grade than she could do now. Lord, she hoped he was a math whiz like her father. Heaven only knew what math tutors cost.

She would have to turn away from the man she loved. The man who said he loved her, who touched her as if she were the most precious thing on earth.

Options. She needed options. If nothing else, she always had the equity in the house. As much as she loved the ocean, she could always sell the house and rent somewhere.

There was always her father.

"Oh hell," she whispered, digging her fingers into her hair and sending a mild ache along her scar. "I'm not that desperate. Not yet anyway."

You could ask John for help. Really share your problems with him. Let him be a true partner.

She shied from the idea. Somehow, dumping her burdens on John was worse than asking her father for money. She needed to come to him as an equal. Being the one who needed more in a relationship was not an option. Hadn't she seen that with her mother? Her father had held all the power in that relationship, and ultimately her mother's neediness had led to her destruction.

Her teeth worried the inside of her cheek, the metallic taste of blood spreading in her mouth.

A muffled knock at the door jerked her out of the miserable reverie, but a peek through the security hole sent her stomach plummeting. She opened the door, and John grinned at her, his hands occupied by a large pizza box and a small stack of DVDs. He leaned forward at an awkward angle and brushed a kiss over her mouth. "Hi. God, I missed you today."

Her fingers clutched the doorknob until her knuckles ached. His hair fell over his forehead, and the boyish grin made her want to drag him inside and wrap around him. All the cravings he'd reawakened and which now she had to rid herself of. "Hi, yourself. I wasn't expecting to see you tonight."

His smiled faltered, and uncertainty flashed in his eyes. "Yeah, it's not a visitation night, is it? I guess I should have called first."

She forced her voice to a noncommittal tone and stepped back from the door. "Well, you're here, and you're bearing food. Come on in."

A slight frown between his brows, he didn't move. "Lanie, I don't have to stay. I thought... well, I thought you might want to see me, too."

The vulnerability in the words slammed her in the chest. She fought for the breath he'd just taken away. Not yet. She didn't have to give him up just yet. Forcing a smile, she took his arm and pulled him into the foyer. "Of course I want to see you. It's just been a weird day. I've got a wicked case of cabin fever."

He didn't look convinced, but he let her steer him toward the kitchen. "Sonny Buck down for the night?"

"He is." She pulled plates from the cabinet and sodas from the refrigerator. "You should see him holding up his head."

His low whistle cut through the room, and she turned to find him holding the hospital statement. "Is this for real? No wonder you're freaked out."

Resisting the urge to slam the plates on the counter, she set them down, placed the sodas next to them and reached for the statement. "Yes, it's for real."

He held on to the paper. "Forty-two dollars for an ibuprofen tablet?"

"Write your congressman. Express your outrage." Lanie dragged the paper from his fingers.

His gaze didn't waver from her face. "That's it, isn't it? You're upset about the money."

A harsh laugh escaped her. "It's a lot of money, John. I'm worried about it. I'm basically unemployed, remember?"

"Baby, we'll handle it." Hands gentle on her shoulders, he pulled her closer. "Together."

She shrugged away from his easy hold. "Don't you get it? It's not just the money. I have no idea what I'm going to do. The simplest math throws me off; I can't dial a right number to save my life—"

"That reminds me!" John snapped his fingers, a grin crossing his face. "I ordered speed dial for you today. All we have to do is program in the numbers you need most, put a list by the phone, and you're covered. Don't know why we didn't think of it before."

Frustration curled in her, burning. He pulled a short list of printed instructions from his pocket and laid it by the phone. Lanie sighed, running a hand through her hair. "That's great, John, but that doesn't solve the big problems."

Flipping open the pizza box, he shrugged. "So we'll handle them as we come to them."

His lackadaisical attitude irritated her further. Didn't he get that this was her life they were talking about here? Speed dial wasn't going to make her a cop again. Without a career, she couldn't be secure. Security was essential—never would she make her mother's mistake of being dependent on anyone.

She picked up a slice of pizza and dropped it on the plate. "I'm glad you're so confident."

The look he shot her was wary. "What?"

She shoved the plate away. “You act like it’s nothing, no big deal.”

He dropped his own slice of pizza, untouched, and sighed. “I didn’t—”

“What would you do if you couldn’t be a cop anymore?”

His eyes narrowed. “In case you haven’t noticed, I’m not.”

The finger she pointed at him trembled. “You made that choice, O’Reilly. I didn’t get one.”

He opened his mouth, closed it, and shook his head. Reaching out, he grasped her wrist and pulled her to him. “The reason for my choice is sleeping upstairs. Yeah, working the records division sucks, but I don’t have to worry about going after a suspect and getting shot. I don’t have to worry about him growing up without me. Come on, Lanie, be realistic. Think about that baby sleeping up there. Would you have gone back to road duty?”

Her anger and resentment faltered. She shook her head, staring into navy eyes soft with understanding. “I don’t know.”

“It’s not completely out of the question.” His other hand slipped to the small of her back, massaging in light circles. “You said yourself that the neurologist said sometimes the problems, like yours with numbers, only last a few months. It’s been two months, baby. Give yourself some time.”

She closed her eyes and blew out a sigh. “I just—”

“Feel overwhelmed,” he finished for her. Giving in, Lanie relaxed into his warmth. His clean, woodsy smell enveloped her. “You’ve got a right to be.”

To her horror, tears pricked at her eyelids, and a lump settled in her throat. She swallowed. “I don’t know what else to be besides a cop. And that statement…”

"We'll work it out," he whispered, rubbing his cheek against her hair. "You're not alone. I'll be here. I promise."

The words scared her death. Promises always ended up broken. Her palms flattened on his back. "I can't ask that of you."

"You're not asking anything of me. I'm telling you what I intend to do." Pulling back, he tilted her face up and smiled at her. "I love you, Lanie. Let me take care of you for a while. That's all you have to do. Let me. Trust me."

Didn't he understand that was like asking her to walk a tightrope blindfolded, not really knowing if the net was there? She shook her head, and hurt bloomed in his eyes. "I don't think I can."

His thumbs smoothed over her cheekbones. Determination darkened his eyes. "I'm not giving up. I won't walk away, and sooner or later, you're going to see you can trust me."

Staring up at him, Lanie wasn't sure what frightened her more—stepping out on faith and learning he'd lied, or learning that he could be trusted. If he stayed true to his word, she'd have no more excuses to hide behind. Nothing left to protect her heart.

Chapter Twenty-Two

"The general rule of thumb is two months' salary." The blonde salesclerk's smile rivaled the brightness of the diamond rings sparkling in the jewelry case.

"Two months, huh?" John lifted an eyebrow at her before he dropped his gaze to the solitaires. Hell, knowing Lanie, she'd rather he just send the money to the hospital. The image of her face on Christmas morning when she'd opened the infinity pendant rose in his mind. Then again, maybe not.

He shifted his weight from one foot to the other. In the glass case, gems glittered in bands of all descriptions—plain, fancy, carved, gold, silver, platinum. He frowned. None of them seemed to suit Lanie or what he wanted with her.

With a sigh, he pushed a hand through his hair. He wasn't even sure what he was doing here—except that sometime during a night of tossing in his bed, the bright idea of asking Lanie to marry him had taken hold of his psyche. Needing a way to show her he was in for the long haul, he'd grabbed the notion and hung on. He didn't have to ask her now—hell, he knew she'd say no—but he could have the ring for when he was more sure of her answer.

But he wanted a ring that was as unique as the woman he loved. Something you didn't find every day.

He glanced up at the patient salesclerk. "Is this all you have?"

She swept a hand down the display case. "This is our collection of traditional solitaires. We also have a selection of three stone bands, gemstone rings, eternity bands—"

"Eternity band?" Not infinity, but close enough.

Her smiled widened, reminding John of a predator sweeping in for the kill. "This way."

"Traditionally, these are considered anniversary bands." She pulled out a tray of rings. Small diamonds encircled each band. "They symbolize the eternity of a relationship."

John eyed a platinum band with rectangular stones and tried to picture it on Lanie's finger. "This is nice."

"You have excellent taste." She lifted the ring and turned it under the light. "Faceted emerald-cut diamonds. Very unique."

"Yeah, she is." He grinned. "I'll take it."

"Lucky as well as unique."

Somehow, he doubted the smiling blonde would think so if she knew the whole, sorry story. If anyone was lucky, he was. He'd gotten a second chance.

In his car, John flipped open the small velvet box and looked at the sparkling band that had cost him more than just two months' salary. Sunlight glinted off the stones, reminding him of the way the early morning light reflected off the waves outside Lanie's bedroom window. He hoped, when the time came, that she would see his intent in the ring, would see that he meant to be there forever.

An unfamiliar feeling curled up in his chest, a lightness he wasn't used to. Maybe something like waiting for Santa Claus felt like. Something a lot like hope.

ଔଓ

Lanie hurried to pick up the ringing phone before it woke Sonny Buck. He'd fussed all day, and she'd finally gotten him down a short ten minutes ago. "Hello?"

"Lanie, it's Dennis." Dennis's voice held professionalism laced with the respect of a long term friendship. Working for someone you'd known since high school had its advantages. "How are you doing?"

"Good. Better." Lanie leaned against the wall, eyes closed, her stomach clenched. Had her leave run out that quickly? She'd kept in touch with the human resources coordinator, but with her penchant for screwing up numbers lately, who knew?

"Great." Dennis cleared his throat. "Listen, I know you're still recuperating, but I talked to Caitlin the other day and she said you're almost back to your old self. She mentioned though that you had some concerns about being ready for road duty again."

Oh, Lord, here it came. Visions of bankruptcy danced in her head. She swallowed hard. "A few, but—"

"I don't want you to worry about that. Haven County takes care of its own—you know that. Anyway, Dee Merida put in her notice yesterday. Her husband is being transferred to Fort Worth, and she's leaving in a month."

"That's too bad. She does an excellent job." Lanie wondered what the departure of the department's media spokesperson had to do with her. The only time she even talked with Dee was if a statement needed to be made regarding one of her cases and the report wasn't available.

"I was wondering if you'd like the position, on a trial basis. Maybe three months, then we re-evaluate, see how it works out.

If you're ready to go back on the road then, great. If you want to stay in the media job, that's good, too. What do you think?"

Relief bubbled in her veins. "I think it sounds great. Thank you for thinking of me."

"All right, then. I'll have Dee get in touch with you, set up some days for her to go over everything with you, and we'll work on the transition."

Still having a hard time believing the opportunity was real, she made some reply she hoped was appropriate and ended the call. The desire to squeal with delight fizzed in her throat. A real law enforcement-based job with mostly predictable hours. Something that would allow her to support the baby and herself and still be there when he needed her. Too good to be true.

In her hand, the cordless phone rang again, and she fumbled it to her ear. "Hello?"

"You sound happy." John's affectionate laughter rumbled against her ear and sent warmth along her veins.

"I am. Oh, John, I've got the best news." Static cut across the line, and she waited for it to clear. "Where are you?"

"Sitting in traffic waiting for an accident to be cleared. So what's the news?"

The urge to dance in wild circles rushed through her again. She laughed. "I'll tell you when you get here."

"What makes you think I'm coming over?" he teased. "It's not one of my nights."

"I'll make it worth your while."

"Really." His voice deepened, and she could just envision the smile quirking at his mouth. "That could be interesting. Tell you what—I'll shower and change and pick up us up some dinner on the way. What are you in the mood for?"

You. She shivered. "Whatever you decide is fine."

"Okay. Hey, traffic is moving again, so I'd better go." Silence vibrated on the line. "Love you, Lanie."

The connection went dead, and Lanie hugged his words to her for a moment, sure that her life was finally going in the right direction.

ଓଃ୪ଃ

"He's asleep. Has he been that fussy all day?"

Lanie glanced up from setting the table as John came down the stairs. "Pretty much, but he's fine once he settles down to sleep. He took a long nap this afternoon, too."

Coming up behind her, he wrapped his arms around her waist and buried his lips in the curve between her neck and shoulder. A stab of desire stung her stomach, and she leaned back into him.

"So what's this great news of yours?" he asked.

"Let's eat first. This smells wonderful." She pulled away from him and lifted the containers of Emerson's crab bisque and seafood pasta out of the bag. "Get some cutlery, would you?"

"You're an evil woman."

"Yeah, but you love it."

"I love *you*," he corrected, trying to pull her back into his arms.

Laughing, she tugged away again. "Food, O'Reilly."

A sober expression flitted across his face, but he reached out a finger, touching the silver chain holding her infinity pendant. A smile curved his mouth. "You're right. We've got plenty of time."

Over dinner, he made her laugh with descriptions of the varied individuals he'd dealt with in the records department that week. Savoring a bite of the sinful bisque, she watched his eyes darken. "What?"

With an almost-shy grin, he shook his head. "It's so good to hear you do that again. I missed your laugh, honey."

She stared into his expressive eyes, her food forgotten. Her tongue darted out to moisten dry lips. "What else did you miss?"

Passion flared in his navy gaze, but he shook his head, chuckling. "Oh, no, you don't. I want to know what's going on. What's the news, baby?"

She pushed her plate aside and leaned forward, eager to share now. "Do you remember Dee Merida?"

He nodded, wrapping strands of pasta around his fork. "Your department spokesperson."

"She's moving to Ft. Worth next month." He looked up, interested, and she grinned. "Dennis called today and offered me the position on a trial basis."

"That's great news." A wide smile creased his face, and he reached out to squeeze her hand before lacing their fingers together. "See, I told you it would all work out."

Heat tingled out from their joined hands. "You love being right, don't you, O'Reilly?"

The smile disappeared. He turned their hands, rubbing his thumb over her knuckles. "It's a rare thing with you, isn't it? For me to do something right."

She didn't want the past between them tonight. Her future stretched before her, not as tarnished as before, and she wanted to share that with him. Leaning close, she feathered her fingers over his jaw. "Don't. It's all behind us."

He didn't look at her, his gaze still on their linked hands. "Is it? I almost got you and Sonny Buck killed." He closed his eyes and pressed their hands to his forehead. "God, I have nightmares about that, about what could have happened."

An ache grasped her throat. Disentangling her hand from his, she cupped his face with her fingers and turned his face up to hers. "But it didn't."

"I love you." Arms wrapped around her waist, he pulled her onto his lap, his face buried against her neck.

I love you. The words trembled on her tongue, but she couldn't force them out. They hovered in her mind, a talisman that once whispered couldn't be taken back. Words that would bestow a power she didn't feel ready to give him.

Her hands drifted down his back, caressing the sloping muscles. She couldn't say it yet, but she could show him. "Come upstairs with me."

His sigh hummed along her neck. "Are you sure?"

She pulled back and smiled. "Very."

ꕥꕥ

A cry from the nursery dragged Lanie from a sated slumber. Sheets rustled, and John brushed his mouth against her temple. "I'll check on him."

Opening her eyes, she watched him pull on his boxer briefs and walk out of the room. Her body thrummed with satisfaction, and she stretched, a most feminine ache between her legs. Smiling against his pillow, she inhaled his scent, still clinging to the cotton case.

She really should ask him to move back in. Her body stiffened a little at the fleeting thought. *Slow down, Falconetti.*

You jumped into living with him before. Just take it a day at a time. No rush to commitment.

Edgy now, she sat up and eyed the clothes strewn about the room. His voice carried from the nursery, soft and soothing, and she slid from the bed. She picked up her clothes and tossed them in the hamper before pulling a T-shirt and yoga pants from the dresser.

His woodsy scent wafted from his shirt when she picked it up, and she couldn't resist rubbing it against her face. Laughing at herself, she tossed the shirt on the bed and reached for his jeans. As she lifted them, his change, wallet and a small box tumbled from the pockets, spilling on the rug.

Throwing the jeans on the bed, she knelt to gather the scattered contents of his pockets. Her fingers closed on the box, the blue velvet smooth and rich under her touch. Gold letters paraded across the box top—*Bennett's.*

Her heart jerked in her chest once before plummeting to her stomach. Oh God. He didn't. He wouldn't have. There was a perfectly logical reason why John O'Reilly had a box from one of Houston's premier jewelers in his pocket, and it had nothing to do with a proposal, a commitment she couldn't handle.

Just put it back. He never has to know you saw it...

Her stomach rolling, she flipped the lid open. Light danced over emerald cut diamonds. The same black fear that had gripped her when she'd opened the hospital statement washed over her. She couldn't handle this. She wasn't ready.

"I guess I should have put that in the top of my closet, too." John's quiet voice startled her, and the box fell to the carpet again.

She stared at him, nerves jerking under her skin. "Your wallet and everything fell out when I picked up your jeans."

Long fingers snagged the box. He knelt beside her, resting on his haunches. Grinning, he reached out and brushed her hair back, hooking it behind her ears. "Do you like it?"

Like it? She didn't know a woman who wouldn't like the exquisite piece. She swallowed hard. "It's beautiful."

"I wasn't going to do this yet." He lifted the lid on the box, and her heart jerked again. "But since you've already seen it... I want you to marry me, Lanie."

"John." She closed her eyes, a sudden rush of tears pushing at her eyelids.

"I know you're not ready now." He took her hand, his thumb rubbing over the knuckles, and she blinked, looking at him. A smile quirked at his lips. "We could go for a trial period. You wear the ring, and we'll see where we are in six months."

"No." The desire to cry sprang up again. She didn't want to do this, didn't want to hurt him.

He snapped the box shut with a quiet pop. "Then I'll hang on to it and in a few months, I'll—"

"No." His smile died, and she shook her head, forcing the tears down. "I don't mean not right now. I mean ever. I can't marry you."

His eyes narrowed, and he stared at her for a long moment. "What the hell?"

"I'm not ready to make that commitment yet. Can you really say you are?"

He surged to his feet, glaring down at her. "We share a child. I'd call that pretty damn committed. What's really going on?"

She scrambled to stand in front of him. "John—"

Visible tension coiled his body. He flung an arm toward the bed. "What the hell was this all about then? You can sleep with me, but not commit to me, is that it? Hell."

He leaned around her for his clothes, shoving his arms into his shirt. Lanie hugged her midriff, hands cupping her elbows. "I don't want either of us to feel trapped."

The glare he shot her way could have frozen the Gulf. "You mean you want to be able to put my ass out when you get ready."

"It isn't like that, and you know it."

"No, I don't." He tugged his jeans up, buttoning the fly. "I'm not your father, Lanie. I don't feel trapped."

"This doesn't have anything to do with him." Helpless, she watched him sit on the edge of the bed and pull on his shoes and socks. "What's wrong with what we have?"

He fixed her with a look. "You *really* don't want me to answer that, do you, honey?"

"John." She sought the placating tone she'd used with hyped-up perpetrators. "We can be together, be a family—"

"No." With deliberate movements, he tied his shoes. He looked up at her. "We can't. I'm not interested in playing house with you again. I want everything. That baby in there, the baby we made, deserves everything. *You* deserve everything."

"I thought we'd found everything." The whisper was so quiet she wasn't sure he heard it. His shoulders heaved with a harsh sigh, and he pushed up from the bed.

"No, Lanie. This isn't everything."

"John, don't go like this." She hated the pleading note in her voice, almost hated him because he made her feel she was letting him down in some way she didn't understand.

"Don't you see?" He shook his head and walked by her to the door. "I can't stay like this. Let me know when you figure out what's missing."

Missing? They had Sonny Buck, and they had each other. They were closer than they'd been before. What did he mean, missing? Filled with disbelief and a desperate anger, she watched him walk out of the room. She didn't follow.

The quiet click of the front door closing carried up the stairs, and the anger twisted through her like a striking snake. Damn him, anyway, for telling her she could trust him, then walking out when things didn't go his way. She closed her eyes against a massive wave of pain and anger.

"I don't need you," she whispered into the emptiness. She didn't. This was why she'd never let herself begin to need him too much, because sooner or later, she'd known it would be over.

All he'd done by walking out that door was prove her right.

ଓଧ୭ଊ

John slammed his desk drawer shut. Tucked in the drawer, the blue velvet box mocked him every time he needed a paper clip. What the hell had he been thinking, buying her a damn engagement ring?

He glanced at the phone, fighting the urge to call her, to give in and take her on any terms she wanted. He reached for the phone and pulled his hand back. They deserved more. He wasn't going to settle this time.

You don't have to marry her to be committed. It's a ring, a piece of paper.

No. There was more to it than that. The memory of standing outside the surgical unit, being told he couldn't see her because he wasn't family, rose in his mind. Another memory assaulted him—Caitlin making the medical decisions because he had no rights. Having to fear losing his son because he and Lanie weren't married.

He wanted more than the ring and the piece of paper—he wanted the vows and the rights that went with being her husband. He wanted to give her the same rights. He wanted to make those vows to her, to promise to always be there. He wanted everything—the good and the bad.

And Lanie wanted... What? Hell, he didn't even know.

Guilt clenched his gut, and he dropped his head into his hands with a muffled groan. Here he sat, bitching and moaning to himself about her not wanting to commit to him, and what reason had he given her? Again, it was all about what he wanted—he wanted her, he wanted them together, he wanted her to marry him.

Not once had he really stopped and thought about what she wanted. Hadn't *asked* her what she wanted, what she needed from him.

And when she balked, he walked out. No, he wasn't her father, but he'd abandoned her all the same when things didn't go his way. Some way to prove himself.

This time he didn't stop himself from reaching for the phone. Her answering machine picked up on the fourth ring. "Lanie, it's John. Honey, we need to talk. If you're there, pick up."

Silence greeted him.

He sighed. "Okay, I'll try again later. And, Lanie? I love you."

An hour and three identical calls later, his nerves sang with tension. He wondered if she was by the phone, listening to his voice, refusing to pick up, refusing to talk to him. Worry shifted over his skin. What if something was wrong?

The chair emitted a loud squeak as he pushed up from the desk. "Joyce, I'm leaving for the day."

Arms crossed over her sagging chest, she pinned him with a look. "Is it an emergency?"

"Yeah. You could call it an emergency."

ଓଓଡ଼ଡ଼

Lanie's vow not to need John lasted until early afternoon. Memories of John's hurt expression and the slump of his shoulders cropped up, no matter what she did to try to forget. With the phone's ringer off, she threw herself into cleaning while the baby napped. Family photos lined the mantel, and she pulled each one down and smoothed a soft cloth over the glass and wood.

She traced a finger over the smile on Caitlin's face in one picture and glanced up at the images on the shelf. In the largest photo, her grandparents sat surrounded by children, grandchildren, and great-grandchildren. Her grandmother had been in the final stages of chemotherapy, and the treatment's ravaging was apparent in her drawn face and smooth head. She gave the camera a weak smile, but Vincenzo Falconetti's gaze lingered on her, an expression of love and utter devotion suffusing his face.

That's what a marriage should be.

Not the mix of need and resentment her parents had shared. Or the wild attraction she and John had once shared.

Lanie shook her head. An example of what marriage should be. Taking the bad with the good.

Love.

Sacrifice.

Devotion.

Basically, everything John had proved during the last two months. Not with words. With actions.

Taking care of their son when she couldn't.

Absorbing her hatred and barbs without comment.

Comforting her when the memories became too strong.

Giving up the job he loved so Sonny Buck would have the security of an available father.

Shame chilled her. *I'm not your father.* No, he wasn't, but she'd judged him that way, simply because of his lingering feelings for Beth.

Fingers pressed against her lips to suppress a tiny moan, Lanie closed her eyes. He'd chosen her. He loved her. He'd become everything she wanted him to be.

And she'd clung to her blind judgment, refusing to see that what mattered wasn't the past—her parents', or even theirs. What mattered was the future, the future John had offered her with a dazzling ring and a lopsided grin, which she had so quickly spurned.

Oh, Lord, what had she done?

ઉ૪ઉ૪

The driveway was empty, but John went to the door anyway and knocked. The house stood silent. He sighed and stared at the spot in the driveway where Lanie's car should be.

She could be anywhere. The store. A doctor's appointment, although he knew Sonny Buck didn't have one scheduled for another two months. She could be having lunch with one of her friends.

The empty house and missing car didn't mean she'd gotten scared and run. Didn't mean he'd pushed too hard and pushed her away. The signs didn't have to mean that, but John would be willing to bet money they did.

He pulled the key from his pocket, shrugging off the tiny stab of guilt. She'd given him the key to use in an emergency. As he saw it, finding her right now constituted an emergency.

Inside, an eerie silence permeated the house. The refrigerator hummed, and the mantel clock ticked off seconds. The portable playpen was missing from the living room. His heart thudding against his ribs, John jogged up the stairs. Her overnight bag wasn't in the closet, and the bathroom counter had been cleared of her toiletries.

He didn't even have to look in the nursery.

Fear and anger churned in his gut. She was gone, and he had no clue where to look. Reason tried to assert itself. She didn't mean to stay gone forever.

She had to come to it in her own time.

He'd pushed, and she'd run.

Well, this time, he'd just wait her out.

ઉ઼ଚ୍ଚ

Sonny Buck grumbled and stretched out his body as Lanie eased him into the car seat. His duck-embroidered hat fell over his eyes, and he fussed harder. With a laugh, she pushed it back. “C’mon, Sonny Buck. Cooperate with Mom. We’ve got to find your dad. I need to tell him what an idiot I’ve been.”

The drive to Houston took forever. She couldn’t find a legal parking spot outside the precinct that housed the records division, and she parked in a slot marked *Official Use Only*. Lifting Sonny Buck to her shoulder, she nuzzled his cheek. “Hopefully, we’ll only be a minute. Want to go see Daddy?”

He chortled, and Lanie hugged his small, warm body as she climbed the marble steps to the precinct house. Nerves clenched in her stomach. What if she was too late? What if he’d decided she wasn’t worth the trouble?

Holding on to the memory of his hopeful gaze the night before, she pushed the doubts down. It wasn’t too late. It couldn’t be.

She eased through the crowded hallway, dodging uniformed officers escorting plaintive suspects and world-weary detectives shooting the bull over coffee. Pushing open the door to the records division, she swallowed and took a deep, calming breath.

The middle-aged woman with brassy red hair and deep frown lines grimaced at her, an expression Lanie supposed was meant to be a smile. “Can I help you?”

Shifting Sonny Buck in her embrace, Lanie glanced around the room. A younger woman sat at one of three desk, entering data into a computer. John wasn’t in sight. “I’m looking for Sergeant O’Reilly.”

The woman harrumphed. “He’s out.”

The hope Lanie had tried to hold on to settled into a cold lump in her stomach. “Do you know when he’ll be back?”

One hand on her hip, the woman pinned Lanie with a long-suffering look. “All I know is he said he had an emergency and not to expect him back today.”

An emergency? Lanie swallowed and backed toward the door. "Thank you."

She traveled the way she'd come, her mind clicking through possibilities. Could his emergency have to do with her? "What now?" she whispered against Sonny Buck's forehead. "Where should we look, kid?"

Stepping outside, she pulled her keys from her pocket. A horrified moan slipped past her lips when she glanced where her car should have been. The spot stood empty. Glancing up and down the street, she saw the taillights flare on a departing tow truck, her car hitched to the back.

With a muttered curse, she held her baby tighter. Could the day get any worse?

ଔଓ

Hours later, Lanie turned onto her street. The baby slept in his car seat, and the setting sun cast long shadows on the sidewalk and lawns. It had taken her two hours and over a hundred dollars to retrieve her car, and her spirits had taken a dive during that time. John's emergency could be anything. She had no reason to think he was looking for her.

She'd given him no reason to do so.

Preparing to turn into her driveway, she braked too hard and stared. His car sat in its customary spot, and sitting on her front steps was John O'Reilly, reading the newspaper, a soft drink can next to his feet.

Joy leapt into her throat, and she forced it down. His being here could mean anything. She pulled into the drive, her hands shaking on the wheel.

He didn't move from the steps, but Lanie could feel his gaze on her while she removed the sleeping baby from the car. He continued to watch her as she walked toward the steps. With deliberate motions, he folded the newspaper and set it aside. Hands linked between his parted knees, he looked at her, not smiling. "Where've you been?"

She wished he would smile. The seriousness made her more nervous, if that were possible. Stalling, she set the car seat on the step next to him and fussed with Sonny Buck's blanket. Finally, she glanced up to find him still watching her with that somber expression.

She looked away, her hands tucked in the back pockets of her jeans. *Tell him*, a little voice whispered. *Tell him you figured out what's missing.* She met his gaze again. "I was looking for you. I went to Houston, to your precinct, but you weren't there."

He nodded. "I was here."

"My car got towed, and it took forever to get it back." She closed her mouth, aware she was rambling, but so nervous her palms were damp, her mouth dry. More than anything, she wished he would reach out, touch her, tell her he loved her.

"Why did you go to the precinct?" For the first time, he dropped his gaze. Uncertainty and hope lingered in his words, and Lanie wondered if he was waiting for her to reach out, touch him, tell him she loved him.

She touched his knee and felt him flinch. "To tell you I want everything. To tell you I love you and I want to wear that ring and I want to marry you. To beg you for one more chance. To tell you that I—"

He didn't give her the chance to finish. His hands shot out and jerked her between his knees, his mouth covering hers. Lanie twined her arms around his neck, her fingers tangled in his hair. She opened her mouth, swallowing his groan. After a long time, she pulled away, smoothing her fingers along his jaw. She smiled, gazing into navy eyes dark with desire. "To tell you I know what matters most. You. Sonny Buck. Us. Our future. That's all. Nothing else."

His lashes dipped, and he caught her to him again. "God, I love you." His arms around her waist, his head against her chest, he sighed. "You don't have to wear the ring yet, Lanie. I'll wait for you. I was an ass last night—"

Her fingers gentle on his jaw, she tilted his face up. "I want to wear your ring, John. I love you, and I want to be your wife. I want you to be my husband, and I want us to have everything."

Doubt lingered in his eyes. "You're sure?"

"Very." She smiled at him, stroking her fingers over his temple. "Let's go to Vegas and find a wedding chapel. I'll make an honest man out of you, O'Reilly."

His eyes flared. "Don't tempt me, Falconetti."

She feathered her lips over his. "I'm already packed."

"You don't want the big wedding with all the trimmings?"

"I want *you.*"

Laughing, he set her back a step and stood. "Let's go."

Lanie wrapped her arms around him, holding on to everything that mattered. "I love you, O'Reilly."

About the Author

How does an English teacher end up plotting murders? She becomes a writer of romantic suspense! To learn more about Linda Winfree, please visit http://lindawinfree.blogspot.com. Send an email to Linda at linda_winfree@yahoo.com or join her Yahoo! group to join in the fun with other readers as well as Linda! http://groups.yahoo.com/group/linda_winfree.

Look for these titles

Coming Soon:

Truth and Consequences -4
His Ordinary Life -6
Hold On To Me -2
Anything But Mine -3
Memories of Us -5
A Formal Feeling -7

An old-fashioned undertaker who asks for lessons in what turns a woman on...what more could any teacher ask for?

Mortified Matchmaker

© 2007 Alexis Fleming

When circumstances force kindergarten teacher Melissa Morgan to take her twin sister's place as proprietor of a dating agency, the last thing she expects is to meet a funeral director in desperate need of lessons in what a woman wants. Despite his quirky behavior and antiquated ideas, Matthew Campbell pushes every one of Melissa's buttons and it's not long before the lessons become more important than finding Matthew a mate.

But how will Melissa react when she finds out Matthew is an undercover federal agent in pursuit of a blackmailer and she's the prime suspect?

Available now in ebook and print from Samhain Publishing.

Printed in the United States
97135LV00002B/331-357/A

9 781599 984216